Dark Obsession

By the same author:

The Bracelet
Cassandra's Conflict
Cassandra's Chateau
Deborah's Discovery
Dramatic Affairs
Fiona's Fate
The Gallery

Please send me the books I have ticked above.

Name ....

Address ....

....

....

....

Post Code ....

Send to: Virgin Books Cash Sales, Random House,
20 Vauxhall Bridge Road, London SW1V 2SA.

US customers: for prices and details of how to order
books for delivery by mail, call 888-330-8477.

Please enclose a cheque or postal order, made payable
to Virgin Books Ltd, to the value of the books you have
ordered plus postage and packing costs as follows:

UK and BFPO – £1.00 for the first book, 50p for each
subsequent book.

Overseas (including Republic of Ireland) – £2.00 for
the first book, £1.00 for each subsequent book.

If you would prefer to pay by VISA, ACCESS/MASTERCARD,
DINERS CLUB, AMEX or SWITCH, please write your card
number and expiry date here: ....

....

Signature ....

Please allow up to 28 days for delivery.

To find out the latest information about Black Lace titles, check out the website: www.blacklacebooks.co.uk or send for a booklist with complete synopses by writing to:

> Black Lace Booklist, Virgin Books Ltd
> Virgin Books
> Random House
> 20 Vauxhall Bridge Road
> London SW1V 2SA

Please include an SAE of decent size. Please note only British stamps are valid.

Our privacy policy
We will not disclose information you supply us to any other parties. We will not disclose any information which identifies you personally to any person without your express consent.

From time to time we may send out information about Black Lace books and special offers. Please tick here if you do <u>not</u> wish to receive Black Lace information. ❑

Dark Obsession
Fredrica Alleyn

BL

This book is a work of fiction.
In real life, make sure you practise safe, sane and
consensual sex.

First Published by Black Lace 1995

2 4 6 8 10 9 7 5 3 1

Copyright © Fredrica Alleyn 1995

Fredrica Alleyn has asserted her right under the Copyright, Designs
and Patents Act 1988 to be identified as the author of this work

This edition first published in Great Britain in 2009 by
Black Lace
Virgin Books
Random House,
20 Vauxhall Bridge Road
London SW1V 2SA

www.virginbooks.com
www.blacklacebooks.co.uk
www.rbooks.co.uk

Addresses for companies within The Random House Group Limited can be found at:
www.randomhouse.co.uk/offices.htm

The Random House Group Limited Reg. No. 954009

A CIP catalogue record for this book
is available from the British Library

ISBN 9780352345240

The Random House Group Limited supports The Forest Stewardship Council [FSC], the
leading international forest certification organisation. All our titles that are printed on
Greenpeace approved FSC certified paper carry the FSC logo.
Our paper procurement policy can be found at www.rbooks.co.uk/environment

Printed and bound in Great Britain by
CPI Bookmarque, Cryodon, CR0 4TD

Chapter One

'*I* can't go to Leyton Hall on my own!' exclaimed Annabel, staring at David in disbelief.

David Crosbie, fifty years old and currently the most fashionable interior designer in the country, smiled at her. 'Of course you can, Annabel. You've done enough renovations with me during the past three years to know what's required.'

'But that was with you,' Annabel pointed out. 'I've never done anything on my own.'

'All the more reason to make a start. You're twenty-three now. When Martin and I retire to the Seychelles you'll be taking over the entire business. How can you do that if you've never worked on your own?'

Annabel ran her fingers through her long brown hair, pushing the unruly curls back off her face. 'That won't happen for years yet! Besides, I thought you'd start me off on something small. Lady Corbett-Wynne probably won't accept a trainee. I wouldn't if I were her.'

'Darling girl, you've graduated from art college with Honours and worked alongside me for over three years. If that isn't good enough for her ladyship then she'll have to go elsewhere. I haven't got the time to disappear into the

Wiltshire countryside for what will undoubtedly be several weeks while she makes up her mind what she wants. I mean, look at her letter! Did you ever see anything less decisive in your life?'

Annabel smiled. 'She does sound a bit unsure, but that's why she'll need you.'

'No, it's why she's getting you,' David corrected her. 'You'll bring fresh ideas and a much younger approach than I would. I'm getting tired of trying to salvage decaying country houses on tight budgets. Give me a London penthouse any day of the week.'

At that moment Martin Wells, David's partner and long-time lover, joined them. He was ten years younger than David and whereas David was tall, slim and grey-haired, Martin was short, sturdy and with a mass of dark hair which looked in permanent need of a cut. Despite their physical dissimilarities they made the perfect couple. David was intense and prone to depression; Martin took life far more easily and had a keen sense of humour that not all of their clients appreciated.

'What's the trouble?' he asked, pouring himself a cup of strong coffee.

'I've just told Annabel I want her to take on the Leyton Hall job,' explained David. 'She doesn't think she's good enough.'

'You're good enough for anything,' said Martin, sinking into a chair with the cup of coffee cradled in his hands. 'God, how much did I drink last night?'

'Too much!' retorted David. 'Did we wake you when we came in, Annabel?'

'I hadn't gone to sleep. I was trying to decide which shade of blue to use in Amanda Grant's bathroom and . . .'

'There you are, that's precisely why I've chosen you for Leyton Hall!' David said triumphantly. 'You live your work. Night and day, awake and asleep. All you think about is interior decorating. From what I've heard you'll

2

need all that enthusiasm for Leyton Hall. I haven't got it anymore, my dear, and that's the truth.'

'It will do you good to get away from us,' said Martin, gradually beginning to feel more like a human being as the coffee took effect. 'You need to meet some young people, socialise more.'

'I don't want to socialise. I love working here with you two. Besides, you're my family. If my parents ever do come to London I doubt if they'll think of looking me up. And if they did they wouldn't recognise me. The last time I saw them I was seventeen!'

'No one would mistake you for seventeen now,' agreed Martin, looking at Annabel with detached interest. She always dressed well, and today she was wearing a navy and white striped jacket that ended about four inches above her knee and two inches below a matching mini-skirt. A crisp white blouse with a navy silk scarf tied in a loose bow at the neck completed the outfit and her slim legs were covered by opaque navy tights. The high-heeled navy shoes emphasised her shapely calves and not for the first time Martin wondered why she seemed to have attracted so few boyfriends during her time with them.

'How am I going to meet young people at Leyton Hall?' continued Annabel. 'Lady Corbett-Wynne isn't young, is she?'

'No, early forties I'd guess,' said David. 'She's Lord Corbett-Wynne's third wife, rather pretty in a delicate way as I recall. Good bone structure too, but not young in the way you mean.'

'There's a son, though,' said Martin. 'I remember the Honourable Crispian very well indeed.'

'There's a girl too,' said David. 'She's Lady Corbett-Wynne's daughter, and I think she was adopted by her stepfather after the marriage. I'm not sure. I can't remember her name, either, but she's probably about your age, and they definitely both live at the Hall.'

3

'It doesn't really matter,' said Annabel. 'I'm not interested in the social side of things. It's the work that interests me.'

'You should be interested in more than work,' said Martin. 'At your age I don't think I found much time for work. That came later, when passion had dimmed!' He looked fondly at David and they both laughed.

Annabel sighed. She loved the pair of them and they'd been kindness itself to her, making her feel part of a family again, but she did wish they'd stop trying to push her into the arms of numerous young men. It wasn't that she didn't like men – she was beginning to think she had a low boredom threshold. No sooner had an affair started than she found herself tiring of the man in question. Recently she'd stopped bothering to take it that far; it only made it more difficult to disentangle herself without unpleasantness.

'Have you asked Lady Corbett-Wynne whether it would be all right for me to take the job on?' she asked David.

'Not yet, but I intend to this very morning.'

'And you really think I could do it?'

'If I didn't I wouldn't give it to you. What you have to remember is that this is almost certainly a very bored lady with money to spend, time to kill and no taste at all. You'll get a virtual free hand. Now, doesn't that tempt you, even if the Honourable Crispian doesn't?'

Annabel giggled. 'I must admit it's the more tempting prospect of the two!'

'One day you'll discover the error of your ways,' sighed Martin in mock sorrow. 'You may know all there is to know about textures, colours and fabrics but when it comes to the pleasures of the flesh you're an innocent abroad.'

'I rather doubt that a few weeks at Leyton Hall will improve my knowledge in that direction!' exclaimed Annabel, picking up her car keys. 'Tell David I'll meet him at the office. We're meant to be seeing Amanda Grant at eleven-thirty, don't let him forget.'

4

Remembering some of the stories he'd heard about Leyton Hall, Martin wasn't sure that Annabel was right. If the rumours had any truth in them then she might return to London a changed woman. He hoped so. In his opinion she needed to realise that there was more to life than turning other people's houses into beautiful homes. That was a very second-hand kind of satisfaction for an attractive young woman.

At the same time as Annabel was driving her way through the busy London streets, the occupants of Leyton Hall were slowly coming awake.

In his third-floor master bedroom, Lord Corbett-Wynne opened his eyes and mentally listed the things that had to be attended to that day. There were the usual estate matters, most of which he suspected his estate manager could handle standing on his head, and also the rather more daunting prospect of telling his wife that he'd invited their new neighbour over to dinner the following Friday evening. Neither of these two tasks caused him any great pleasure, but the third did – the matter of the new girl working in the stables. He'd caught sight of her the previous afternoon, her rounded buttocks tightly encased in jodhpurs as she mucked out Solomon's stall. She'd looked up at him and smiled in what he could only describe to himself as a knowing way; it was the knowledge behind the smile that he intended to find out about this very morning. At the prospect his heavy, flaccid penis began to stir and he felt a thrill of excitement go through him. There was nothing he enjoyed more than breaking in his new grooms.

In the west wing of the house, Lady Corbett-Wynne had been awake for several hours. Her maid Mary had brought her Earl Grey tea and two slices of toast at eight-thirty and since then she'd been lying staring at the ceiling wondering whether today would be the day she'd hear from David Crosbie. She did hope so. She couldn't wait to get her redecorating scheme under way. Running her hands absent-mindedly down the sides of her slender body she swung her legs out of bed and rang the bell.

Mary could run her bath, and then she thought that she might take a stroll round the grounds before attending to her needlepoint. For a brief moment it crossed her mind that at forty-four she was rather too young to be spending all her waking moments in solitary pursuits, but the alternative was far worse. At the memory of her husband's amorous attentions, most of which had been bizarre and brought her no pleasure at all, she shivered. She was better off as she was now, but just the same there were times when she found herself imagining what it might be like if another man, more thoughtful and attentive to her needs, were to take her in his arms. Perhaps touch her where her fingers were roaming now, just between her thighs, the touch feather-light and undeniably sweet.

A tap on the door interrupted her thoughts and she quickly withdrew her hand and lay back on the bed again, astonished at her own behaviour. It must be the time of year, she thought as Mary began to run her bath. May was such a lovely month, and it always promised so much.

Back on the third floor, Lady Corbett-Wynne's daughter Tania was also awake, but unlike her mother she wasn't alone. She was lying crouched on all fours, her weight supported on her arms and legs while her stepbrother, the Honourable Crispian Corbett-Wynne, groaned beneath her as she clenched and released her internal muscles around his bursting erection. His hands cupped her firm upthrusting breasts tightly and when she ground her buttocks down hard against his lower abdomen he squeezed even harder, so that she whimpered with the delicious pressure.

'Let me come, damn you!' muttered Crispian.

Tania laughed. 'Not until you apologise for flirting with Amanda last night.'

'I wasn't flirting, I was simply being polite. You know

what Pa's like. He wants me to marry her; surely you can't blame me for making civilised conversation.'

His stepsister's green-grey eyes were bright with malice and she suddenly sat upright facing away from him, ruining the steady build-up of tension that her skilled muscle movements had been arousing.

'I think I'll go for a ride before breakfast,' she announced, and before Crispian realised what was happening she'd slid off him and was standing at the foot of the bed. 'You'd better get back to your own room,' she said sweetly. 'What would your papa say if he found you here like this?'

Crispian glared at her. 'You can't just leave me now!'

'I most certainly can. Perhaps we'll finish later, after breakfast?'

'I've got to go to some boring meeting with Pa and the estate manager.'

'Too bad!'

'You're a bitch, you know that, don't you?' muttered Crispian thickly.

Tania picked up a brush and pulled it through her short auburn hair, smoothing it down into a pageboy style. 'That's why you love me,' she declared.

Crispian stood behind her, his erection nudging against the cheeks of her bottom. 'Bend over,' he whispered. 'Let me take you like this. You want it as much as I do.'

Tania shivered. He was right, she did want him, but he would have to wait. She liked to be in control, to keep him waiting until she drove him over the edge and he lost control. That was when she enjoyed it best; when he forgot everything except the sensations. 'Later,' she repeated as she started to dress. 'Run off to Papa now. You don't want to annoy him again, do you?'

'I can't afford to annoy him again,' retorted Crispian. 'If I'm not careful he'll cut off my allowance, and then what would I do?'

Tania laughed. 'You'd have to find a job. Or marry a rich wife.'

'You know I'll never marry anyone except you,' Crispian said, suddenly fierce.

Tania's eyes turned cold. 'But I'm not good enough for your papa, am I? My mother was good enough for him, but he has his sights set higher for his son and heir.'

'That's because your mother's a lady, and you're not!' Crispian taunted her.

Tania didn't care. She knew that if she was more like her mother, Crispian wouldn't be so enthralled, and she had no intention of leading the kind of life her mother did, shut up in the west wing doing needlepoint. She'd rather die.

Tania Corbett-Wynne was in another man's thoughts that morning, apart from her stepbrother's. As Sir Matthew Stevens walked around the Old Mill, a rambling seventeenth-century stone millhouse whose land adjoined Leyton Hall, he was thinking about the auburn-haired girl he'd seen riding near the boundary of his land. She'd glanced sideways at him the previous day when she'd passed him in the lane, as well.

Recently widowed, Matthew saw all women as a challenge. Since he stood six feet tall, had dark curly hair and a tanned face with an interestingly enigmatic expression he rarely had any difficulty in overcoming any initial opposition. Once he'd made his conquest he lost interest. It was rather like fox-hunting he supposed; it was the chase that provided the greatest thrill.

Whistling for his labrador which had gone off after an interesting scent, he wondered whether or not Tania would present much of a challenge. He doubted it, but it would still be worth the hunt. She was bound to know one or two interesting little tricks, and if she didn't then he'd teach her some of his. Cheered at the prospect, and knowing that he would be dining with her family three days later, Matthew strode on. He loved May mornings.

At one o'clock when the estate meeting was over, Crispian and his father returned to the Hall for lunch. To the surprise of both of them, Crispian's stepmother was waiting in the dining room. It was rare for her to venture forth from her own wing these days unless they were entertaining, and her husband immediately thought something must be wrong.

'What is it, Marina?' he asked testily. He always became testy when unsettled.

She raised her perfectly arched eyebrows in a genteel expression of surprise. 'Am I not allowed into the main part of the house? Strange, I imagined I lived here.'

'Of course you live here, damn it, but it's pretty difficult to remember that since you persist in shutting yourself off from the rest of us these days.'

'I wanted to talk to you about redecoration,' said his wife. Her voice sounded far more assured than she really felt.

Her husband's face turned sullen. 'I've told you, we can't afford to spend a fortune. Things are hard enough as it is at the moment. Only this morning we were discussing . . .'

'If you remember,' his wife said in an icy tone, 'I do have a considerable amount of money of my own. *Some* of that money I would happily use to civilise your family seat a little. Having failed with the human members I thought I'd turn my attention to the Hall itself.'

James, who could think of very little apart from the young groom he was due to see straight after lunch, did at least grasp that Marina was willing to spend some of her own money and he forced himself to smile at her.

'In that case I'm sure we could find a way,' he assured her.

'I've also managed to secure the services of David Cros-

9

bie,' his wife said, with what seemed to James to be a deceptively sweet inflection.

'Good God! How much money are you planning to throw away?' exploded James. 'You must be mad. He's the most expensive man in the country.'

'He is also the best. However, it isn't quite as bad as it seems. His assistant will be coming in his place. He assured me over the telephone this morning that she was highly qualified and extremely gifted. She will arrive on Friday morning and stay in the guest rooms for however long it proves necessary.'

'A female! How old?' asked Crispian.

Marina glanced at her stepson with distaste. 'It never crossed my mind to ask.'

Crispian grinned. 'I don't suppose she'll be young. Never mind, more fodder for you, Pa!'

'Your father's taste runs to young women,' his stepmother responded in a crisp manner. 'In any case, the lady in question is here to work on the house, not provide the gentlemen with entertainment.'

'Talking of entertainment,' her husband said swiftly, grateful for the lead-in, 'I've invited our new neighbour over to dinner on Friday. He's Sir Matthew Stevens, the one whose wife died a few months ago. I think he was knighted for services to industry or something like that. Anyway, now that he's living at the Old Mill I thought we should have him over. You can manage that, dear, can't you?'

'Of course. Do you want him to be the only guest, or had you intended inviting others to keep him company?'

James shrugged. 'Hadn't really considered it. Tell you what, invite this designer woman to join us and that will make the numbers equal. He probably isn't up to large dinner parties yet, still in mourning most likely.'

'I thought mourning had gone out of fashion,' remarked Marina, turning to leave the room. 'I can't imagine you'd be grieving for very long if I were to die.'

Crispian snorted with laughter. 'She's got a point,' he remarked as soon as his stepmother had left the room. 'Why should Sir Matthew be in mourning?'

'Don't suppose he is, but I couldn't be bothered to think of any other people to invite. As for your stepmother, I might mourn her more if she were a proper wife to me.'

'Lucky for you we keep a full stable,' retorted Crispian. 'No shortage of nubile girls around!'

'I wish you'd take more interest in nubile girls, in the plural, rather than one extremely nubile but totally unsuitable girl!' commented his father.

'You live your life and I'll live mine,' said Crispian, flushing with annoyance. 'After all, Tania's mother was good enough for you.'

'When Marina dies, most of her money goes to that son of hers. Since he's married with children of his own that won't leave very much for young Tania. You need to marry money, Crispian. Screw the girl as much as you like, but for God's sake find yourself a wife. You heard Robert today. We need an injection of money into the place.'

'Perhaps you can open the place up to visitors once Step-mama's had it decorated,' suggested Crispian. 'Got to go now. Urgent appointment, if you know what I mean.'

His father made a sound of irritation and watched his son hurry away. He knew only too well what he meant.

Crispian tapped on his stepsister's door and felt a rush of relief when she called out for him to enter. She would know it was him, he thought with a wry smile. No one else in the house ever tried to go into Tania's room. She regarded it as her very own, a private retreat from the world, only shared with those closest to her, and even then only by invitation.

As usual the room was in chaos. Her riding boots had been pulled off and thrown carelessly against a chair, her jodhpurs and hacking jacket lay in a heap in a corner of the room and a trail of underwear led from the burgundy coloured damask curtains at the head of her bed to the adjoining bathroom.

Tania however was looking immaculate. Crispian's heart started to pound loudly in his ears as he took in the sight of her. She was clad from head to toe in an olive-green figure-hugging bodysuit that totally covered her legs and trunk but left bare her arms and an inviting semicircle of creamy white flesh at the base of her neck. Matching three-quarters length silk gloves and very high-heeled shoes completed the outfit, while her auburn hair had been gelled and teased into exciting disarray.

She was lying across her bed, her full lips pouting provocatively, and he started to unbutton his check shirt. 'Leave it,' she said sharply. 'I'm in charge today.'

Crispian swallowed hard and swept his long fair hair back off his forehead. When she behaved like this he always had an overwhelming urge to take her by force, and sometimes he did, but looking at her almost cat-like eyes he knew today it would be best to do as she said.

She slid off her bed and walked over to him, standing on tiptoe so that she could reach his top button. His breath quickened at the brush of her gloved hands against his chin as she struggled to unfasten the button; he stared down at her.

Tania moistened her lips with her tongue and slowly unfastened all his buttons. To his surprise she didn't remove the shirt but instead walked round behind him and pressed her silk-clad body against him, letting her hands wander round until the silk gloves reached his bare midriff. She pressed down lightly with her fingertips and he sighed softly.

For several minutes she let her fingers move up and down his chest and he thought he'd go out of his mind if she didn't do something more. She moved round to the front of him and unfastened his brushed cord trousers. Easing them over his hips she drew them down until they reached the floor and then stood up again.

12

She stared into his eyes and he saw the gleam of sexual arousal flickering deep in their depths. Slowly her arms reached up and she pressed on his shoulders until he at last gave in to her and sank slowly to the floor. Once he was prone at her feet she removed his shoes and socks and then finally his cords. 'Bend your knees up,' she whispered.

Again he obeyed, his excitement now so great that his erection was straining against the waistband of his boxer shorts. Tania stepped carefully over him, then lowered herself onto his body and leant back against his legs. The caress of her bodysuit against the naked patches of his skin was all the more arousing for being intermittent, and Crispian reached up to grab her by the waist.

'Don't touch me!' snapped Tania. 'If you do I shall stop.'

Crispian muffled a curse and felt the points of her high heels touch the cheeks of his bottom through his boxer shorts. At this reminder of her absolute control his penis swelled yet more and he thrust upwards against her body.

With a tiny laugh Tania turned herself around so that he could no longer see her face, and her gloved hands lifted the constricting waistband so that his engorged glans was at last free. For several seconds she let her gloved fingers tease it, watching with interest as clear fluid filled the tiny slit in the top and began to seep over the purple head and down the sides.

'What an eager boy,' she murmured, then she bent her head and flicked her tongue delicately at the fluid, until it was all gone.

Crispian felt a tightness in his testicles and the end of his penis started to tingle. He ran his hands over Tania's small, firm buttocks and let them stray against the material that covered the cleft there.

At once Tania stood up. 'I said, don't touch me!' she reminded him. 'Now you've spoilt it. You'll have to wait until tonight.'

To his amazement she started to walk away from him,

but he was too quick for her and his right hand shot out and grabbed her round the ankle. 'I am not waiting until tonight,' he said breathlessly. 'In fact, I'm not waiting more than five minutes.'

Tania kicked out, but Crispian had anticipated the move and she failed to make contact. Instead she lost her balance and fell in an awkward heap on top of him.

Crispian laughed, grabbed her by the wrists and then forced her to the floor, so that now he was the one straddling her body. She looked up at him, her eyes bright with excitement.

Crispian let his hands roam over her covered breasts and at once the large nipples that he knew so well pressed against the material. He licked at them, then sucked both material and nipple into his mouth while his hands moved down lower and stroked his stepsister's hipbones.

This time it was Tania whose breathing became ragged. 'I'm meant to be in charge,' she protested, but he knew that it was only a token protest. Her body's responses told him that. Pulling off his boxer shorts he let his erection press against her lower belly through the bodysuit. 'Don't you want this?' he teased.

Tania didn't answer him. Her body was pulsating within the confines of her outfit and her need for him was making her ache in her belly and between her thighs. She felt one of his fingers stray along the creases of her inner thighs and shivered. He smiled down at her, the smile not entirely kind.

'Where shall I touch you next?' he asked softly.

Tania's hips bucked in reply as she tried to brush her moist vulva against his hand. 'Not just yet,' he murmured, and then he wrenched at the scoop neck of the bodysuit and before she realised what was happening he'd torn it open so that her breasts and rib cage were totally exposed.

Crispian loved her breasts. They were large considering how slight the rest of her was, but they were also firm and creamy white with a faint dusting of freckles in the valley between them. Burying his head there he nipped at the tender flesh and then let his teeth graze over the surfaces of both breasts while at the same time his hands were sliding down beneath her buttocks lifting her against him so that she could feel his excitement more clearly.

Between Tania's thighs her bodysuit was wet with excitement and he laughed as she desperately strained against him. At last, when he sensed that neither of them could wait any longer, he tore the suit right off her, dragging it down over her legs without thought for anything except their final pleasure.

Tania moaned with relief and then she felt Crispian's hands turning her face down on the faded, threadbare rug. Immediately she raised her bottom high into the air. Crispian slapped her buttocks lightly with his fingertips and reached across to the box that she kept at the foot of her bed. From it he withdrew what he wanted and Tania suddenly felt the delicious touch of cool jelly being spread around her rear opening.

Crispian took the slim, smooth latex probe out of its box and slowly inched it into his stepsister's lubricated opening. She whimpered with ecstasy as she felt it invading her, and when he turned the switch and it started to squirm and gyrate against her sensitive inner walls she felt the wonderful tightness deep inside her, while sparks of desire flashed upwards through her belly.

'Lift yourself higher,' Crispian muttered hoarsely, and Tania strained to obey. Her whole body was throbbing now with the mounting tension and when Crispian finally slid his penis between her sex lips, penetrating deeply into her second opening, she felt her muscles bunching as they prepared for orgasm.

'Wait for me,' muttered Crispian, his own climax dangerously near, but Tania didn't want to wait and she tightened her vaginal muscles around him to increase all her sensations. Tendrils of excitement were snaking across every inch of her and she was no longer aware of her stepbrother, only her own body. The rectal probe continued its relentless squirming and she teetered on the edge of blissful release.

Realising that she either couldn't or wouldn't wait, Crispian started to thrust frantically in and out of her, until he knew that he was about to pass the point of no return. At that moment he reached round beneath Tania, his fingers swiftly locating the moist, swollen clitoris standing out proudly from its covering. As he felt his seed rushing upwards through his shaft he grasped the clitoris between the tips of two fingers and squeezed firmly.

For Tania this sudden fierce sensation, so different from the other, softer feelings that were washing over her body, proved the trigger for release as well and with a scream of excitement her body tightened and she bucked violently with the intensity of the explosion that shook her from head to foot.

Trapped deep within her, Crispian felt her well-trained muscles contracting even more furiously around him as her body became lost in the blissful spasms of orgasm, and even though his own climax was over her muscles kept him trapped until her body was finally quiet. Slowly he withdrew, but when he went to remove the probe from her back passage Tania made a second protest. He moved it gently within her. 'What is it?'

'Leave it there. I think I can come again,' she said huskily.

'There's no time,' replied Crispian, and without any warning he withdrew the implement from between her rounded buttocks.

Tania collapsed onto the floor, then turned her head to look at him. 'Why did you do that?'

'Because I wanted to.'

She wriggled sensuously against the rug. 'I'm not finished.'

Crispian laughed. 'I'm afraid I am.'

Tania rolled onto her back and stared up at him and

16

immediately he knew that he wanted her again. 'Give me five minutes!' he protested.

'Use the crop on me,' she whispered. 'Please!'

Dark excitement filled Crispian's brain. 'Are you sure?'

'Of course I'm sure. You can tie me up first if you want,' she added, knowing how much he liked that.

Crispian felt his hands starting to shake. 'All right, I'll . . .'

There was a sudden tap on the door. The two of them looked at each other in surprise, but it was Tania who pulled herself together first. 'Who is it?' she asked in a lazy drawl.

'It's your stepfather. Is Crispian in there?'

Tania had difficulty suppressing a giggle. 'In where?'

'In your room,' James said furiously.

'Sorry, no. Perhaps he's taken one of the horses out.'

'I've checked the stables. He's in there with you, isn't he?'

'No,' drawled Tania. 'Now go away. I'm trying to rest.'

'When you see him, tell him I want him in the stable block straight away. We've got a mare coming this afternoon for Solomon to cover and no one's got a damned thing ready.'

'Okay,' said Tania. 'If I see him I'll let him know.'

They both stayed very quiet until James's footsteps had died away along the corridor. 'Blast,' muttered Crispian. 'I'll have to go. We can't afford to mess up on this. Solomon brings in a fortune.'

'He should put you out to stud, you'd probably bring in a fortune too!' laughed Tania.

Crispian began to pull on his clothes. 'We'll finish tonight,' he promised.

'I might not be in the same mood tonight,' said Tania, slowly getting up from the floor and walking towards her bathroom. 'In fact, I'm almost sure I won't be. Maybe tomorrow.'

Crispian caught hold of her shoulder. 'Why do you do

17

this? Why can't you be honest and admit that it's what you want to do all the time?'

'Because it isn't,' lied Tania, who knew very well that this was the best way to keep Crispian bewitched. 'Sometimes I like a rest. Run off to your papa now, he's waiting, remember?'

Crispian left. Sometimes he wished that Tania didn't have such a hold over him, but as yet he hadn't met anyone who could excite him in the same way as she did, or who took such delicious delight in the more outlandish practices that enthralled him. He couldn't imagine ever meeting anyone to match her.

'You mean, you've told her?' asked Annabel at the end of the day.

David Crosbie nodded. 'She took it very well. I explained that you would soon be in great demand and that this gave her the opportunity of being one step ahead of everyone else. She'd be able to boast that you'd done Leyton Hall long before you were famous. She's probably planning to claim credit for having asked for you by the time you've finished.'

'But what if she doesn't like my ideas?' protested Annabel.

'She'll like them. She'd probably like anyone's ideas, but in your case she's getting a genuine bargain, far more than she deserves.'

Annabel sighed. 'You don't know what she deserves. She might be a very nice, knowledgeable lady.'

'And pigs might fly.'

'I've got a feeling I'm not going to enjoy myself very much,' said Annabel. 'I hope I'm not there long.'

'It shouldn't take more than three weeks at the outside,' David assured her. 'Martin and I will take you out for a meal tonight, to celebrate your first solo venture. How about that?'

Annabel smiled. 'It sounds more like a bribe to me, but a very nice one.'

'Good, then that's settled.'

It was nearly midnight when the three of them returned from the promised meal, and Annabel felt pleasantly cheerful after the delicious food and excellent wine. 'I hope the food's like that at Leyton Hall,' she sighed. 'Then the three weeks would fly by.'

'It isn't,' said Martin, glancing at David, who busied himself pouring them all brandies. 'Hasn't David told you we spent a weekend there once ourselves?'

'No,' said Annabel in astonishment.

'Well, it wasn't a great success, that's probably why he kept quiet. The food was dreadful, and the company even worse.'

'David, is this why you won't take on the commission?' Annabel asked accusingly.

For once David had the grace to blush. 'Not exactly, darling. Let's just say that the countryside and I are not entirely at ease with one another.'

'But you do know Lord and Lady Corbett-Wynne?'

'Yes,' David admitted reluctantly. 'That's to say, I've talked with them. I wouldn't for one moment suggest that I *know* them.'

'Why didn't you tell me that before?'

'It wasn't relevant,' retorted David, beginning to sound irritable. 'I really don't know why Martin's mentioned it now.'

'Of course it's relevant!' she exclaimed. 'For heaven's sake, tell me what they're like.'

'Pretty typical of their kind. Lord Corbett-Wynne's tall, heavy-set, with greying hair and one of those florid, rustic complexions. He manages to get to the House of Lords about once a month, the rest of the time he's busy with Leyton Hall. At least he's busy with the girl grooms at Leyton Hall!'

'What about his wife?' asked Annabel, intrigued. 'Doesn't she mind?'

'She's probably grateful!' laughed Martin. 'As I remember she's one of those fine-boned, beautifully turned out women who seem totally asexual. It would be difficult to imagine her in the throes of any sexual passion, don't you agree, David?'

'Possibly, certainly not with that husband of hers anyway. Her daughter's the exact opposite. According to her stepfather she's quite a handful. Not that he went into any detail, but he certainly gave that impression.'

'And the son?' asked Annabel.

'Gorgeous!' declared Martin. 'You'll fall for him immediately, Annabel. He's tall, fair-haired and tanned, with that deliciously languid air that's so irresistible.'

'I'm sure I'll be able resist him,' retorted Annabel. 'Whose son is he then?'

'Don't you listen?' asked David, clearly wanting to change the subject. 'He's the Honourable Crispian Corbett-Wynne, heir to Leyton Hall. Tania, his stepsister, is Lady Corbett-Wynne's daughter by her first marriage. That husband died or got himself killed jumping a hedge, something like that.'

'If you stayed there you must have been a friend of theirs, so why aren't you doing the Hall for them?' asked Annabel.

'I'm tired,' said David shortly. 'I'll leave you two to finish your drinks and lock up. Sleep well, Annabel.'

After he'd gone she turned to Martin in surprise. 'What's all that about?'

Martin laughed. 'David's embarrassed. He used to know James – that's Lord Corbett-Wynne – quite well, which is why we were invited there soon after he remarried for the third time. Unfortunately it was a disaster.'

'Why?'

'Because no one had told Tania about David and me. She thought we were just business partners and made a very blatant and somewhat drunken pass at him. Before he could explain, her stepbrother was trying to make something out of it, threatening to take David outside and thrash him with a riding crop, all very melodramatic!'

Annabel laughed too. 'I can't imagine David being threatened with a thrashing!'

'We left the next morning. David said we'd been called back to London unexpectedly, and everyone accepted that. Probably Tania had been told the truth by that time and they were all glad to see us go.'

'But it didn't stop Lady Corbett-Wynne asking David to do the Hall for her.'

'She might not have known what went on. Even then, which was early on in the marriage, she seemed to be quite separate from the rest of them. She was always retreating to her own rooms. I liked her but thought she'd made a disastrous marriage. They were the most mismatched pair I've ever come across.'

Annabel wrapped her arms round her knees. 'It's beginning to sound more interesting now. I wish David had told me earlier.'

'He really does want you to start taking on some work of your own,' explained Martin. 'I suppose he thought that if he told you about our social disaster you'd think you hadn't been given the job on merit.'

'Maybe. Anyway, now that I know more about them all it makes it more real. I think I'm beginning to look forward to it, although that might be the champagne and brandy!'

'It will certainly be an experience for you,' said Martin. He looked thoughtful.

Annabel nodded happily, blithely unaware of exactly what kind of an experience it would turn out to be.

Chapter Two

*I*t took Annabel over an hour and a half to drive from London to Wiltshire, and then a further half-hour to find Leyton Hall. David's sense of direction was never good, and as far as Leyton Hall was concerned he seemed to have tried to put its location entirely out of his mind. As a result she was more than three-quarters of an hour late arriving.

She was agreeably surprised by the Hall itself. Having expected a dilapidated and conventional country house she was taken aback to discover that it was a large, well-maintained home built at the end of the eighteenth century in the Palladian style of architecture. The south-facing front of the house had beautiful flanking pavilions and, although it was clear that there had been renovations from time to time, the occupants had maintained the harled walls with stone dressings round the windows and doors.

On the ground floor there were two three-light Venetian windows with traditional low-pitched triangular gables above them. The normal mouldings were well represented by bands of stone set flush with the wallface. The West Wing had corbelled turrets at the corners of the roof while wisteria and honeysuckle grew up the walls.

All this, together with the profusion of rhododendrons, azaleas and orange-stemmed birch trees that she had driven past along the approach to the Hall, cheered Annabel up. If the exterior had been so lovingly and tastefully maintained then it seemed likely that her job would be easier than she'd anticipated.

As soon as the car stopped the front door opened and six dogs came tearing down the steps towards her. They were a strange assortment. Two heavy basset hounds, their long ears flapping out behind them, were leapt over by a pair of springer spaniels. Two imposing grey Weimaraners approached more cautiously but in a far less friendly spirit, their ears back and their legs stiff with suppressed aggression.

Annabel opened the car door and the Weimaraners growled low in their throats. She froze, knowing that her fear would be plain to the dogs but unable to contain it. She'd never liked dogs, large or small, and had no idea how to handle the situation.

'Come here, you stupid animals!' shouted a voice from the doorway, and to Annabel's relief a young man emerged from the shadows. He was tall and slim with high cheekbones and a wide, thin-lipped mouth that was open at that moment in a welcoming smile which revealed perfect, gleaming white teeth. His long, fair hair was swept back off his face and a pair of light-blue eyes surveyed her with interest.

'You needn't be afraid of them,' he drawled, 'they only attack after dark!' Annabel laughed, hoping it was a joke.

'Who is it?' asked a light feminine voice, and then the young man was joined on the steps by an auburn-haired girl with equally stunning bone structure and an incredible figure, accentuated by the tight brown jodhpurs and fitted white silk shirt she was wearing.

'No idea,' said the young man.

The girl's eyes assessed Annabel's physical attributes for

23

a moment. 'I suppose you're the decorator Mama's brought down from London,' she said at last.

'I'm the interior designer, yes,' said Annabel.

'She will be pleased. At last she'll have some meaning to her life! I'm her daughter, Tania Corbett-Wynne, and this is my stepbrother Crispian.'

Annabel held out her hand. 'I'm Annabel Moss; I work for David Crosbie.'

'Classy name for a classy lady,' commented Crispian. 'Let me take your cases for you. Where's Step-mama put her, Tania?'

'On the third floor. She has the guest rooms along the corridor from me,' said Tania, shooting a swift glance at Crispian.

'In that case I'll let George take them up. No need to strain my back in the pursuit of politeness!' His eyes creased at the corners when he smiled, and as he took a case from Annabel's hand his fingers brushed lightly against hers.

'Mother's been waiting hours,' said Tania as the three of them went through the front door into the lobby that led to the hallway. It was an attractive room in its own right, the walls covered in hunting prints, the oak shelves full of trophies, cups and photographs of various family members winning prizes for riding and other sports. Riding boots and wellingtons littered the floor; a narrow marble-topped table with a vase of lilac and mimosa on it added the only touch of femininity.

'I know I'm a bit late,' apologised Annabel. 'My directions were rather vague. David got the wrong turn-off the main road.'

Tania smiled. 'I remember David Crosbie. Did he tell you he'd stayed here?'

'Yes,' said Annabel. She added calmly, 'Perhaps I'd better meet your mother now.'

'I hope you've brought some smart clothes with you,'

said Crispian as he walked away. 'We've got a small dinner party tonight, and you're making up the numbers.'

Tania laughed at the look of dismay on Annabel's face. 'Don't tell me you were expecting to eat with the servants? Interior designers are very important people in my mother's world! Come on, I'll take you over to the West Wing. Mama never ventures out of there unless forced. Probably terrified my stepfather will leap on her and demand his conjugal rights!'

As they made their way through the main part of the Hall Annabel noticed a strange smell that seemed to be made up of a mixture of woodsmoke, saddle-soap and beeswax polish. Once they were in the West Wing this vanished, replaced by the scent of sandalwood potpourri.

Tania tapped on a panelled oak door. 'It's your tame designer, Mama.'

'Please come in,' called Lady Corbett-Wynne, and Tania pushed on the door. As it swung open she rested a hand lightly on Annabel's arm. 'My stepbrother's very handsome, don't you think?'

'Yes, very,' said a startled Annabel.

'I thought you'd like him, the women all do. Well, just remember this. Keep your hands off him, he's mine, all right?'

'I've come here to work,' said Annabel, keeping her voice low so that Lady Corbett-Wynne couldn't hear.

'Oh sure, but you'll play too, everyone does at Leyton Hall. I'm only warning you not to play with Crispian. You probably wouldn't enjoy it if you did; he likes to play rough.'

'Come in,' Tania's mother repeated irritably, and her daughter drifted away, glancing back at Annabel with a deceptively sweet smile as she vanished out of sight.

The drawing room of the West Wing was beautiful. The cream walls had green-stencilled leaf designs on the upper sections and the reproduction furniture all toned perfectly. At the windows plain white linen curtains were tied back with matching green cords. The slim woman with ash-blonde hair sitting in the winged chair by the window seemed to have been designed to live in just such a room.

'Welcome to Leyton Hall,' she said, rising slowly to her feet. 'I do so hope that we can work well together.'

'I'm sure we will,' Annabel said warmly, glancing around the room.

'I'm sure we will too. David spoke very highly of you.'

Annabel sat on the sofa, and the two of them began to talk.

James Corbett-Wynne had seen Annabel arrive from his bedroom window, and like his son was pleasantly surprised by her youth and the fact that she was very attractive. She reminded him of a well-bred filly, which was the highest compliment he could pay a young woman.

The young woman with him at this moment wasn't in the least like a well-bred filly, but she was exactly the kind of girl he enjoyed. Sandra had come to work in the stables from Bracken Manor, the home of James's closest friend, and she'd come highly recommended. 'Full of enthusiasm, willing to have a go at anything,' had been Richard's exact words, and James was about to test the truth of this himself.

Sandra, a short, fair-haired girl with rounded hips and full breasts, stood in front of him in her working outfit of corduroys and check shirt and waited for him to speak.

'Settling in all right?' he asked casually, as though it was perfectly normal for an employer to interview his new groom in his bedroom.

'Very well, thank you, your lordship,' she said meekly, well aware that meekness was the last thing he was going to want of her before the interview was out.

'Good, excellent! No trouble with discipline? Miranda can be a bit of a handful.'

'She exercised very well this morning,' replied the

groom, wondering what Lord Corbett-Wynne would look like without his clothes on.

'You're a good disciplinarian yourself then, are you?'

Sandra gave a small smile. 'I like to think so, sir.'

'Excellent. Take off those clothes, let's take a look at you. Richard recommended you very highly.'

'I enjoyed my time with him,' Sandra said truthfully, her heart starting to beat more rapidly at the memory.

She peeled off her corduroys and edged her white lacy knickers down over her legs with her thumbs. Then she stood in front of Lord Corbett-Wynne clad only in her check shirt. He walked round her slowly, pausing only to run one large hand appreciatively over her rounded buttocks. 'Promising,' he murmured. 'Now the shirt.'

The groom unbuttoned the shirt and slid it off her shoulders. Beneath it she was wearing a half-cup bra that scarcely controlled her large breasts. James swallowed hard and forced himself to stand still in front of her. 'That too,' he muttered harshly.

Sandra lowered her lashes, feigning innocence in a way she knew he'd like, and then unfastened the bra before bending forward from the waist and letting it drop to the floor, leaving her breasts hanging downwards, the long nipples showing dark brown against her skin.

'Perfect,' whispered her new employer, reaching out and pulling softly on the already erect tips of the nipples. 'I've something here I'd like you to put on.' Scarcely able to wait, he drew a black leather harness out of his wardrobe. 'Hurry up!' he said sharply, and as Sandra started to put it on Lord Corbett-Wynne began to strip off his own clothes.

By the time he was naked, Sandra had managed to adjust the harness to fit her. Two thongs ran from front to back between her thighs while a leather strap encircled her body just below her hip bones. From a metal link in the middle, two more thongs led up to each of her breasts and

27

then divided to encircle them before fitting round her neck in a halter.

Her lush curves were accentuated by the tight straps. Her face was flushed with excitement while her nipples stood out proudly, eagerly awaiting whatever was to happen.

'Delicious!' muttered James, and as Sandra watched he began to pull on a black leather harness of his own. His body was heavy but firm and the straps over his large shoulders joined up with a band of leather just beneath his nipples. From the round metal circle in the middle, a leather strap continued down the middle of his abdomen until it met up with one that sat on his hips. From this join a strap similar to the one between Sandra's thighs ran between the cheeks of his bottom and up over his pubic hair. But a tiny pouch allowed his testicles to nestle comfortably there while he slid a chrome link, set in the middle of the strap, over his already hardening penis and settled it at the base of the shaft. It would enable him to maintain his erection for far longer than normal.

Finally he handed the groom a padded leather eye mask, a leather-plaited whip, and what looked to the groom like a short dog leash with a tiny leather collar at one end and a loop at the other. 'For you,' he said shortly. 'Now, let's see what you can do.'

For a moment Sandra hesitated. She'd grown used to her previous employer's ways, but had no real means of knowing whether or not this man standing in front of her, his sexual excitement clear, shared the same taste. Deciding that if he didn't she wouldn't have been recommended, she sharpened her voice.

'What would your wife say if she knew I was here?' she asked harshly.

James's penis stirred visibly. 'She'd be very annoyed,' he said softly.

'Because you were being naughty, isn't that right?'

'Yes, yes!' he said in a thick voice. 'I'm always being

naughty. That's why she won't have anything to do with me any more.' He started towards Sandra, his hands reaching for her temptingly heavy breasts, but she flicked her whip lightly across his exposed abdomen and he stopped with a swift intake of breath.

'Don't move until I say you can,' she said firmly. Then she took the padded eye mask, climbed onto the end of the vast bed and signalled for Lord Corbett-Wynne to move towards her. He immediately obeyed, turning his back so that she could slip the covering over his eyes. Once he was in darkness his excitement increased and a tiny drop of clear fluid appeared at the tip of his straining penis.

Sandra knew then that this man was no different from Richard in his needs and desires and gave a small sigh of satisfaction. She would be happy in her employment, and secure too. Men like this hated change in women, the journey from passivity to authority.

'Use the leash,' muttered the naked man in front of her.

'Be quiet,' she said shortly, privately wondering what on earth she was meant to do with it, and then as he thrust his hips forward slightly, she realised. Stepping down from the bed she strapped the collar-like end round his erection just beneath the swollen glans and then grasping the other end in her hand, tugged lightly on it, leading him round the room as she would a horse.

He was breathing heavily now, and after a moment Sandra raised the leather-plaited whip and brought it down in a swift stinging blow across his shoulders. He groaned with excitement and reached blindly for her, his heavy arms making contact so that he was able to pull her towards him. Then his face was nuzzling desperately at her exposed breasts and she felt his tongue sweeping upwards until it located a nipple. Once it was found he drew it into his mouth and sucked, gently at first but with increasing pressure, and Sandra grew damp against the thongs between her thighs.

His teeth grazed the nipple in his excitement and she knew that he must be stopped – that was what he would expect, even though she really wanted him to continue. 'How dare you?' she demanded, flicking the whip at him and pushing him off with all her strength.

'Let me! Let me!' he choked, lunging forward again, but she stepped backwards and tugged on the strap attached to his penis, pulling it down from where it was resting against his lower belly.

'Aah!' sighed the Lord of Leyton Hall in blissful satisfaction.

Sandra's own body was beginning to throb with sexual desire. She loved this as much as the men did and just wished that her satisfaction counted for more, although at the end it was always worth the wait. Still leading her prisoner by the leash she moved towards the bed and lay on her back. 'You may use your mouth on me,' she said crisply, 'but only your mouth. If you use anything else you'll be punished again. Is that clear?'

'Quite clear,' agreed James, delighted at the girl's understanding of the complexities of the game, and then he was using his tongue on her outspread legs, working slowly up the inner calves and around the backs of her knees. Finally he managed to crouch awkwardly on the bed so that he was able to lick and suck at the tender creases of her inner thighs.

Sandra's body started to tremble. He was better than Richard had been, more subtle, and she felt herself swelling with excitement, but then one of his hands tried to push at the straps covering her sex and she hastily brought the whip down over his back. 'No hands!' she reminded him.

'But I can't reach you!' protested her employer.

'Later,' she assured him, and reluctantly he moved on up her body until eventually every available inch of flesh was damp from his skilful ministrations. When his tongue swirled inside her ear she could hardly stand the waiting any longer herself.

'Hands as well,' she conceded and at once his large hands were moving blindly over her, cupping her heavy breasts and at the same time he moved further up the bed until he was able to angle his painfully hard penis between them and then he started to massage her breasts against his erection, almost sobbing with excitement.

Sandra's breasts were tight and tingling and she could feel the leather straps between her legs growing more and more damp. She desperately longed to be touched there, to have the straps pushed aside and feel her employer's clever tongue against her straining flesh. But that wasn't part of the rules.

Lord Corbett-Wynne was rapidly approaching the point of no return. The tip of his penis was throbbing and his testicles felt tight in their leather pouch. Just before he passed that point Sandra pulled unexpectedly on the leash, jerking his manhood upwards and away from the stimulation of her magnificent breasts.

'No!' he shouted furiously. 'I was ready then.'

'Well, I wasn't,' said Sandra coolly, relishing her role and aware that if she could dominate him even more than he'd expected she might well be able to reach a powerful position in his house. 'I want you to stimulate me more first. Remove the straps between my thighs.'

'I can't,' he muttered. 'I've still got the blindfold on.'

'I expect you to do it with the blindfold on,' she said calmly. 'What's more, I expect it to be done quickly.' And with that she flicked him again with the whip.

James Corbett-Wynne wasn't sure that he liked this turn of events. He'd been so close to satisfaction that his testicles were now exceedingly painful and all he wanted to do was come between the girl's magnificent breasts.

The whip flicked over his back once more, but this time it didn't just sting, it hurt, and he felt a surge of almost unbearable arousal, greater than anything he'd had for a long time. 'Hurry up!' Sandra said irritably.

He knew that this was as an important moment. If he did as she said and let her dictate the way the game went, then he would be in her power. But it was so deliciously thrilling that he hardly hesitated for a moment and as he reached blindly down her body, fumbling for the metal loop that held her straps in place, he knew that he was lost.

Once he'd managed to unfasten the thongs he turned himself round on the bed until he was poised above her, facing her feet. Carefully he lowered himself to take his weight on his elbows and then he reached under her thighs and pulled them apart.

Sandra sighed with satisfaction as she felt him opening her outer sex lips and immediately he began kissing the entire vulval area, his lips teasing her moist, needy flesh. She shivered as she felt a climax beginning to build and then his tongue was swirling around her clitoris, flicking against the side of the tiny stem before stabbing more firmly along her inner channel.

Her hips began to move of their own accord and her body brushed against his. He moaned in protest, terrified that he might come before she gave him permission and aware that, if he did, unlike her predecessor this girl wouldn't hesitate to punish him.

Then, as the long-awaited pressure built steadily in Sandra, her employer slid two fingers into her vagina while at the same time drawing her clitoris into his mouth and letting his teeth graze very softly against the incredibly sensitive bud.

With a wild scream of satisfaction Sandra's body exploded into a climax and as she bucked wildly beneath him she reached up and closed her right hand around his thick, swollen member. He gasped, and when she moved her hand rapidly up and down he tried to move so that he could come over her breasts, but she wouldn't let him and he was forced to stay where he was as his orgasm rushed through him and the thick white liquid spilled out of the crimson glans and fell onto Sandra's still trembling belly.

As soon as he'd finished James tore off his blindfold and climbed off the bed. He didn't look at the groom lying replete on his bed but started to remove his harness and dress again. 'Hurry up and get back to the stables,' he said shortly. 'You might be missed.'

'Yes, your lordship,' said Sandra, meekly aware that at this moment he would want her gone as quickly as possible. But she knew that she'd soon be sent for again, and intended to keep him in thrall for as long as possible.

Once the door had closed softly behind her, Lord Corbett-Wynne sank down on his bed. Richard had been right. This girl was something special.

Sandra walked along the corridor well satisfied physically and mentally. She scarcely noticed Annabel, who was making her way to her room after her talk with Lady Corbett-Wynne, but Annabel noticed her and wondered what one of the grooms was doing wandering around on the third floor.

Because her head was still full of the ideas they'd been discussing it took Annabel a few minutes to really appreciate her bedroom, which at first glance seemed cold and sparsely furnished. However, there was a made-up fire in the grate, which she decided she'd have lit in the evening, and the bed was a gleaming imitation Jacobean four-poster, the wood warm and well polished. The one window in the room was set in a tiled alcove and through the tiny latticed panes she could see the courtyard where some of the horses were being returned to their stables.

The carpet had once been rich-coloured and thick, but it was now thin and dull, as were the brocade chair and day-bed. Although vast, her wardrobe looked to be on its last legs and she found she had trouble closing the doors.

The ceiling was covered in a giant mural depicting a hunt in full cry. It was beautifully painted and at first she didn't notice that several of the ladies on horseback were bare-chested and exceptionally well endowed. She looked more closely and made out figures apparently copulating in the bracken as the hunt went by. 'Bizarre!' she muttered to herself, wondering who'd chosen to ruin the decoration with such a tasteless touch.

A small door at the far side of the room led down two steps into a bathroom that took her breath away. It was tiny, but the rich wood panels gleamed in the light of the candles that surrounded the old fashioned deep basin and mirrored shelf, while a three-sided copper bath fitted into the far corner. A crimson Persian rug covered the strip of floor between the bath and the basin, and ruby red towels hung over heated rails beneath the small rectangular window. Annabel hoped that Lady Corbett-Wynne didn't intend to try to modernise this room. It was quite perfect.

Returning to the bedroom she took her notebook out of her briefcase and started to jot down the main points of their conversation. She'd only just begun when there was a knock on the door.

'Yes?' called Annabel.

'It's me, Tania,' came the reply. 'May I come in?'

Annabel opened the door. 'Please do. I was just admiring the bathroom.'

Tania smiled. 'Great, isn't it! Crispian and I have some fun in there with our visitors, I can tell you.'

Annabel didn't quite know how to reply. 'Was there something you wanted?' she asked after a pause.

'Crispian wondered if you'd like to join us for afternoon tea. Dinner won't be until nine tonight, it helps stave off the hunger pangs.'

'Sounds lovely,' agreed Annabel.

'Wonderful! We'll be in the music room, that's on the first floor, second on the left when you reach the bottom of the stairs. Don't bother to change, Crispian adores businesswomen in suits.'

Annabel hadn't thought of her long-line caramel jacket

worn over a short skirt and beige blouse as a suit and immediately felt over-dressed, particularly in comparison with Tania, who had changed into a short, pale-blue A-line dress, was bare-legged and had a pair of scruffy trainers on her feet.

'What about tonight?' she asked. 'Is dress formal then?'

'Frightfully formal. We've got a new neighbour, Sir Matthew Stevens, a widower, coming over, and Step-papa's bound to want to impress him. I can't imagine why. He's new money too.'

'New money?'

Tania smiled. 'Sure, you know, he made a fortune exploiting the masses and got knighted for services to industry. Not much different to Crispian's grandfather who was given Leyton Hall in return for donating enormous chunks of his ill-gotten wealth to charity. You didn't think we'd lived here for generations, I hope? If so, you've been brought here under false pretences. My mother's the genuine article. That's why she's so neurotic I expect, generations of inbreeding, but Step-papa's a very different story.'

'Oh!' Annabel said feebly. She was fascinated, but didn't think that Tania should really be telling her all this, especially as she'd only just arrived. 'Your mother's got exquisite taste,' she said quickly. 'Her ideas for the Hall are lovely.'

'Sure, but her taste let her down when she chose her second husband, don't you think? No, better not answer that, after all he can always send you packing if he doesn't like the way you do things. Mother might pay the bills but the house belongs to him! See you in a few minutes, right?'

'Right,' agreed Annabel, somewhat overwhelmed by the auburn-haired girl's flow of conversation.

It was nearly twenty minutes before she made her way to the music room as it took longer than she'd expected to write up her notes. When she pushed open the door she didn't notice the grand piano at the opposite end, or the numerous antiques that littered the rather battered tables and sideboards around the room, because her whole attention fastened on to what was happening in the middle of the room.

Tania and her stepbrother were locked in a passionate embrace, their heads together as they kissed with all the pent-up hunger of lovers who'd been kept apart for years.

They didn't hear Annabel come in. While they'd been waiting Crispian had mentioned that he thought Annabel was very attractive. Tania's response had been to throw one of her temper tantrums, and as usual he'd only been able to stop her by taking her in his arms, but once he'd done this his feelings had taken over and now all he was aware of was her mouth.

At the first touch of his soft, supple lips against hers Tania had gone weak at the knees, and then he'd sucked gently on her lower lip until he'd felt her tongue pressing against his mouth, delicately insistent as she tried to run it over his teeth.

He parted his lips to let her and almost at once their tongues were locked in a familiar erotic battle, Crispian allowing his tongue to probe in and out of her mouth in a gradually increasing rhythm that made Tania remember the way he would penetrate her between her thighs. Sighing, she wrapped her arms round his neck and he began to kiss the corners of her eyes, the tip of her nose, the lobes of her ears and then finally, blissfully he moved his mouth to the side of her neck and nipped tenderly at the exposed flesh.

Tania's legs started to shake and when his arms began to stroke her hips and buttocks through the fabric of her dress she edged backwards towards the settee, suddenly desperate for a quick, urgent coupling. It was then that Annabel, standing red-faced and silent in the doorway, cleared her throat.

Tania groaned in annoyance as Crispian gently released her and turned to greet the newcomer. 'Annabel!' he said.

'Sorry, completely forgot you were joining us for tea. Have a seat. Tania, ring the bell for Susan, there's an angel.'

'I'd rather have a stiff brandy,' muttered Tania, her whole body hot with desire.

Crispian smiled at the discomforted Annabel. 'Found your way all right then?'

'Er, yes,' responded Annabel, uncertain whether she was more shocked by what she'd seen or the way her own body had responded to it. Her breasts felt tight against her blouse and her mouth seemed swollen, as though Crispian's lips had bruised them with his passion.

He saw her bright eyes and the delicate stain of pink on her cheeks and knew that he'd have her before she left Leyton Hall. No doubt she'd only be a diversion, but an interesting one, and he'd enjoy telling Tania about it. Their sex together was always given extra spice when he was bedding another woman.

The maid arrived with the tea and plates of sandwiches and cakes. Crispian ate hungrily but neither Tania nor Annabel had much appetite and both of them had difficulty in holding their cups steady.

'What does your boyfriend think about you spending three weeks with us?' asked Tania, her eyes cold.

'I'm fancy-free at the moment,' confessed Annabel. 'My work takes up most of my energy these days.'

'What a waste,' murmured Crispian. 'Tania and I always find time for play.' He grinned boyishly and Annabel found it impossible not to smile back at him.

Tania crossed her legs, revealing thighs that, although slender, were surprisingly muscular. 'Do you ride?' she asked.

Annabel shook her head. 'I've never tried, but I don't like horses very much, or dogs either,' she added, noticing that the two bassets she'd seen on her arrival had now come into the room.

'I hope Dopey and Dozey don't bother you?' laughed Crispian. 'They wouldn't hurt a fly.'

'They certainly look harmless,' agreed Annabel, still trying to rid her mind of the image of this slender fair-haired young man locked in such a torrid embrace with his own stepsister.

'They're more reliable than men,' retorted Tania.

'The visitor tonight,' said Annabel. 'What's he like?'

'Out of your league,' drawled Tania. 'He's in his mid-forties, I should think, and definitely a man of the world. Quite attractive really, tall with lots of brown curly hair and one of those interesting faces that make you think he's seen and done almost everything.'

'Sounds fascinating,' said Annabel.

'Not to me!' exclaimed Crispian. 'I hate competition.'

'I've seen him a couple of times when I've been out riding,' explained Tania. 'I wouldn't mind trying him out.'

Annabel glanced at Crispian to see what he thought of this, but he didn't seem very interested. 'Pa was interviewing his new groom this afternoon, Tania,' he said after a pause. 'I hope she was up to the mark!'

As Tania laughed, Annabel remembered the girl in corduroys that she'd seen walking along the corridor on the way to her bedroom. 'Does your father have an office on the same floor as our bedrooms?' she asked with interest. 'If so, I think I must have seen the girl.'

Tania giggled.

'He interviews them in his bedroom,' said Crispian, looking directly into Annabel's eyes. 'He has special requirements of the grooms, and that's the only place he can really test them out.'

Annabel understood him, but his words made her stomach move in a strange way that was rather pleasant. She'd had the same feeling when watching Tania and Crispian together. 'Really,' she said calmly, hoping he couldn't tell how much all this was disturbing her.

'Not shocked, are you? My stepmother won't let him near her, he has to get his pleasure somewhere.'

'Yes, of course. Well, anyway, it really isn't any of my business,' Annabel said stiffly.

'What kind of men do you like?' asked Tania.

'I don't think I've got a particular type,' mused Annabel. 'Most of my boyfriends have been quite tall, but apart from that they didn't have anything in common.'

'I hope they were all good in bed,' remarked Crispian.

This time Annabel couldn't stop herself from blushing. 'Most of them,' she murmured, trying to sound as casual as he and his stepsister did about all this.

'You always get a few who are no good, it's such a bore,' murmured Tania. 'I wish men came labelled, marks out of ten or something. That way you could save such a lot of energy finding out for yourself, don't you agree?'

'I suppose so, yes.'

Crispian stood up. 'I think I'll have a sleep before I get ready for dinner tonight. Meetings about the estate exhaust me. How about you, Tania?'

'I'm not sleepy,' Tania said slowly, 'but I wouldn't mind a lie-down.'

Annabel swallowed hard. 'I really ought to have another word with Lady Corbett-Wynne before dinner.'

'Fine, run along then,' said Crispian. 'Just make sure you're there for dinner. I can't wait to see you in an evening dress. They're so feminine. It's hard to make out what you're really like under that efficient suit!' He laughed, and when Tania started to laugh as well, Annabel left them.

As soon as she'd gone Tania turned to her stepbrother. 'Let's go upstairs,' she said huskily. 'If I have to wait any longer I'll die, I swear it.'

Crispian took her hand and drew her against him. 'Me too. Do you think we shocked our visitor?'

'Who cares, she's only an employee anyway.'

'True, but a very attractive one. Your room or mine?'

'Yours,' said Tania. 'I want to use the frame.'

Once they were in Crispian's bedroom Tania stripped

39

off her dress and G-string, the only undergarment she was wearing, while Crispian fetched the frame. He'd built this himself from spare wood found around the stable block when it was being modernised. It sat on the floor but arched over the foot of the bed.

Tania lay on her back on the bed and then her step-brother eased the frame beneath her lower body, strapping her legs into stirrups before sliding a pillow beneath her hips. Knowing that once the game was underway she might start to struggle he also took the precaution of fastening her wrists to the far corners of his bed with long silk scarves. Then he drew a chair up to the foot of the bed just behind the frame, his eyes level with her exposed sex.

For several minutes he sat and studied her in silence while Tania trembled gently with excitement. Her whole body felt hot and ready to explode, but sensing this he refrained from touching her at all which drove her wild.

'Start!' she screamed. 'Don't just look at me.'

'I like looking,' he murmured, reaching out one hand and tugging very lightly on her lower pubic hair. The movement of flesh caused by this touch sent tiny tingles of arousal up through Tania's lower abdomen and she whimpered with need.

With a low laugh Crispian allowed both hands to touch her, tenderly taking hold of her outer sex lips and pulling them apart to expose the shining pink inner tissue. The cool air brushed against her heat and Tania made a guttural sound of contentment, which quickly turned into a wail as he allowed her sex lips to close again.

'Do keep your voice down,' he said in amusement. 'I'm sure Annabel wouldn't be so vocal in her enjoyment.'

'Touch me!' shouted Tania, squirming against the frame beneath her and trying to force her vulva nearer to his clever hands.

Crispian leant forward and slid his hands up over her abdomen and then down again before once more opening and closing her outer sex lips. She was quaking now, her whole body racked with desire, but she knew that he could make the game last an eternity if he wanted and this knowledge made her need all the sharper.

Crispian let his hands travel upwards over her body again, but this time he lifted her breasts and then rolled the large nipples between his fingers. As Tania's breathing grew ragged he pressed her breasts together and drew his flat tongue across each nipple in turn, moving from left to right in slow, steady sweeps until her breasts were swollen and throbbing with excitement.

Just as she was about to climax from this stimulation alone, Crispian stopped and sat down in his chair again, leaving her frantic for further touches on her needy breasts. Now he turned his attention back to the area between her thighs. Bending his head, he licked her inner thighs, letting his tongue linger in the creases of the joins, and then he reached for a vibrator and held it high in the air.

'Would you like me to use this, Tania?' he teased as she squirmed helplessly on the frame, her legs unable to move.

'Yes!' she gasped.

'Where?'

'Anywhere,' she shouted, knowing that if she chose her favourite place he'd only ignore her and use it somewhere else.

'Anywhere?' he queried, and then he was letting it touch the tightly stretched skin of her arms and she shrieked at him in frustration. 'No, not there!'

'Sshh!' he cautioned her. 'Pa might hear.'

'I don't care if he does,' she groaned.

'Well, I do, so keep quiet,' said Crispian, and then she felt him parting her outer sex lips again and this time he let the head of the slender vibrator move in tiny circles just above her frantic clitoris.

Tania felt as though he was applying an electric current to her as shockwaves of delight coursed through her and the familiar tight knot of an impending climax began to form behind her clitoris. He allowed the vibrator to play in the same spot until she was gasping, urging herself on in the climb towards release, but just as she was about to come he removed the stimulation and the delicious tremors slowly faded, leaving Tania close to tears of frustration.

Crispian was enjoying himself. He always liked having Tania strapped to the frame and at his mercy, but today it was even more exciting because he was imagining having Annabel in the same position some time soon.

Leaning forward he opened up his stepsister once more and this time he let his tongue run up and down her soaking inner channel, now and again easing the clitoral hood back so that he could flick the stiff tip of his tongue directly against it. Each time he did this Tania's legs went rigid in the stirrups and her eyes started to roll back with ecstasy, but he never allowed her to topple over into an orgasm.

For Tania the thrilling torture was almost unbearable and she could hear herself screaming at him to hurry and let her come, but the more she screamed the slower he worked. Just when she felt certain that she couldn't bear the relentless teasing a moment longer, Crispian lubricated one finger with some soothing jelly and slid a hand beneath Tania's bottom. Then he let his tongue slide in and out of her incredibly moist opening while his lubricated finger moved in and out of her back passage in exactly the same rhythm.

Now the tightness was all over Tania's body and her breasts were so swollen she felt as though they might burst unless she came quickly. Her neck was covered with a pink flush of arousal and there were beads of perspiration between her heavy breasts.

Keeping his tongue and finger working together, Crispian let his spare hand slide up his stepsister's rippling belly until it reached her left breast. He massaged it softly for a moment and then his fingers gripped the nipple hard and he extended it as far as possible, still massaging it firmly.

For Tania this final touch was all that she needed. Now it felt as though the electric current between her thighs had joined with another one from her breasts; every muscle in her body seemed to bunch and coil before finally exploding as his tongue swirled round and round inside her. As the climax gripped her, Crispian felt her internal muscles tighten around his tongue and the walls of her rectum clenched violently as he slid a second finger inside her there.

Tania was only aware of the fact that Crispian was filling her everywhere, either with his hands or his tongue, and she screamed with delirious delight at the shattering explosion he'd finally allowed to course through her.

When she'd finished she waited for him to unfasten her from the frame, but instead he stood up and let his trousers fall to the floor as he pushed himself into her, moving hard against the tender flesh, his hands gripping her fastened hips.

'I want you to come again, when I do,' he muttered.

'I can't!' wailed Tania.

Muffling a curse, Crispian slid his hand across her body until it was resting on her pubic bone. Then he allowed his fingers to stray lower and as his own orgasm approached he beat a slow steady tattoo just above her still-swollen nub and immediately she felt her body racked by a second climax. Crispian threw his head back in triumph as he felt her contracting around him at the exact moment that he came.

Along the corridor, Annabel heard his shout of triumph and wondered what the noise was.

Chapter Three

At eight-thirty in the evening, Annabel heard a gong sound in the distance. Assuming that this was intended to summon them downstairs, she left her bedroom and walked straight into Crispian, who was coming out of Tania's room, adjusting his cufflinks. The conventional dinner suit accentuated his fair good looks and Annabel wondered briefly what he'd be like as a lover.

He looked at her appreciatively. 'Very nice,' he murmured, his eyes approving as he took in her bronze-coloured silk taffeta dress with thin shoulder straps, and a neckline that left her upper chest entirely bare. Two large imitation roses covered her breasts and the bodice of the dress was fitted at the waist before flaring out into a full skirt.

'Those roses wouldn't be large enough for Tania, but they look great on you!' he said with a laugh. 'Let me take you down. We have drinks in the library before dinner.'

'What about Tania?' asked Annabel.

Crispian chuckled. 'Tania's late as usual! She's only just getting dressed. At the moment her look is definitely what you might call sexily tousled.'

His blue eyes stared into Annabel's and she had a

sudden image of the pair of them entwined on a bed, their fine-boned limbs writhing in ecstasy. When Crispian put a hand on her bare arm she jumped with surprise.

'Daydreaming?' he enquired as they walked down the stairs.

'I'm afraid so. It's a fault of mine.'

'About the house, or its occupants?'

Annabel glanced at him from beneath lowered lids. 'The house, of course. Why would I daydream about the occupants?'

'Why indeed? Pure conceit on my part; I was hoping you might be daydreaming about me.'

The library was rather a shock to Annabel. It was small, cluttered and in total chaos. Books were stacked untidily on the shelves and a small stepladder had been left resting against them. The once-splendid carpet was again threadbare, and holes in the sofa and chairs had been disguised by the simple tactic of throwing lion skins, complete with their heads, over them.

In the midst of this mess Lady Corbett-Wynne looked totally out of place. She was wearing a pale-blue crepe and silk organza evening dress which had a wide shawl collar, tightly fitting long sleeves with large, turned-back cuffs, and a tight waistband that emphasised her slim figure. The skirt hung in long folds to the floor and her only jewellery was an emerald necklace, and what looked to Annabel like a chain of emeralds and diamonds that she'd fastened to the waist of the dress. This hung half-way down her skirt, rather like an old-fashioned chatelaine's key chain. Her fair hair was drawn back off her face and fastened with a diamond clip.

'There should be rushes on the floor,' Crispian whispered in Annabel's ear. 'Don't you think she looks like one of those historical ladies of the manor?'

'I think she looks beautiful,' Annabel whispered truthfully, wondering what on earth this withdrawn, aristocratic looking woman could possibly have in common

45

with her large, florid-faced husband standing next to her, who apparently enjoyed the attentions of his girl grooms.

'Where's Tania?' Lady Corbett-Wynne asked sharply.

'No idea,' replied Crispian. 'I thought I ought to bring Annabel down, since no one had thought to tell her where we met up.'

'Very good of you, my boy,' said his father, glancing uneasily at his wife. He then walked towards Annabel, his hand outstretched. 'Don't think we've met yet. Lord Corbett-Wynne, the man whose home you're planning to tear apart.'

'I hope you don't really believe that,' replied Annabel. 'Your wife wants me to help her redecorate some of the rooms, but I'd never do anything to spoil the atmosphere of the Hall.'

'Then you can leave this room alone,' he said shortly. 'This is my favourite place. Somewhere a man can come and think.'

'I didn't know you did much of that, Pa!' laughed Crispian. 'Annabel, what can I get you?'

'Sherry, please.'

He crossed the room to the drinks cabinet, which looked like an old-fashioned gramophone box but opened up to reveal numerous bottles. 'Any particular sherry?'

'Amontillado if you've got it.'

'Drink is one thing we're very well-stocked with, isn't that right, Step-mama?'

Lady Corbett-Wynne flushed. 'I'm sure I don't know. It's your father who's the drinker around here.'

'Damned shame you don't drink more,' said her husband. 'Might loosen you up a bit.'

His wife shot him an icy glance, but at that moment the door opened and the maid announced the arrival of Sir Matthew Stevens. Sherry glass in hand, Annabel turned to look at the dinner guest and at her very first glance her stomach tightened and she felt a pulse beating in the side of her neck.

46

She had no idea why. He wasn't conventionally handsome and his brown curly hair had one or two threads of silver in it. But his face was tanned and rugged and there was a sense of great strength and masculinity about him that she found almost irresistible. As he walked towards Lady Corbett-Wynne and started to greet her, he brushed against Annabel's skirt. For a brief moment he turned to look at her. His grey eyes were unfathomable, but when he gave her a swift impersonal smile she felt ridiculously pleased, like a child given an unexpected present.

Crispian watched Annabel closely. He recognised the signs of physical attraction immediately, and although surprised – he couldn't see anything all that special about the newcomer – he'd heard rumours about the man's success with women and Annabel's response made it plain that these were most likely true.

Matthew himself was hardly aware of Annabel at their initial meeting. He was far more interested in Lady Corbett-Wynne. Her delicate appearance intrigued him, as did the cool exterior she presented to the world. Always eager for a challenge, he felt that to break down her resistance, and capture her so that he could feel her slenderness against him, actually physically penetrate the facade she used like a shield against men, would give him tremendous satisfaction. And if he was any judge of women it would bring equal delight to her.

None of this was apparent in his polite greeting, but he let his eyes hold hers for a fraction longer than necessary and once he'd been handed his drink he stood very slightly closer to her than she might have expected.

Despite remaining calm and serene, Lady Corbett-Wynne was experiencing very similar sensations to Annabel's, except that she didn't recognise them for what they were and wondered if she was ill. Her stomach was turning in a decidedly uncomfortable manner and her mouth was strangely dry.

'I'm afraid my daughter's a little late, Sir Matthew,' she apologised. 'It's a fault of hers.'

He smiled. 'I've seen your daughter out riding. Any girl as attractive as that is automatically forgiven for being late.'

'Unfortunately she relies on that,' responded his hostess. 'I've tried to teach her manners, but she simply refuses to believe that they matter.'

'You should use your time teaching her some morals,' muttered Lord Corbett-Wynne.

His wife turned her head sharply towards him. 'Crispian of course has no need for such guidance?'

Before he could reply the door opened and Tania came into the room. It was quite an entrance, Annabel conceded to herself. She was beautifully made up, her eyes well-defined with kohl and her lips carefully shaped with pencil and lipstick into a cupid's bow, but it was the dress that really took everyone's breath away. Ruby-red in colour, it seemed to match the lighter tones of her auburn hair, which was sleeked back for the evening, and the sheer old-fashioned glamour of the satin bias-cut dress with diamanté clasps and halter neck was stunning.

Lady Corbett-Wynne, however, seemed oblivious of the impact her daughter's entrance had made. 'You're late,' she said coldly.

'Sorry, Mother,' said Tania, her tone of voice making it clear that she wasn't. 'It took me ages to wash my hair and bath, someone had used all the hot water, as usual. I think you should get the plumbing in this place seen to before you start on the decorations.'

'Well, since you are here I'd like to introduce you to –'

'We've already met,' interrupted Tania.

'When?' asked her mother.

'When I was out riding. Isn't that right, Sir Matthew.'

Annabel noticed that, although Sir Matthew nodded and smiled in agreement, he wasn't quite as appreciative of

Tania as might have been expected, and quickly turned his attention back to her mother.

Tania didn't like this. 'God, I could use a drink. Isn't anyone going to offer me one?'

'Dinner's ready,' said her stepfather. 'We've all been waiting for you.'

'I'm sure you can wait five more minutes while I have a quick gin. Crispian, be an angel and pour me one, would you?'

'How could I refuse?' he asked with a lopsided smile. His father and stepmother glanced briefly at one another. And Annabel wondered if they were both aware of how close their offspring really were.

'Even if you know my stepsister, I don't suppose anyone's thought to introduce you to Annabel,' murmured Crispian as he poured out Tania's gin.

'How rude of me,' said his stepmother, turning towards the waiting Annabel. 'Sir Matthew, I'd like you to meet Annabel Moss. She works for David Crosbie and comes highly recommended by him. You've probably heard of David?'

'Good heavens, yes. I knew him a few years ago. We ran with the same crowd but then I moved away. I haven't seen him now for about three years or more. Is he still with Martin?' he asked Annabel as he lightly took her outstretched hand.

'Yes, yes, he is,' she said in a low voice, hoping that he couldn't feel the way her hand was trembling in his. It was utterly ridiculous, and she didn't know what was the matter with her, but all she wanted was to get this man into bed with her, to feel his strong, capable hands on her breasts, thighs, and buttocks. She'd heard of instant physical attraction, but never believed in it. Now she knew that it could happen. The only trouble was, he clearly didn't feel the same.

'Good. What are you planning to do with the Hall?'

'I really don't know yet. I only arrived this afternoon

and although Lady Corbett-Wynne and I discussed some provisional ideas, they were just a starting point.'

'I'm sure her taste will prove impeccable,' replied Sir Matthew. He then turned away from Annabel and started talking to his hostess again.

'Bad luck!' whispered Crispian as he passed behind Annabel. 'It seems he likes the more mature woman!'

Annabel flushed, mortified that anyone had realised how she felt.

'Do come along,' Lord Corbett-Wynne said irritably. 'I'm famished and Susan told us dinner was ready over ten minutes ago.'

'Sorry, Step-papa,' drawled Tania. They all moved towards the door.

The dining room was large and dark. Old family portraits adorned the walls and the suspended lights over the dark mahogany dining table had navy-blue shades with gold braids over them. Annabel found herself seated between Lord Corbett-Wynne and Sir Matthew, which rather pleased her, with Tania and Crispian opposite her.

The damask table cloth was immaculate and the pure crystal glasses shone, while the eighteenth-century pistol-handled cutlery added a wonderful touch. Small vases of freesias were placed along the centre of the table and their scent drifted in the air, masking the musty odour that seemed to be present in all the rooms of the Hall.

The first course was delicious, smoked salmon in saffron aspic, and was accompanied by an excellent Chablis. Annabel found that the presence of Sir Matthew on her right seemed to have removed her appetite but she managed to force most of the light fish down.

'Tell me what you think of my place then,' said Lord Corbett-Wynne as Sir Matthew talked softly and intimately to the lord's wife. 'Like it?'

'I think it's got tremendous character,' said Annabel with total honesty. 'I'd want to keep the atmosphere too. I had thought in terms of very subtly shaded surfaces and

I'd use artificially faded fabrics, anything too obviously new would clash horribly.'

'Do you admire Marina's wing?' he demanded abruptly.

'I like the French romantic style,' Annabel said carefully, 'but it has to be used in the right rooms.'

'Seems to keep her happy. She's a romantic type of woman, of course. Are you?' He pushed his face close to Annabel's.

'I don't think so,' responded Annabel, who felt anything but romantic with her sexual desire for Sir Matthew occupying every spare thought.

'Glad to hear it. Ruins everything that does. She's not a physical woman, you see,' he added, dropping his voice. 'Now me, I'm very physical. I have needs, if you take my meaning.'

Remembering his son's comments, Annabel took his meaning only too well, but she kept her face expressionless and didn't answer him.

'A man needs someone to warm his bed now and again,' persisted her host, his hand reaching beneath the tablecloth and gripping her left knee tightly.

Annabel glanced down the table to where Lady Corbett-Wynne was sitting but she was still in intimate conversation with Sir Matthew and totally oblivious to anyone else at the table. As Annabel moved her legs to one side her right foot pressed against Sir Matthew's. Although he continued to keep his gaze on his hostess Annabel felt the pressure returned softly.

'Not engaged, are you?' asked Lord Corbett-Wynne, draining his glass of Chablis and refilling it before the waiting maidservant had the opportunity.

'No,' said Annabel with a polite smile. 'I think perhaps I'm too fussy.'

'Doesn't do, doesn't do! It's astonishing the number of women I've bedded who've turned out to be extraordinary once you got them going. Be more adventurous, my dear, that's my advice to you.'

Across the table Crispian looked at Annabel and grinned. 'Ignore him; he's only hoping you might decide to try the more mature man. Isn't that right, Pa?'

Annabel shifted uneasily in her seat, still worried about Lady Corbett-Wynne. Crispian understood her fear. He leant across the table, narrowly avoiding knocking over one of the vases of freesias. 'Don't worry about Stepmama, she couldn't care less what he does as long as he leaves her alone. Besides, it seems she's having a good time for once in her life.'

Annabel could see that for herself. She only wished it wasn't with the first man to have literally set her own pulse racing.

The second course was rather over-cooked pheasant, served with parsnips, carrots, and game chips. The vegetables were horribly undercooked and this time Annabel could scarcely eat more than a few mouthfuls.

'Not hungry?' asked Sir Matthew as the plates were removed.

'Not really.'

'You ought to take more exercise. Are you naturally pale, or is it the company?' he asked with a smile.

'I'm always pale. In fact I only get colour in my cheeks when I've got a temperature.'

He looked thoughtfully at her. 'I'm sure I could bring some colour to them without making you ill in the process.'

Annabel knew that he could, she only wished that he'd put his hand on her knee as Lord Corbett-Wynne had done. But he didn't, contenting himself instead with resting his hand on the top of Annabel's arm. 'You must come and look over my place before you go. Some of the ground-floor rooms are in a sorry state. I'd like your advice on them.'

'With pleasure,' responded Annabel. 'I'll be here for at least three weeks, so there's no rush.'

'Well, don't leave it until the last minute. We might need

to spend a little time discussing things,' he said quietly. Then his fingers travelled in a slow line down her arm and over her hand before he picked up his spoon for the dessert.

After that he spent the rest of the meal talking to his hostess again. Annabel began to wonder, as she fended off more and more suggestive remarks from her host, whether this was the way the family always behaved or if the presence of Sir Matthew had brought about some kind of change.

After the delicious fig-fritters, the men tucked into stilton and port but Annabel sat back and sipped at her orange muscat dessert wine. This wine was new to her and she decided she'd get David to try it.

At last the meal was over, and they withdrew to the library again for coffee, although now the evening was clearly drawing to a close and Tania kept looking at her watch.

'What's the matter?' whispered Crispian as he passed behind her. 'Are you bored?'

'A bit. Mother hogged Sir Matthew's attention, and you hardly said a word to me,' she hissed.

'How can I when Pa's about? You know how he feels about us! Tell you what, why don't we go to the stables later, have ourselves a different kind of party?'

Tania's eyes gleamed. 'Even better, why don't you get our house guest to come along and look at the horses? She's pretty worked up already. I think Sir Matthew's had an effect on her. She might even enjoy herself once we persuade her to join in!'

Crispian looked startled. 'Is that wise? Suppose she says something to your mother?'

Tania's lip curled. 'Not scared, are you? What could she say? That she'd joined us for a threesome and felt Mama ought to know?'

Crispian could feel his own excitement growing, but it was always this way with Tania. She didn't seem to have

53

any sense of self-preservation, and sometimes he wondered what would become of them both.

'Go on,' Tania urged him. 'It will be fun.'

'Okay,' he said swiftly. 'Leave it to me. You go on ahead in about twenty minutes, get things prepared, and then I'll bring her round a bit later on and we can "bump into each other"!'

Tania laughed excitedly. 'Heavenly!'

'Crispian, I thought you were going to fetch another bottle of port,' said his father. It was evident that he was irritated.

Crispian deliberately caught Annabel's eye and gave her an intimate smile. 'Sorry, Pa, forgot. Annabel, let me show you where our cellar is.'

'Annabel doesn't need to know her way to the cellar,' Lady Corbett-Wynne said sharply. 'I'm sure she has no interest in it whatsoever.'

Annabel hadn't, but the blood coursing through her veins had more than a passing interest in Crispian, especially since it was plain that for this evening at least, Sir Matthew's charms were being directed at his hostess and not his fellow guest.

When Tania finally slipped out of the room only her stepfather noticed her go, and he merely gave an inward sigh of relief. She unsettled him. Normally he would have found her blatant sensuality highly erotic, but the knowledge that his son was besotted with her when he was meant to be out and about finding himself a wealthy wife took the edge off her charms.

In any case, he sensed that she wouldn't enjoy the kind of sex he liked, and she lacked the fragile allure of her mother. If he had his way he'd get her married off, but to his annoyance his wife stood firm over that, telling him that she had no intention of pushing her daughter into the kind of mistake she'd made.

Eventually the day's activities and a long evening of heavy drinking took their toll and Marina, who was listening with rapt interest to Sir Matthew's description of his latest equestrian acquisition, despite having no interest whatsoever in her husband's horses and having long since given up riding, gave a tiny polite yawn behind her hand.

Immediately Sir Matthew looked at his watch. 'Good Lord, is that the time? I must be on my way. Thank you both for a delightful evening. It's been a long time since I've had such agreeable company.' He took Lady Corbett-Wynne's hand in his, letting his fingers caress her palm.

She shivered, but didn't remove her hand, merely smiling politely. 'We enjoyed it too,' she said warmly. 'I'm afraid we don't entertain as often as we should, but perhaps once the Hall has been redecorated that will change.'

'Didn't know it had anything to do with the wallpaper,' grumbled her husband. 'Thought you disliked all my friends.'

Sir Matthew looked sympathetically at his hostess, at the same time wondering what would be the best way to make his next move.

'You must come over and see my Dalmatian's litter of pups,' he said with a smile. 'Two of the dogs are already taken, but I'm sure I could find one that you'd like out of the rest.'

'Step-mama loathes dogs,' said Crispian.

'Nonsense,' responded Marina, her palm still warm from the soft pressure of Sir Matthew's fingers. 'I think a little spotty dog would be enchanting.'

Her husband laughed. 'A little spotty dog! God, you can tell she doesn't know a damned thing about animals, can't you!'

'She knows Dalmatians have spots,' said Sir Matthew calmly. 'Just ring me, Lady Corbett-Wynne. I'm usually free in the afternoons.'

'I will,' she said softly, 'and please call me Marina.'

He nodded, and knew that providing he was careful he was well on his way to a satisfying seduction.

Crispian ran a finger down Annabel's bare spine, ending at the top of her zip. 'Fancy a walk?' I could do with some air before going to bed.'

Annabel nodded, said her goodnights and then followed him along a passageway and out through a side door into the grounds. She breathed in the cool evening air with satisfaction, but then shivered slightly. The contrast with the library, where a log fire had burned in the grate, was marked and her evening dress wasn't meant to keep her warm.

'Here, wear this,' said Crispian, and he draped his evening jacket over her shoulders. She pulled it tightly round her and they walked along the gravel path towards the stable block.

'Did you enjoy the evening?' he asked, merriment clear in his voice.

'It was certainly interesting,' conceded Annabel. 'I wasn't sure at one point whose hand was on my knee.'

'Almost certainly Pa's. Sir Matthew doesn't look like a groper; he's got a far more subtle approach. Good-looking, the women seem to think.'

'Quite attractive,' agreed Annabel, her heart pounding at the thought of what he might be like in bed, with his hands on her breasts and his mouth covering hers.

They came to the corner of the stable block and here Crispian turned so that Annabel found herself with her back against the wall while he stood in front of her, his hands resting on the wall above her shoulders.

'You looked bloody attractive tonight,' he said huskily, bending his head towards her.

Although it was Sir Matthew who'd stirred her into sexual awareness, Annabel found Crispian very attractive, and when his mouth softly touched her lips she found that she responded instantly.

Slowly he eased his jacket off her and ran his hands down her back, pressing her closer to him until her hips were thrust against his upper thighs. He moved his hands across her naked shoulders, down her arms and then over her hips and all the time he continued kissing her slowly and sensually, moving his mouth to the delicate skin beneath her ears and at the base of her throat.

'Let's go into one of the empty stables,' he said at last as he broke free for a moment.

Annabel went willingly, suddenly needing more than just kisses and light caresses. She wanted more intimate contact, wanted to feel pressure on her breasts and above all some kind of stimulation between her thighs where she was damp and aching.

The stable smelt of leather saddles and fresh straw but Annabel didn't care. Crispian took a rug off a peg and spread it over the straw before laying her down on her back. He then eased her stockings off her legs, pushed the full skirt of her evening dress upwards and crouched between her legs, lowering his head to her most intimate parts.

She was wearing tiny silk bikini briefs and when Crispian let his tongue glide over the material she nearly spasmed on the spot at the delicate pressure. He allowed his tongue to play around the edges of the bikini, gliding into the creases of her thighs and then across the small strip of silk again before tugging at the edges with his hands and finally pulling them down her legs and over her feet.

Annabel sighed with satisfaction as she felt his arms pushing her knees apart and his hands gripping her thighs, but suddenly she opened her eyes in astonishment as another pair of hands slid circles of rope over her ankles and then she was being spread-eagled even wider as her feet were pulled outwards.

Struggling to sit up she saw Tania expertly fastening the ropes to two conveniently situated wooden poles. 'Don't worry,' said the auburn-haired girl, her eyes glittering. 'No one will come along and spoil your fun. We often use this

57

place and there's never been an interruption, has there, Crispian?'

'Let me go!' exclaimed Annabel, hitting out at Crispian, but he only caught her hands and pushed them backwards. 'Tie her hands as well, Tania. I need to concentrate.'

'You can't do this!' protested Annabel.

'Of course we can, and it's fun. Just you wait and see,' Tania reassured her, pulling some more rope round the slim wrists and fastening the other ends round two metal rings in the stable wall. 'There, you look lovely. We should have taken her dress off first though, Crispian.'

'Just cut the straps,' said her stepbrother.

Annabel tried to protest, to tell them that the dress was expensive and she didn't want it ruined, but then Crispian's head moved back between her naked thighs and she felt his fingers opening her up so that his tongue could move up and down the cleft between her sex lips and she started to tremble.

While he was working, Tania was cutting the thin straps of Annabel's dress and then she peeled the bodice back off her breasts. 'Nice,' she said approvingly. 'Not very large, but firm. What do you think, Crispian?'

He swirled his tongue around Annabel's rapidly swelling clitoris for a moment and then lifted his head to examine her exposed breasts. 'Very nice,' he agreed. 'Use the suction cups on them.'

Annabel began to struggle against the ropes, but he slid a hand up beneath her dress, massaging her abdomen and carefully filling her with an incredibly warm, melting sensation that overwhelmed her fear and focused her thoughts back to the delicious feelings he was arousing in her.

Tania placed two clear plastic cups over Annabel's breasts and then pressed on the attached bulbs. Immediately a strange sucking feeling coursed through her breasts as the blood flow increased and Tania was able to watch as the other girl's soft mounds swelled and her nipples grew pointed and tight.

Knowing what was happening above him, Crispian now fastened his lips firmly round Annabel's clitoris and began to suck slowly on that, so that it felt as though his mouth and the cups were working in unison. She gasped with excitement and felt her belly tighten.

Her thighs trembled violently and she felt them pressing against Crispian's cheeks as her climax approached. Alerted by this, Crispian slowly eased the amount of pressure against the tiny mass of nerve endings giving her such delight and very slowly her body ceased its climb towards orgasm.

She whimpered in frustration, but there was nothing she could do because of the way they'd tied her up.

'You nearly came then, didn't you?' he asked.

'Yes,' she said breathlessly. 'Why did you stop?'

'We've got a guessing game we like to play,' said Tania, easing one of the suction cups off Annabel's left breast and running her fingers slowly round the swollen globe. 'When you've finished it, then you get your climax.'

The finger moved lightly, softly, circling the tight flesh before moving over the surface and teasing the already painfully hard nipple. 'The cup worked well on you,' commented Tania. 'I think I'll put it back on for a while.'

Annabel moaned, half with pleasure and half with despair because the sucking sensation of the cups was making her whole body turn to jelly and she longed for firmer stimulation. A hand closed tightly over her breasts, squeezing the nipple in a firm but arousing movement that she loved.

'Did you want to say something?' Tania enquired as she started to replace the cup.

'No,' muttered Annabel.

Tania laughed and bending down she let her mouth close around the bright-red protrusion, sucking on it just as her stepbrother had sucked on Annabel's clitoris. 'There, that's nice, isn't it?'

Annabel sighed. It was perfect, exactly what she'd needed, and her whole body started to quake. 'Oh dear, too much I think,' murmured Tania, removing her mouth and sliding the cup back in place. 'I mustn't spoil the game.'

Crispian lifted Annabel's buttocks off the straw a little so that he could flick the point of his tongue across the delicate area of skin between her front and back passages. She caught her breath in surprise and then let the incredible feelings wash over her. After a few moments he lowered her onto the straw again and then his tongue slipped into her sex, and he curled it upwards until the tip lightly brushed the area near her G-spot.

Annabel felt her legs begin shaking violently again and at once he stopped, squeezing her buttocks with his hands for a moment as he sat upright to talk to her.

'Annabel, I'm going to trace the outline of some letters on you with my tongue. You have to work out what the letter is. I shall do six, and when you've got them all right then you can have your climax, all right?'

'Trace it where?' she whispered.

'Why here of course!' His tongue slid up and down her damp channel and at the same time his hand moved onto her lower abdomen, gently massaging palm downwards towards her sex. Due to her mounting excitement Annabel's clitoris had retreated behind its protective hood and he knew that this movement always brought it out again. Sure enough after a few moments it reappeared and he touched the base of its stem tenderly with his tongue causing the bound girl to quiver and groan.

'Do it harder!' Annabel begged him. 'Flick more firmly.'

'Not yet; wait until the game's over. Now, tell me what this letter is.'

As his tongue began to trace the outline of a letter of the alphabet on her frantic, pulsating flesh, Tania removed both the suction cups and then picked up some pieces of straw. These she drew all over the highly sensitised breasts, sometimes letting the tip of a piece of straw into the tiny indentation at the top of the nipples. Each time she did this a streak of excitement darted through Annabel's whole body, distracting her from what Crispian was doing.

She found it almost impossible to work out the pattern his tongue was making because the experience was so arousing that all she could think about was sheer mounting pleasure and the terrible pressure that was building deep in her belly.

'Come on, what is it?' asked Crispian after a time.

'A?' asked Annabel, who had no idea at all.

'Wrong. Now you pay a forfeit.'

'You never said anything about a forfeit!' she exclaimed.

'Must have forgotten. Tania, what shall it be?'

'The clitoris ring,' said Tania.

Crispian laughed excitedly. 'Brilliant. Have you got it?'

'Of course,' murmured Tania, leaving Annabel's breasts and moving down to her stepbrother. She handed him a minute copper ring and kissed the nape of his neck before running her hands over the front of his trousers. 'My, you're almost as excited as Annabel!' she said lightly.

'She's so gorgeous,' he muttered. 'And just think, she's here for three weeks.'

Annabel felt like screaming at them both. Her whole body was frantic with desire. They were arousing her, giving her pleasure and playing with her like a pampered pet, but refusing her the one thing she so desperately needed and there was nothing she could do about it. As for ever joining them again during her three weeks, she decided they were mad if they honestly thought she'd agree after this.

'Open her up,' said Crispian. Tania's cool hands parted Annabel's outer sex lips again and then Crispian's hand returned to her now swollen stomach and he repeated the massaging movement he'd used earlier. As soon as her clitoris showed itself he licked the copper ring and then eased it over the engorged mass of nerve endings so that it was firmly captured, unable to retract any more and a perfect target for any stimulation he or Tania chose to offer it.

'This time I'll just use a piece of straw,' said Tania. Annabel felt a delicate prickling sensation as the other girl drew a thin piece of straw over the clitoris, moving it very slowly upwards, and then she licked her finger and pressed lightly downwards against the tip of the nub.

Annabel writhed and bucked, trying to escape the strange, insidious pleasure that deepened with every passing second even though Tania didn't increase the pressure or move her finger in any way.

'Careful,' cautioned Crispian. 'She's about to come.'

'Let me!' screamed Annabel, no longer caring who heard. 'Do it once more. That's all it needs, one more touch.'

'Sorry, still six letters to go,' Tania said coolly.

This time Annabel concentrated fiercely, ignoring Tania's hands that were massaging what felt like oil into her over-stimulated breasts and causing hot sensations to envelop her upper body. 'D!' she screamed.

'That's right, well done,' Crispian congratulated her, and he kissed the base of her belly, pressing his mouth down and moving her clitoris within the tight ring. She felt her abdominal muscles start to contract, felt the glorious swelling towards climax as her legs stiffened. Tania suddenly tugged sharply on Annabel's hair and the pain distracted her at the vital moment. Again the longed-for orgasm evaded her, and this time she felt close to tears.

'Come on,' Crispian urged her. 'Only five to go, and you'll get better as you go along. Everyone does.'

Once more he began to trace a letter and this time she got it straight away, and then the next three letters came easily so that she was only left with one more to guess.

'You're a quick learner,' said Crispian. 'This is thirsty work, Tania. Got any wine?'

'Don't stop now!' Annabel said; she was nearly shouting.

He gripped her breasts in his hands and she shuddered with pleasure as his strong fingers massaged them in the way she loved. 'Sorry, have to have a top-up. Pour it on her breasts, Tania. They feel rather warm after the suction cups.'

Annabel tensed in anticipation and all at once ice-cold Chablis was poured onto her breasts. To her astonishment Tania and Crispian lapped at one breast each. Their mouths and tongues were so different that it made the experience incredibly sensuous and Annabel could hear herself whimpering with delight.

When her breasts were fully engorged, Crispian and Tania stopped lapping at them and leant over the frantically squirming Annabel. 'Do you want me to untie you?' asked Crispian. 'You could go back to the house. I don't want you complaining to Pa that we kept you here against your will.'

'Don't stop!' Annabel pleaded, totally lost in the sensations the stepbrother and sister had aroused and no longer caring in the least that she was tied up and spread-eagled on a bed of straw. Even the slight prickling of the rug against the bare skin of her shoulders and legs only added to her general excitement.

'You're enjoying the game then?' he persisted, his blue eyes staring into hers, as though trying to penetrate her thoughts.

'Yes! Yes! Please, don't leave me like this.'

'My, my, who'd have thought you'd be quite so enthusiastic! I can see we're going to have an exciting three weeks,' laughed Crispian, and then to Annabel's relief he slid down her body and at last his head was between her thighs again.

Tania continued to pour wine over the other girl's

breasts, but now she sucked more firmly at the swollen globes, enjoying the gentle tremors that were running through her.

Crispian allowed one finger to drift slowly up and down Annabel's damp inner channel and, once it was lubricated by her secretions, he slid it carefully into her vagina and heard her give a tiny gasp of pleasure. Bending his head he ran his tongue lazily along the tissue surrounding her encircled clitoris and then pressed upwards with his finger, holding it firmly against her G-spot while his other hand rested softly on the base of her stomach. When he felt her abdominal muscles start to tense he pressed down more firmly. The tight pressure deep inside the fastened girl increased and he heard her breathing quicken with excitement as her body started to reach the point of no return.

Tania could tell how close Annabel was to climaxing and she deliberately let some of the wine spill into the other girl's armpits, the cool liquid sparking further tremors of delight through her upper body.

Annabel felt as though there was a long piece of cord running the length of her body from behind her clitoris, throbbing within its copper ring, to her breasts, and the cord was steadily tightening, pulling the various sensations closer and closer together while between her thighs the hot heavy pressure throbbed and spread.

With one hand pressing her belly and a finger stimulating her G-spot, Crispian finally allowed his tongue to swirl around the stem of Annabel's clitoris and at once her belly arched upwards against his hand.

'Oh yes, stay there, please!' she cried in delight.

He hadn't expected her to be so responsive or so vocal and could feel his own excitement rising as he waited until her thighs were quaking violently, her stomach swollen and hard against his hand and her breathing ragged. Then, and only then, did he at last allow his clever tongue to dance across the swollen and fastened clitoris and as he did so a searing flash of exquisite pleasure tore right through Annabel and at last her whole body was convulsed in orgasm.

She heard herself screaming with pleasure, felt her head twisting and turning on the straw and her arms and legs writhing within the ropes but she didn't care. All that interested her was the wonderful thrill of explosion, the glorious release of carefully calculated sexual tension. It was the best climax she'd ever had, and at one stage she wondered if it was ever going to end as her body continued to be shaken by tiny after-tremors of pleasure, but finally she was still and lay in an exhausted heap on the straw.

'I hope that made up for a rather boring dinner,' said Crispian as he and Tania unfastened the ropes.

Dazed, Annabel got to her feet, leaning against one of the poles as her legs threatened to collapse beneath her. 'It was incredible!' she said breathlessly.

Crispian glanced at Tania, who nodded her head in answer to the unspoken question. 'Perhaps you'll join us again, some other time?' he asked.

Thinking of the excitement of the night and the unbelievable sensations she'd experienced, Annabel knew that she wanted more. 'That sounds like a good idea,' she said with a tiny smile.

Crispian gave her a long, level look and there was a mixture of admiration and appreciation in his eyes. 'We look forward to it,' he said lazily. 'Sleep well.'

'Aren't you coming back to the house?' asked Annabel.

Tania stood by her stepbrother and put her arm through his, resting her head against him. 'We've still got one or two things to do here,' she said huskily.

As Annabel turned away she was aware that the pair of them were already kissing, but to her astonishment she didn't mind. She wasn't concerned about what they did, or what they meant to each other. For the first time in her life she'd enjoyed a sexual experience without emotional commitment, and she intended to enjoy some more before she left.

David Crosbie would be surprised at how well she was getting on with the occupants of Leyton Hall, she thought to herself with a smile.

Chapter Four

*T*he following day, Marina Corbett-Wynne awoke and realised that for the first time in several years she felt happy. For a moment she simply lay in her bed, which was draped with eighteenth-century lace, and savoured the sensation. Then she tried to analyse it. Why, after all this time, should she be happy? Almost before the question was formed she knew the answer, as a picture of Sir Matthew Stevens sprang into her mind.

He was a handsome man, but she'd met many other handsome men who hadn't had the same effect on her. He was well-built and rugged looking, but so had her husband been once, and even then she hadn't felt the way she'd felt about their visitor last night.

No, she thought to herself, nice as all of that was, what had really attracted her was the sense that Sir Matthew understood women. She was quite certain that, in the unlikely event of there ever being anything physical between them, he would be able to give her starved body the kind of pleasure that she secretly longed for.

As she thought about this her hand strayed over her flat stomach and lingered in her pubic hair, pressing down softly. She rotated her palm and felt an almost forgotten tingling sensation start up beneath her hand. Startled, she snatched it back and lay with both arms at her sides, shocked by what she'd done.

When the maid came and ran her bath, Marina rejected the conventional silk blouse and pleated skirt selected for her and picked out a draped chiffon dress in ice-cream pink instead. She knew that it flattered her, and since Sir Matthew had invited her to go and look at his litter of pups, she might as well go there looking her best.

'Isn't there any bath oil left?' she asked as she walked across the pale grey floorboards and climbed into the deep, marbled, claw-footed bath. Opposite, the large window was draped with bright sea-green curtains, drawn up into soft folds to let in the light. The walls were also sea-green with a looping stencil pattern around the top, and once she was in the water and the oil had been added the maid drew a cream muslin screen around her before leaving.

Marina sighed with pleasure. She loved her bathroom: it was so tranquil and there was nothing in its design or the furnishings to remind her of her husband, his horses or, more to the point, his strange desires. Remembering the harness that had blighted their sexual relationship right from the start she shuddered to herself.

Her first husband had been the sexually dominant one in the marriage. To learn that her second husband wanted her to lead him round the room like one of his own horses had shocked her, and within a few months even the small amount of sexual desire she'd initially felt for him had died.

She knew about his grooms but, as long as he kept them in his own quarters and no one outside the family knew, she wasn't concerned. At least it kept him from her bed. But although she didn't want him she realised now that her body wasn't ready to remain celibate for the rest of her life. At forty-four she was still in her sexual prime; all she needed was someone to bring her to life again. She couldn't help hoping that Sir Matthew might be that man.

Once she was dressed she sent for Annabel, asked her to look over the music room, the dining room and the lobby and then dismissed her. The girl seemed competent, if a little heavy-eyed this morning, and for once restoring Leyton Hall wasn't top of Marina's list of priorities.

'I'm going for a walk,' she told her husband, putting her head round the library door and shuddering at the chaos.

His head came up sharply. 'A walk? Are you ill?'

'I do have legs,' she said coolly. 'Unlike you, I prefer to use them for walking rather than riding.'

'First I knew of it,' he muttered. 'Besides, you've got a slender waist, lovely little breasts and a tight bum, too, but you don't seem interested in using those.'

'You are unspeakably coarse,' retorted Marina. 'Please save that kind of talk for your stable girls.'

He flushed. 'What about your designer? Who's going to look after her?'

'I'm going for a walk, not a holiday abroad. By the time Annabel's looked over the rooms I shall be back. We can talk about them then.'

'As you like. I'm taking that new filly out for a ride later on. Don't know if I'll be back for lunch or not.'

'I assume you mean the horse and not that new girl, Sandra,' his wife said smoothly, and before he could think of a reply, she'd gone. Sighing, he went back to studying the pile of bills in front of him. They weren't very reassuring and he decided that later that day he'd talk to Crispian again about finding a rich wife. They desperately needed a fresh injection of money and Marina's was so cleverly tied up that it could only be touched with her approval.

At the same time as he was trying to console himself with thoughts of a ride later that day, with Sandra for company and probably a little stop somewhere secluded, his wife was walking towards The Old Mill.

As she approached, Sir Matthew's car drew up alongside her and he wound down his window. 'On your way to see me, Lady Corbett-Wynne?'

She felt her heart fluttering. 'Yes, as I was passing I though I might as well look at your litter of spotty puppies.'

Knowing full well that she couldn't have been passing because there wasn't anywhere else for her to go along that particular road, Matthew's pulse quickened. He hadn't expected such a speedy response to his invitation and was glad that his planned business meeting had been cancelled.

'I was off to London,' he explained, indicating his smart grey suit, light blue shirt and grey tie. 'Luckily they called me on the car phone to say the meeting had been cancelled. Hop in. There's no point in you walking on your own.'

Secretly grateful because she didn't enjoy any kind of physical exercise, Marina smiled prettily at him. 'Well, I suppose you're right, but it seems a shame to waste this lovely morning.'

'You'll get plenty of air on your way back,' he replied, and smiled to himself at the look of distaste that flashed briefly over her normally carefully controlled features. His assessment had been right, he thought. She wasn't really a country woman at heart. Leading her into the house, he called for his housekeeper to bring them tea and biscuits. 'Unless you'd like something stronger?' he added in an aside.

Marina shook her head, wishing that the palms of her hands didn't feel quite so sweaty and hot. 'Tea will be lovely. Do you have Earl Grey?'

'Afraid not. Now that I'm on my own, as long as it's hot and strong I'm content,' apologised Sir Matthew.

Marina smiled at him. 'Hot and strong sounds perfect,' she said politely and then blushed as she realised what she'd said.

Matthew kept his expression neutral, touching her gently on the elbow as he ushered her towards one of the large armchairs in the room. Marina sank back in the deep cushions and glanced about her.

It was a nice room, warm and lived-in. A tall grandfather clock stood in one corner and she liked the reassuring ticking sound. Prints of landscapes and dogs decorated the walls while the original fireplace was untouched and laid with wood logs ready for the evening. Vases of flowers stood on each of the two tables, and both windowsills were full of potted plants, all flourishing. Marina wondered if Matthew's long fingers attended to them, or whether this was his housekeeper's doing.

Matthew sat opposite her, relaxing on the sofa and crossing his legs as he smiled into her eyes. 'Once we've had the tea we'll go and look at the pups. I'm afraid they're not ready to leave their mother yet though.'

Marina shook her head. 'Of course not. I'm not even sure that I'll be able to take one, I mean we already seem to have too many dogs, but . . .'

'They're sweet to look at,' he said gently.

As the housekeeper brought in the tea tray and Matthew started to pour, Marina found that she was shooting quick glances at him all the time from beneath lowered lids and when he caught her eye she felt her tongue flick out to moisten her suddenly dry lips.

Sir Matthew held her gaze for a moment longer and then looked away. He knew that she was attracted to him, but also knew that if he made the wrong move or did the wrong thing he'd frighten her away. She had to be handled carefully, and he found this very arousing.

When he handed her the cup he made sure that his fingers briefly brushed hers, and then pointed out an antique rag doll on his mantelpiece. As he pointed, he let his other arm rest casually on her shoulders for a fleeting moment, withdrawing it before the contact could alarm her. For Marina that touch triggered an almost overpowering need to feel herself wrapped in his arms, and she tried to imagine how it would feel if he kissed her.

'Come on,' said Matthew, draining his cup. 'Let's go and look at the little pups.' He put out a hand to assist his visitor to her feet and as his strong fingers closed round hers she shut her eyes for a moment, feeling a rush of blood to her face and neck.

When they walked out through the doorway Sir Matthew stood to one side to let her pass. Their bodies brushed against each other, another moment of fleeting contact that stirred Marina's starved senses. By the time they reached the heated outhouse where the Dalmatian bitch and her litter were kept, Marina's legs were wobbly and she was finding it hard to breathe deeply enough.

'There you are,' said Matthew, opening the top half of the divided door of the puppy area. 'What do you think of them?'

He stood directly behind her as she looked, allowing his breath to move strands of her fair hair, and although he wasn't touching her, Marina felt as though he were. She could sense every part of him; his hands, his broad chest and his strong thighs, all so close it was unbearable.

'They're sweet!' she exclaimed, and at that moment the pups' mother decided to bark at the unknown visitor. With a tiny squeal of surprise Marina stepped backwards and at once her imaginings became reality as their bodies collided and his arms went around her.

'It's all right,' he said softly. 'She won't hurt you. She's only protecting her young. No one will hurt you here,' he added, feeling her trembling.

Marina didn't reply. She simply stayed with the back of her body pressed against him and relished the sensation. Hesitantly he allowed his hands to move slightly up and down along the sides of her body from beneath her armpits to just below her hips, and the caress was wonderfully tender.

'You didn't really come about the pups, did you?' he asked.

Marina hesitated. He was right, she wasn't in the least interested in the puppies, but to admit as much was beyond her. To her surprise, she found that she couldn't deny it either – it seemed too ridiculous when this man, the first she'd found attractive for many years, so clearly understood her, and she decided to keep silent.

Matthew bent his head and kissed the top vertebra of her spine, sending a thrill of excitement through her. Then he turned her towards him and kissed her on the tip of the nose, as though she were a small child. 'Let's go back inside,' he said softly. 'My housekeeper will have gone by now; we'll be quite alone.'

For a moment she froze, uncertain that this was what she wanted. She had terrible visions of it all going wrong. Of being asked to dress up in something extraordinary, have handcuffs put on her wrists, or worse still, to discover, once her clothes were off, that this man she wanted so urgently didn't find her attractive.

'What's the matter?' he murmured, his hands cupping her face.

'I don't want it to go wrong,' she confessed, her eyes looking nervously away from his.

'It won't go wrong. How could it? Relax, sweetheart, leave it all to me.'

Still trembling, she allowed herself to be led into the house, feeling a tremor of apprehension as he locked the door behind them and then drew the curtains. 'Better to be certain of our privacy,' he murmured, and then at last he took her in his arms and began to kiss her.

No one had ever kissed Marina Corbett-Wynne in the way that Matthew Stevens now did. His mouth plundered hers, but softly, tenderly, and when his tongue eased between her parted lips and swirled over her gums she sighed and relaxed against him even more.

Emboldened by this he let his tongue invade her further, and suddenly she found that she was responding in the same way, her tongue darting inside his mouth as she felt her excitement increasing.

Matthew's arms gripped her firmly and as they kissed he skilfully unfastened the tiny buttons down the back of her carefully chosen pink dress. Then, when he'd finished he stepped back from her a little and eased it off her shoulders so that it fell in a heap around her ankles. Marina stared at him, anxiety clear in her wide eyes as he studied her. 'You're beautiful,' he whispered. 'Take off the rest of your clothes for me.'

She went rigid, and shook her head. 'I'm sorry, I can't. You do it.'

Matthew put out a hand and with the middle finger drew a line down her body from her chin to the valley between her breasts. 'I'd much rather you did it, then I can admire you as I watch.'

Marina swallowed. The atmosphere in the room was electric. Her need and his desire were almost physically present and she realised that if she didn't do as he asked something would be lost.

'I want to watch you,' he said. 'Seeing a beautiful woman undress is very arousing.'

His voice was deep, a soft chocolate voice, she thought to herself, and the words increased her desire. Hesitantly she reached for the waistband of her slip and then, bending forward from the waist, allowed it to drop to the floor to join her dress. She stepped out of it and Matthew admired the curve of her slender legs and the way her high heels pushed out her buttocks in a provocative way; an effect which was totally at odds with her normal appearance. He could feel his penis growing hard already. Her hesitancy and slight awkwardness were an aphrodisiac in themselves.

Marina's left hand drifted down the naked patch of skin between her stocking top and high-cut panties as she wondered whether or not the stockings should come off next. The movement, involving the slight downward tilt of her shoulder, meant that the slender strap of her camisole slipped down the top of her arm. At this hint of disarray Matthew's mouth went dry. She'd been so perfect, so cool and composed the night before, and now she was stripping for him, her slim, desirable body coming alive beneath his gaze. Without taking his eyes off her he began to remove his own clothes.

Once the shoulder strap had slipped, Marina decided to remove the camisole top next. She peeled it over her head to reveal a tiny, see-through lace bra that failed to conceal the rosy pink nipples beneath.

'Go on,' muttered Matthew, discarding his tie and unbuttoning his shirt. 'You're just as incredible as I'd imagined.'

His words encouraged her. Slowly she unfastened her stockings and rolled them down her legs until finally she had to step out of the high-heeled shoes that were giving Matthew such pleasure. Once the stockings were off he looked directly into her eyes. 'Put the shoes back on again, please,' he said with a catch in his voice. 'You look so sexy in them.'

She'd never been told she looked sexy before and without hesitation she slipped the ivory-coloured shoes onto her bare feet and then removed her panties. As she bent over to step out of them her tiny, tight buttocks were thrust out and Matthew could hardly stop himself from running a hand over the delicious curve.

Finally all that Marina was wearing was her bra, and all at once she became conscious of her nakedness. Without thinking she thrust the leg nearest to Matthew forward so that her thigh hid her most secret part from him. This unconscious piece of teasing brought his straining and now naked erection fully upright until it was resting against his stomach, its head swollen and red.

Marina saw that he too had undressed and found that she couldn't stop looking at the clear evidence of his desire for her. 'Take off the bra, Marina,' he reminded her. Almost in a daze she obeyed, and then at last he stepped towards her and reaching out he let his hands cup the undersides of her tiny breasts. 'Are they sensitive? Do you like them caressed?' he asked in a low voice.

'Yes, oh yes!' she murmured, and to her delight he let his strong capable fingers play over the rapidly swelling globes, touching them lightly at first but with increasing pressure until he finally let himself caress the delicate nipples and watched them grow into small, pale-pink peaks. Unable to remain so detached he pulled her unresisting body against his and felt those tiny nipples brushing against the dark hairs of his chest as he rubbed her close.

Marina suddenly began to struggle against the pressure of his arms. She felt as though he was crushing her and all her fears and doubts started to return. Immediately Matthew released her, gently pushing her back into the armchair she'd sat in earlier, when she'd arrived.

He pulled her legs straight and slid her down the chair a little until she was half-lying and half-sitting. She looked at him apprehensively, and he wondered what she'd heard about him, or whether it was simply the result of some ham-fisted lovemaking by her husband. Whatever the reason, he was determined to make this special for both of them.

'I'm going to touch you all over,' he whispered, and Marina felt herself shaking with nervous excitement. 'Only little touches,' he continued, 'and I want you to tell me if they excite you or not.'

Her long fair hair, carefully piled on top of her head before she left Leyton Hall, had now fallen down around her face and neck, and he pushed it back behind her ears before lightly stroking his thumbs twice over her temples. She sighed with satisfaction and her whole body started to relax again.

'Was that good?' he asked.

'Yes,' she whispered.

Next he touched each of her eyelids in turn and when she gave a contented sigh he ran his thumbs down each of her cheekbones. This touch sent strange tingling sensations down the sides of her neck and he saw that her nipples,

76

which had become quiescent again, were beginning to stiffen. 'Nice?' he asked.

'It's all nice,' she said with a slow smile.

'You must say which you prefer,' he insisted, but Marina knew that she couldn't because so far it was all delightful.

His thumbs and fingers went on to stroke her nose, lips and chin before moving to her shoulders. Here he used one finger only and ran it along each of her naked shoulders in turn, stroking twice over tiny two-inch areas until she felt that she wanted to scream with pleasure.

'Quite sensitive, I think,' he said to himself, watching her nipples rise to taut peaks, and he proceeded to repeat the process along her inner arms, paying particular attention to the soft insides of her elbows.

As he swirled his fingers there Marina felt her internal muscles start to move, slowly stirring as though awakening from a long sleep, and her stomach, although flat, felt swollen and hard.

Her eyes looked huge and the pupils were dilated, while her mouth was moist and pliant. Matthew knew that if he took her at that moment she would quickly climax. His own body was clamouring to possess her but he also knew that by prolonging the foreplay the end result would be even better for them both, and she was such a novelty that he decided to savour the moment.

He stroked her hands, her fingers and the highly responsive flesh across her hipbones. Then he caressed her legs, the backs of her knees, her calves, ankles and finally the high arches of her fine-boned feet until he reached the toes. There he let a finger play across the pad beneath every toe until Marina was squirming restlessly in the armchair, every inch of her except for her stomach and genitals brought to fever pitch by the incredibly slow and sensuous process.

To her shame she felt damp between her thighs, something that had never happened to her before, and she tried

77

to clench her thighs together so that Matthew wouldn't realise.

He allowed his hand to rotate in soft circles across her abdomen and used the other hand to part her legs so that he could cup her sex, pressing gently but firmly against the entire area. The arousing pressure sent sharp darts of excitement up behind Marina's pubic bone and across her lower belly and without realising what she was doing her legs fell apart and Matthew's fingers brushed against the opening of her sex-lips and felt her dampness. Marina closed her eyes.

'Look at me,' he commanded in a gentle tone. 'Please, Marina, open your eyes.'

Reluctantly she did, and he gazed deeply into them, his fingers straying softly through her pubic hair and just touching her slowly opening labia. 'That's a compliment to me,' he assured her. 'Don't be ashamed of your sexuality.'

'But I hardly know you,' she protested, aware at once of how ridiculous this sounded since she was sitting naked and open to him in the armchair of his drawing room.

'We're adults, and we're enjoying ourselves, that's all that matters,' he assured her. 'Now, can you kneel up and lean against the back of the chair? Rest your arms on the top of it and move your knees back a little.'

As Marina got into position, Matthew knelt between her outspread thighs, putting his arms round her waist and pulling her buttocks back towards him until the angle was just as he wanted it.

'Rub your breasts against the material of the chair,' he whispered. Reluctantly Marina shifted her weight slightly, but once her nipples had felt the stimulation of the raised pattern on the brocade she got more and more excited and started breathing heavily as her breasts became engorged with blood.

Once she was lost in the sensations Matthew took his throbbing erection in his right hand and swirled it slowly around the excited woman's outer sex-lips. As they parted for him he did the same within the inner lips, teasing her damp and trembling flesh before letting the tip of his penis rest against the opening of her sex.

Driven almost out of her mind by the incredible feelings between her thighs, Marina waited for the sudden thrusting that her two husbands had always seemed to enjoy so much, but to her delighted surprise Matthew didn't do this. Instead he eased his penis inside her a little way, circled his hips and then withdraw, while at the same time his free hand located her clitoris and he carefully stroked the side of the shaft.

Suddenly all the pleasure Marina had experienced up to this point seemed to run riot. The small sparks of excitement turned into piercing darts of intense sensation like electric currents running through her. There was an aching tightness just below where his finger was massaging her that seemed to get worse with every movement he made.

She closed her mouth tightly to stop herself from moaning aloud as her body began to clamour for a release from the almost frightening tension that was consuming it. Her breasts had never been so full and hard; her stomach muscles had never been so tight and when he slid his penis back into her a little further than the first time it seemed as though she was melting between her thighs.

Matthew worked slowly and steadily, gradually allowing more of his erection to slide inside her, and sometimes on the inward stroke he would hear her breath snag in her throat as he brushed against her G-spot. He tried to make sure that each time this happened his fingers also touched the stem of her clitoris.

Now Marina was certain that she was going to burst. Even through closed lips she could hear herself making strange, unintelligible sounds and her hips and thighs were trembling from unsatisfied sexual tension.

At last Matthew inserted the full length of himself and when he did so, he realised that his own self-control was going. Suddenly his hips took on a life of their own and he found himself thrusting fiercely into the slender woman.

He felt her body tightening, saw her head go back as the tendons of her neck strained with tension and he quickly drummed his finger against the side of her clitoris. This, combined with the friction caused by his movements and the quick touches of his erection against her G-spot, splintered Marina's starved body into a thousand pieces.

The tight muscles felt as though they had gone into cramp-like spasms and she was flooded by a rush of warmth as the dreadful aching sensation exploded deep within her. Her whole body twisted into shattering contortions until finally she slumped exhausted and bewildered over the back of the chair.

Matthew fell forward as well, but he was careful to put his hands on either side of her so that she didn't have to take his full weight against her. After a moment he eased her round and, seating himself in the chair, lifted her slight frame so that her buttocks were across his naked thighs. She leant against his shoulder, her skin damp from their lovemaking, and he stroked her softly as her breathing slowed and her pulse gradually returned to normal.

'It's been a long time for you, hasn't it?' he said gently.

Marina nodded. 'I married for the first time when I was nineteen,' she explained. 'He was a very sweet man, but neither of us were at all worldly. We'd been friends since we were children and the marriage was probably as much for our parents' benefit as our own. As for James, well, I imagined him to be something he wasn't, and then tried to change him to what I'd thought he'd be. Sex has never been in the least pleasurable for either of us, and these days he finds his enjoyment elsewhere.'

Matthew had heard all about that, and knew very well the kind of enjoyment Lord Corbett-Wynne craved, but he kept silent. He had no wish to humiliate the lord's wife at a moment like this. 'But you've had other lovers?' he asked.

'None. I've never met anyone I was attracted to, until now.'

'I'm very flattered, Marina. Last night at dinner, all I could think about was what it would be like to make love to you.'

'And now you know,' she said softly.

He smiled. 'Now I know, and it was even better than I'd imagined.'

She sighed. 'I don't think I've ever been in love before.'

Luckily for Marina she didn't see the look of astonished panic that crossed her lover's face. She was delicate and beautiful and he knew that he'd enjoy making love to her for some time yet – there was so much she had to learn. But she wasn't the kind of woman he would ever fall in love with.

He was a robust man who enjoyed far more variety and excitement in his sex life than Marina Corbett-Wynne would ever wish to provide. He doubted if he'd marry again, but if he did it certainly wouldn't be to someone like her.

'I don't think I've ever been in love,' he said carefully. 'Not even when I was married.'

She turned her face up to look at him. 'But in that case, how could you make love to me so tenderly?'

'Because I find you sexually desirable, and I enjoy making love to beautiful women. I also like you, very much indeed.'

Marina wasn't stupid; she understood that he was warning her. If their affair was going to continue then it would be on the clear understanding that it was a purely physical relationship, with no prospect of any long-term emotional commitment.

Only a couple of hours earlier she would have been shocked at the idea. Now it was different. Already her body was responding to his rhythmic stroking, and she knew that once wasn't enough. She had to have him again; not today – she had to get back to Leyton Hall – but soon and on any terms.

'I have to leave,' she said quietly. 'Annabel, the girl from London, might need to see me but I'd like to come and look at your litter again, if I may?'

Relieved at the way she'd taken his words, Matthew hugged her tightly, covering her neck and face with kisses. 'I'd be very disappointed if you didn't,' he assured her.

As she was about to leave, an idea struck Marina. 'What did you think of my daughter?' she asked slowly.

Matthew's eyes narrowed. 'Your daughter?'

'Yes, Tania. Don't you think she's attractive?'

'Very.'

'She seemed to find you attractive as well.'

'Are you suggesting a threesome?' he queried.

Marina flushed. 'Certainly not! I was merely wondering whether, in the long term . . .'

He nodded, understanding how convenient such a marriage would be if Marina was anxious to keep him close to hand. 'I don't think she'd be very interested,' he said slowly. 'I'm told she likes slim, fair-haired young men like Crispian.'

Marina's eyes widened in shock. 'What do you mean?'

'Nothing at all, except that I'm not slim and fair-haired.'

She took an anxious step towards him. 'What have you heard? Tell me, I must know.'

He caught hold of her hands and kissed her again. 'Marina, stop it. What do you think I might have heard?'

The touch of his lips on hers had already assuaged her anxiety. 'Nothing,' she said lightly. 'I misunderstood.'

'I wish I could run you back,' said Matthew with a smile, 'but somehow I think that might give the game away, don't you?'

'Well . . .'

'Besides, I know you like walking,' he added.

Marina nodded, wishing she'd never made up the lie.

'You must try riding again,' he suggested as he stood in the doorway. 'If you went out riding it would increase the number of times we could meet. Besides, I'm told ladies find it very sexy.'

'I don't know,' she said hesitantly.

'You've got a man there who could teach you, haven't you? Give it a go. Riding a horse with Chinese loveballs inside you is one of the most incredible sensations possible, or so one of my girlfriends told me.'

Between her thighs Marina felt a faint dampness beginning again, and she pressed her hands to her increasingly hot cheeks. 'I really must go now, Matthew. It was wonderful. You'll never know how much it meant to me.'

'And to me,' he assured her as he watched her walk away.

Once she'd gone he closed the door and poured himself a scotch. He'd enjoyed the encounter: her nervousness and lack of experience had been touching and he always enjoyed giving pleasure to women. All the same he knew that after time she would bore him, unless he could encourage her to experiment more.

If all the rumours were true her daughter wasn't in the least averse to trying almost anything, but somehow he didn't think her mother was the same. Surprisingly he had a sudden mental picture of the girl Annabel, and the way she'd looked at him the previous evening. He thought that later on he might see if she was interested, and if he could get Marina to join them then that would be even better.

'A man can dream,' he said aloud as he sipped at the whisky.

Annabel hadn't had a chance to dream. She'd been busy all the morning jotting down copious notes about the rooms Lady Corbett-Wynne had wanted her to see. Her biggest problem was going to be incorporating her employer's personal taste into Leyton Hall without losing its original atmosphere. Cream drapes and delicate furniture were all very well in their place, but that place certainly wasn't the music room of Leyton Hall.

As she was finishing, Crispian came in through the front door. 'Good morning,' he said brightly. 'Quite recovered this morning?'

Annabel nodded. 'Yes, thank you.'

'I've got something for you. A little memento of last night.' He held out his hand and there, in the middle of his palm, lay the tiny copper ring that had encircled her clitoris in the stable.

Annabel felt a warm heaviness in her belly and struggled to keep her breathing even. 'Thank you, Crispian, very thoughtful of you both,' she responded, picking it up and slipping it into the pocket of her linen slacks.

'What are you doing tonight?' he asked.

'Having an early night.'

'Alone?'

'I prefer to sleep alone,' Annabel said coolly.

Crispian smiled. 'If I joined you first you might sleep more soundly later.'

Annabel sighed. 'You may be surprised to learn, Crispian, that I always sleep well.'

Crispian shrugged. 'Only trying to be friendly. I thought, since we all got on so well last night, that you might not be averse to my company again.'

'I'm not, but tonight I'd prefer to sleep. I'm sure Tania will keep you company if you get bored.'

'I never get bored,' Crispian assured her. 'See you later then. I've got to spend the afternoon teaching the daughter of one of Pa's friends to ride. Bloody boring but she's going to be very rich one day and it will keep the old man quiet if he thinks I'm seriously looking for a suitable wife!'

Annabel couldn't help smiling. It was impossible to dislike Crispian or to deny his potent sensuality, and despite her protests she had felt a thrill of excitement at the thought of another evening's pleasure. Watching him walk away from her she had the pleasant suspicion that he hadn't taken her refusal too seriously.

Chapter Five

*L*ord Corbett-Wynne was smiling too. He could think of nothing he'd rather be doing on such a lovely morning than riding through the Wiltshire countryside on his favourite bay gelding with a pretty groom alongside him, her shapely thighs gripping the sides of the piebald mare. He watched appreciatively as Sandra's buttocks rose and fell against the saddle, and he thought to himself that she had one of the best seats he'd ever seen, in more ways than one.

Well aware of his approval, Sandra took care to use her thighs more than was strictly necessary as she urged the piebald on or slowed it a little, and all the time she was waiting for the move that she was certain would come. So certain in fact that she'd taken the precaution of slipping a few items in the pockets of her jodhpurs. Lord Corbett-Wynne had proved so enthusiastic at their first meeting that she was starting to wonder just how far she might be able to enslave him.

The previous evening she'd lain in bed imagining herself as Lady Corbett-Wynne but, in the cold light of day, had decided that was unrealistic. All the same, if she could keep him enslaved she might well progress from being just another of his girl grooms to a favoured mistress, which would suit her rather well as she was quickly tiring of the messy jobs she was required to do around the horses. Mucking out and rubbing down were starting to lose their appeal. She would quite happily settle for a small cottage somewhere near the Hall and regular visits from Lord Corbett-Wynne.

If her employer had known of her dreams he could have disillusioned her immediately. The whole attraction for him was the fact that she *was* a groom. He loved the scent of hay and stables on his girls, and without their tight-fitting jodhpurs and rubber boots his senses would have been far slower to be aroused. As it was, he could barely control himself as he continued watching Sandra rising and falling in the saddle.

After a time they entered a copse and the horse track led them beneath some low-hanging trees and then out into a small clearing. It was a spot that Lord Corbett-Wynne knew very well. He pulled his horse up and dismounted. Sandra noticed that the horse immediately wandered off and started nibbling at the grass nearby, and she realised that this must be a regular stopping-off point for him.

'Are we stopping?' she asked with assumed surprise.

'Thought we'd have a spot of lunch. You did pack the sandwiches in the saddlebags, I hope?'

Sandra swung a leg over her horse's back and dismounted, making sure she gave him a very good view of her buttocks as she did so. 'Of course, just as you asked.'

'Good, good!'

The sun was shining down on them and Lord Corbett-Wynne decided that it would be better to sit beneath one of the horse chestnut trees and eat in the shade. Not that he was really hungry, at least not for sandwiches, but it was always difficult getting the girls to understand exactly what he wanted of them at this point. In fact, one or two of them never did enter into the spirit of the thing in the way he liked. He just hoped that Sandra wouldn't disappoint him.

Well-primed by some of the other stable girls, Sandra felt fairly confident that she could make this the best lunch he'd ever had in the copse. The only difficulty lay in timing. She had to be sure that the moment was right before she changed from subservient employee to dominant female. She decided to test the ground.

'I hope you're not going to eat with dirty hands,' she snapped suddenly.

Lord Corbett-Wynne's mouth opened slightly in surprise, but then he felt a delicious thrill of excitement run through him and shook his head meekly. 'Of course not,' he murmured.

'Wipe them on your handkerchief, then,' continued Sandra, her own excitement surfacing now that she knew it was going to be all right. She watched as her employer took a clean white handkerchief out of his pocket, carefully licked it and then wiped it over his hands.

She held out the wrapped package of sandwiches. 'Would you like something to eat now?' she asked softly.

He nodded eagerly. 'Yes!'

Sandra snatched the sandwiches away. 'You didn't say please. Haven't you learnt any manners yet?'

Lord Corbett-Wynne felt his penis start to stir. 'I'm sorry,' he muttered, hanging his head.

'You'll be sorrier before I've finished with you,' retorted Sandra, throwing the sandwiches to the ground. 'Take off your trousers.'

For the first time her employer hesitated. Although secluded, the copse wasn't on his land, and there was always the possibility of other people using the bridle path to reach it.

'Hurry up,' Sandra said irritably. 'If you don't do as I say you'll have to go straight home.'

He didn't hesitate any longer, but fumbled with the fastenings on his trousers, letting them fall to the ground and stepping out of them. Sandra nodded in satisfaction, but at the sight of the swelling in his Y-fronts she frowned. 'What's that?'

'I'm sorry,' he apologised, but despite his words the swelling was increasing visibly.

With a sound of irritation Sandra drew a long piece of cord from her pocket. 'Put your hands behind your back,' she said fiercely. Again he hesitated, but when she turned as though to fetch the horses he quickly obeyed and he could feel his erection straining against the restricting underpants.

Sandra made him kneel on the ground and then fastened the other end of the cord around the tree trunk, leaving him on a leash about three-feet long. Once he was at her feet she caught hold of his hair, pulling his head up until he was staring up at her. 'Now you know why you're being punished, don't you? It's because you haven't any manners, right?'

'I forgot my manners,' he agreed eagerly.

'And you know you need to be punished?'

'Yes! Yes!' Lord Corbett-Wynne could hardly wait, but he was incredibly stimulated by Sandra's skill at prolonging the game, and the waiting heightened all his senses. He only hoped he could control himself well enough.

Sandra bent down and very slowly unbuttoned his shirt, easing it off him with tantalising slowness until finally he found himself in nothing but his underpants as Sandra gently trailed her riding whip over his bare shoulders and across his naked stomach.

He was so hard now that it hurt, and when Sandra bent down and opened his underpants to release his erection he gave a gasp of relief. She looked at the purple tip, the veins standing out on the thick stem and felt a heady sensation of power rush through her. Dropping to her knees in front of him, she very casually started to take off her short-sleeved cotton top. As she peeled it over her head Lord Corbett-Wynne realised for the first time that she was naked beneath it, and at the sight of her breasts with the nipples already hard he thought that his pleasure was going to spill over.

Sandra watched him struggling to control himself; saw his abdominal muscles straining to subdue his excitement. When she thought that he'd mastered himself she took the rigid penis in her hands and then placed it between her breasts.

Lord Corbett-Wynne made a tiny sound, half-protest, half-pleasure, as he realised what she was going to do, and then he felt himself being massaged between the tight globes and heard Sandra's breathing start to quicken with pleasure as she rolled her swelling flesh around his soft, velvet tip.

Lord Corbett-Wynne felt his testicles drawing up beneath him. Tiny pricking sensations started up beneath the head of his glans and he knew that if she didn't stop quickly he would spill himself all over her and the fun would be ended.

As soon as his head started to go back and the tendons of his neck began to tighten, Sandra stopped the stimulation and rose to her feet, leaving her employer still kneeling with his huge penis standing up proud and hard.

'You can't have your pleasure until I've had mine,' she said shortly. The tethered man made a strangled sound of protest, which she ignored, and then he had to watch as she stepped back until she was clearly in his line of vision. She pushed her jodhpurs down below her knees and he was forced to look at the tantalising sight of the snow-white G-string nestling between her sex-lips.

'Pleasure me with your mouth,' she instructed him, and then she moved slowly forward until she was standing over him and he lifted his head, desperate to inhale her delicate musky perfume and taste her glorious femininity. Sandra moved her G-string to one side and waited.

Lord Corbett-Wynne began by letting his tongue tickle the crevices of Sandra's thighs until her legs began to tremble, then he pressed his mouth against her pubis and very lightly ran his tongue around the throbbing, soft tissue beneath. She felt her clitoris swelling and her body desperately wanted to feel his tongue against it, but when she moved herself into position his tongue refused to do as she wanted. Instead it moved lower and jabbed into her sex, drumming hard against the walls of the opening.

Sandra gasped and began to run her hands over her breasts, which were also screaming for stimulation. That was the only disadvantage of this game, her employer's hands were tied and she had to fondle herself.

She was very damp now and he used his tongue to spread her secretions up and down her inner channel but still without touching the clitoris itself. Then, when she could bear it no more, Sandra heard herself shouting at him. 'Move higher! Use more pressure!' she screamed, totally lost in the glorious climax that she could feel building within her.

The bound man let his mouth fasten around the slippery little bud and started to suck, slowly at first but with increasing pressure until Sandra's thighs moved to press tightly against either side of his face as her whole body began to quake. Keeping her clitoris firmly between his lips, Lord Corbett-Wynne suddenly moved his head rapidly from side to side, almost knocking Sandra off-balance as her legs were forced to move as well.

Now the feelings were running out of control. Her nipples were hard peaks of desire, her belly felt tight and warm and every muscle in her body started to tense as the pressure built behind the imprisoned bud.

She felt herself shaking, felt the wonderful wet, warm sweetness of the imminent orgasm and yet, maddeningly, it still remained balanced on the edge. She tried to move herself around, to change the pressure and topple herself over the edge.

Her employer, though, was an expert, and knew perfectly well what she needed. Despite his desire for his own climax he was enjoying this brief moment of power as the groom shook frantically and made tiny sounds of despair as she trembled on the verge of satisfaction. Finally he released the nub from the relentless suction, curled the sides of his tongue around and then brushed almost imperceptibly the side of the tiny stem.

That final, feather-light touch was exactly what was needed and with an ear-splitting scream Sandra climaxed, pressing herself down on her employer's face as her body went into a series of violent spasms.

When she was at last still, Lord Corbett-Wynne moved his head away and gratefully took in deep breaths of air. His own climax was once again dangerously near; he'd had to use all his self-control to avoid coming at the same time as Sandra and now all he wanted was his own satisfaction.

Sandra moved shakily away from him and glanced at his straining penis. 'I think it's time to see to you,' she said briskly. 'Is that what you'd like?'

'Of course it is!' snapped her employer, who was desperate for release.

Sandra's eyes widened. 'I hope I'm not going to have to punish you again,' she said menacingly. If anything his erection stiffened further as he quickly apologised. No one had ever taken the game to such extremes before, and he wasn't quite certain if he liked it or not, but his body didn't seem to share his doubts.

'That's all right, then,' murmured Sandra, and to her employer's delight she wrapped her whip round the end of his erection and then bent her head. As he tensed in anticipation she moved back and looked thoughtfully at him.

'I'm not quite satisfied yet,' she murmured as he stared at her in astonishment. 'I think I'll pleasure myself at the same time. Just make sure you don't come before I do, or I really will be cross.'

Carefully she sat down, removed her jodhpurs and

spread her legs out so that she could use her hands on herself. Then she made him kneel up until she could take him comfortably into her mouth. 'Excellent, now let's see how well we get on,' she said with a thin smile, and finally he felt her mouth on him.

Sandra let her left hand slip between her own thighs while her right grasped the base of her employer's erection. Bending towards him she let her tongue run up and down the top of the shaft while her hand alternately gripped and released the lower part. As she bent forward her pelvis tilted and she was rocked against the ground. This, combined with the delight of her fingers playing along the damp inner flesh, quickly excited her.

She was amazed at how swiftly she became aroused again after her first climax and, carried away by this, quite forgot that she was meant to be concentrating on Lord Corbett-Wynne. She rocked back and forth more quickly, letting the head of his penis slide in and out of her mouth, sometimes keeping her lips closed around the tip of the glans until the last possible moment so that he felt an incredible tugging sensation that seemed to be relentlessly drawing his seed upwards.

As the groom's fingers worked more and more urgently between her thighs, slipping in and out of her vagina and round and round in wonderfully arousing circles just beneath her clitoris, so her fingers worked more busily around her employer's shaft. Lord Corbett-Wynne's breathing was harsh as he strained to keep his climax at bay, but the sight of Sandra's open mouth and flushed cheeks, and the sound of her muffled cries of excitement, were too much for him.

Just before Sandra's body finally convulsed in the throes of her orgasm she sucked firmly at the fastened man's glans. Letting her tongue dip into the tiny slit at the top, she swirled it round briefly before drawing her head away, her bare buttocks moving fiercely against the lush grass as the sexual tension peaked.

Tiny tremors shook Sandra's body and she cried out with pleasure. 'I'm coming, I'm coming!' she screamed, and unwittingly she shattered Lord Corbett-Wynne's control so that he came first, spilling himself into her eager, hungry mouth with a deep groan of satisfaction.

Seconds later Sandra's body was once more shuddering in the throes of pleasure and tiny beads of sweat rolled down between her breasts as she slumped back on the grass, legs splayed out on either side of the still-fastened man.

Lord Corbett-Wynne let himself collapse too, so that he was now kneeling back on his haunches as his pulse and breathing slowly returned to normal.

'Magnificent!' he declared enthusiastically.

Sandra opened her eyes and stared at him. She sensed that if she could do something special now, something no one had ever thought of doing to him before, then he would be totally enslaved. Her mind raced and at last she smiled at him, but it wasn't an entirely pleasant smile.

'You came first,' she said accusingly.

'Only just,' he blustered. 'Not many men would have lasted like I did.'

Sandra touched his now limp penis and he flinched. 'I've known men who last longer,' she informed him. 'In fact, I seem to remember saying that if you came first you had to be punished. Isn't that right?'

'It's time to get back,' said her employer, but behind the command she sensed a hint of unease.

'Not yet. Naughty boys have to take their punishment, even when it's late.'

James Corbett-Wynne stared into the girl's eyes and knew that if he really wanted to go back all he had to do was say so. She worked for him – he could sack her if he liked and she wouldn't dare complain – but the truth of the matter was he suddenly didn't want to go back. He wanted the game to continue, even if it wasn't what he'd originally planned.

'That's not fair,' he said sulkily, and with a surge of delight Sandra knew she'd won.

Slowly she continued to fondle his flaccid penis, but it only retreated further and his testicles were shrivelled and empty, looking strangely vulnerable. 'I think you'd really like another orgasm,' she said with a smile.

James Corbett-Wynne looked at her in astonished disbelief. When he'd been young he hadn't needed very long between orgasms, but these days it was different and he had the feeling that any attempt at a repeat performance would be a painful failure.

'Not really,' he said quickly.

'Of course you do, and it shouldn't prove difficult for a big strong man like you. Here, you can play with my breasts first. That should get you started.'

'I don't think . . .'

'I shan't untie you until you've had another climax,' said Sandra with a light laugh. 'It might be awkward if we had to stay out here for the whole afternoon. I'm sure we're not the only people who use the horse track.'

Even as she spoke Sandra was sitting up and moving towards James. As she brought her body up against his, he felt her soft breasts rubbing against his chest, the nipples slowly hardening with the contact. He longed to have his hands free so that he could use them but knew that there was no chance she'd allow that. He moved his torso from side to side, increasing the friction between them until he felt each globe swelling and growing firmer.

Slowly Sandra rose to her feet, letting her breasts brush against his chin, mouth and eyes. He opened his mouth, trying to lick one of the nipples, but she swayed away and moved behind him so that she could gradually lower herself as she allowed her breasts to travel down his spine, finally coming to rest at the top of his underpants.

Although he felt excited and aroused there was no flicker of life from James's penis and he began to panic. Sandra moved round in front of him again and her hand wandered down inside his pants so that she could fondle him. Even his testicles seemed to shrink from her fingers and she gave a soft chuckle low in her throat.

'Suck on my nipples,' she suggested, positioning herself in front of him, and he quickly obeyed, drawing each of them into his mouth in turn and applying the same suction-like pressure that he had used on her clitoris. Sandra was soon damp between her thighs again, but this time she ignored her own pleasure. The excitement lay in forcing a second orgasm from her employer.

Finally, as her cries of excitement began to rise and the veins in her breasts became more pronounced, James's penis started to stir. It moved slowly, gradually increasing in size until it was semi-erect, but it refused, in spite of his frantic excitement at the situation, to grow any more.

Sandra knew what to do. She took one of the uneaten sandwiches and carefully lubricated a finger with the butter, then she tugged down her employer's underpants and with her other hand very lightly stroked his perineum. At the same time she started licking the tip of his penis.

'Kneel up,' she whispered, 'and part your knees more.'

Her mouth and fingers were working delicious magic on him and she could feel the sexual tension in him as he obeyed her, his whole body trembling with a mixture of excitement and fear. Sandra's own excitement was growing rapidly too and she knew that if she could make him come she'd climax as well. Deftly she increased the pressure of her tongue on his penis and as he gradually hardened she slid the prepared finger round the back of him, parted the cheeks of his bottom and let her greased finger slip into his anus.

As it slid inside him, searching gently for his prostate gland, James Corbett-Wynne knew that she was going to succeed. He felt her reach her goal and then she was touching the incredibly sensitive gland, massaging it lightly, exquisitely but remorselessly and he felt his testicles tighten once more.

Sandra's own breathing was ragged because she knew that this second climax would tear right through him, bringing him a new kind of ecstasy, an ecstasy so intense it would be almost painful, but she was sure that this was what held the key to her success.

As his erection hardened it started to hurt and James made a brief sound of protest that was quickly stifled as she continued the dual stimulation and her finger brushed insistently at the minute bliss-inducing gland.

Suddenly, with almost no warning, his thigh muscles went stiff, his belly cramped and then the wonderful hot tingling spread all over the top of his erection. Within seconds he could feel the thick liquid rushing up through the swollen stem of his manhood, and then it was spilling out over Sandra's breasts as her right hand pumped up and down the stem until she had extracted every last drop and with a shout of agonised delight he slumped backwards onto the grass.

As he lay there Sandra's hands strayed once more between her already damp thighs and within seconds her busy fingers had tumbled her aroused and excited body into its third climax, a climax mainly brought about by the wonderful feeling of power the whole episode had given her.

When he was recovered, Lord Corbett-Wynne got slowly to his feet. 'Untie me at once,' he said curtly. 'We have to get back to the Hall.'

This time Sandra knew that he had to be obeyed; her moment of authority was over, but not for long if she had her way. Meekly she unfastened the cord from his wrists and then as he dressed himself she removed it from the tree, curled it up and put it back in her pocket. It had been a good move to bring it along, she thought to herself.

'Hurry up and get dressed,' her employer said abruptly. 'Someone might come along at any minute.'

Sandra wondered why that hadn't bothered him earlier, but she quickly pulled her clothes on and just as the pair of them were preparing to mount there was the sound of hooves and a rider came into view.

'Lovely day!' called Matthew Stevens, reigning his horse in.

Lord Corbett-Wynne gave a silent prayer of thanks that the man hadn't arrived a few minutes earlier. 'Certainly is,' he agreed with enthusiasm, remembering exactly how good a day it had been.

'Saw your wife earlier; she's been looking at the pups I mentioned yesterday,' continued Sir Matthew. 'Pity she doesn't ride.'

'Quite,' agreed James, who was delighted that his wife was no longer interested in horses. 'Still, once your nerve's gone that's it. At her age she's probably right to stay well clear. Horses sense nerves – like dogs in that respect.'

Matthew, whose sharp eyes had taken in the fact that Sandra's shirt wasn't buttoned and her employer only had one sock on, nodded as he tried to hide his amusement. Clearly James Corbett-Wynne wasn't going to provide any incentive for Marina to try riding again; it would only cramp his style. 'Hope to see you soon,' he concluded as he dug his heels into his horse's sides and rode out of the clearing.

'Who was that?' asked Sandra, rather taken by the newcomer.

'Sir Matthew Stevens, he's a new neighbour of ours. For heaven's sake get your shirt fastened; I hope Matthew didn't notice anything.'

Sandra shrugged, did up the buttons and remounted her horse. She didn't much care if he had noticed; it wasn't likely to bother him and he might even be interested in her himself. She knew from experience that a lot of the county set enjoyed sexual liaisons with girl grooms.

Her employer was relatively silent on the ride back but Sandra wasn't perturbed. It was always like that after sex games with any of them; they tried to pretend it hadn't happened, but after a day or so they were back for more.

Once they arrived back she took both sets of reins and went to rub the horses down. As she was about to go she turned to Lord Corbett-Wynne, as though a thought had just struck her. 'If a vacancy came up in the stables, I wonder if you'd consider my sister, sir?' she said demurely. 'She's having to leave her present job as the horses there are all being sold and it would be nice if we could work together. We're very alike,' she added meaningfully.

Despite his total exhaustion James felt a frisson of excitement. 'How old is she?' he demanded.

'Eleven months older than me. She's *very* experienced,' she added.

'Worked together before, have you?' he asked, his eyes boring into hers so that she understood he wasn't talking about mucking out stables.

'Yes, sir, and we gave total satisfaction.'

James nodded. 'I'm sure you did. Very well, I'll keep it in mind. I'll have a word with Jerry. He's in charge of the stables. Tell you what, ask him to come and speak to me at five-thirty, in my study.'

'Thank you, sir,' said Sandra, lowering her eyes to hide her triumph. Together she and Melanie would be invincible, and Lord Corbett-Wynne would get excellent value for money.

At four-thirty Tania and Annabel met in the music room, where afternoon tea was served. Annabel had spent the past hour trying to speak to Lady Corbett-Wynne about her ideas, but to her surprise she'd been turned away repeatedly with a variety of rather weak excuses. Her ladyship had been resting, bathing or was simply too busy, according to her maid. This seemed extraordinary considering her desire for someone to look over the Hall at the first possible moment.

'Had a good day?' asked Tania, lolling on one of the sagging chairs, her legs bare beneath her cotton skirt.

'I've been busy,' responded Annabel. 'This room's taken

up most of my time. It certainly needs something doing to it, but your mother's ideas and mine aren't quite in tune.'

'What does she want? Chintzy curtains and lace drapes?'

'Regency-striped wallpaper and brocade curtains. I had something much more subtle in mind. I thought that if the walls were –'

'Save it for her,' drawled Tania. 'I couldn't care less what the bloody place looked like. I wonder how Crispian got on with that frightful Amanda? I bet she did nothing but talk pigs to him. She's heavily into pig breeding!'

Annabel laughed. 'Isn't that rather unusual for a girl?'

'Not for that family; they're all mad as March hares. Unluckily for Crispian, they're absolutely rolling in money, so Step-papa says he should ignore the batty streak and think about the dosh.'

'Well, I suppose he's got to marry someone,' murmured Annabel.

Tania glared at her, her eyes sparkling dangerously. 'Why? Not all men get married. Besides, he's already in love.'

Annabel wished she'd kept quiet. 'Yes, but that can't come to anything, can it?'

'I don't see why not. We aren't related, you know. If we'd met at a hunt ball instead of being thrown together by our parents' marriage we'd have been considered a good match.'

'Really?' asked Annabel.

Tania pulled a face. 'No, not really. I'm not rich, you see, that's the big problem. My mother's rich, and one day my brother will be rich, but I haven't anything of my own, so theoretically I should be trying to marry money too. Perhaps I'll marry Amanda's brother and we can all four have a really close family relationship!' She gave a peal of laughter but there was no amusement in her eyes. 'I'll never let him go,' she said quietly when the laughter had died away. 'I know how to keep him and I intend to do just that, even if it means this house falls down round our ears due to lack of money. We suit each other. He'll never want another woman like he wants me.'

Luckily for Annabel one maid brought in a tray of sandwiches and another followed with a pot of tea in an antique silver teapot with a mismatched set of chipped bone-china cups and saucers, which saved her from having to reply.

'You can pour,' said Tania, suddenly sounding sulky.

As Annabel poured the first cup the door opened and Lord Corbett-Wynne walked in. 'Hope I'm in time for tea,' he remarked cheerfully. 'Take it young Crispian's out at the Fitzwilliams'?'

'Yes, scratching a pig's back, most likely,' snapped Tania.

'Pig's back? Don't know what you mean.'

'Yes you do. Amanda Fitzwilliam's potty about pigs; well, potty full stop, really.'

'Rubbish, she's a damned fine filly. I'd like some tea, my dear, and a couple of those delicious sandwiches too. Missed lunch today, too busy riding to eat.'

Tania gave a smothered giggle and her stepfather glared at her. Annabel handed him his tea and sandwiches, gave another cup to Tania and was just about to sit down when Lady Corbett-Wynne walked in. Everyone looked astonished.

'What brings you here, Mama?' asked Tania. 'Don't tell me you wanted our company!'

Her mother smiled placidly and Annabel thought that her employer looked a great deal less tense than on the previous day. 'I thought it would be nice to have tea with Annabel; she and I have some things to discuss and I've been too busy to see her. I also wanted to ask you, James, about whether or not we still employ that dark-haired youth in the stables?'

'Jerry, you mean?' growled her husband.

'Probably; the thing is, I've decided that I'd like to take up riding again.'

There was a stunned silence, broken eventually by James, who seemed to Annabel to be less than pleased at the announcement. 'Nonsense!' he said briskly. 'You know full well that last fall nearly killed you. What's the point in risking your pretty little neck for something you never enjoyed much in the first place?'

His wife glanced at him in amusement. 'This "pretty little neck", as you put it, was never in danger; I simply had a heavy fall. I was also once considered quite a good rider, which is probably where Tania gets her talent from. Not that I have any desire to take part in any kind of competitive riding at my age. I would merely like to be able to go for a ride in the countryside.'

'But you hardly ever go out in the air!' blustered her husband. 'If you've suddenly decided you need a healthier lifestyle, why not try walking? It's a damned sight safer.'

'Is there some reason why you don't wish me to ride?' asked his wife.

James looked swiftly away from her searching gaze. 'Of course not! Only thinking of you, my dear.'

'That's very thoughtful of you, but despite your concern I'm quite sure I'll be in safe hands with this Jerry person. You're always telling me that we have the most skilled stable staff in the country.' At this her husband's face went an even darker shade of red and he mumbled a token agreement before taking a large bite out of a rather small sandwich.

Marina turned her attention to Annabel. 'I'm so sorry I've been busy this afternoon, my dear. Tell me, have you come to any conclusion about this room yet?'

Annabel nodded, trying to swallow the remains of her sandwich in a hurry and ending up coughing as a result. Lord Corbett-Wynne was quickly at her side, patting her enthusiastically on the back, his fingers lingering there a little longer than was necessary after she'd recovered.

'I tried to visualise the room as you suggested, Lady Corbett-Wynne,' she said at last, 'but to be perfectly honest

I don't think it would look right. Everything needs to be lightened, and Regency-stripe wallpaper gives an extremely heavy look to a room. I thought that if the walls were painted a very soft blue-grey colour it would be possible to incorporate your brocade curtains, but only if they were looped right back off the windows. A carpet of naturally faded blues and pinks would look wonderful. You'd then have considerable choice for your furnishings because there'd be so many colours in the walls and carpet. Also, I don't think it's a good idea to have everything matching. In a house like this it just doesn't look right. Part of the charm of the Hall is –'

'It's no good talking to my wife about the charm of this house,' exploded Lord Corbett-Wynne. 'She hates the place. If she had her way she'd tear it apart and fill every room with spindly bits of French furniture and lace curtains. She should live in a harem, except she wouldn't like the life!' Laughing heartily at his own joke, he subsided into silence again.

His wife raised her eyebrows. 'Have you quite finished, James?'

He wiped his eyes on his handkerchief, remembered wiping his hands on it earlier in the day before Sandra punished him and to his astonishment felt his penis stir. 'Quite finished,' he said hastily.

'Good. Well, Annabel, it isn't really how I'd imagined it, but I can see what you mean and it is difficult to imagine my husband looking at home in a tidy room. So your suggestion about odds and ends of furniture is probably a sensible one.'

Annabel leant forward in her chair. 'I didn't mean odds and ends, Lady Corbett-Wynne, I simply meant that . . .'

To her amazement her employer waved a hand in the air dismissively. 'As you like, Annabel. I've been assured that you're very talented and, considering the amount I'm paying you, I hope that's true. Tomorrow afternoon we can discuss the dining room. I trust you're in favour of modernising that?'

'I think that different lighting and . . .'

'I want the entire room changed,' Lady Corbett-Wynne said firmly. 'I hate eating there at the moment, such a dark depressing place. Perhaps a little Italian influence wouldn't come amiss.'

Annabel was so shocked she couldn't think of a reply. She knew it would be sacrilege to attempt any major changes to such a beautiful room, but now was clearly not the moment to say as much so she nodded, hoping that by the next day she could think of some kind of compromise, although she had no idea what it would be.

'Talking of the dining room,' continued Marina, 'I thought we might have a dinner party on Saturday week.'

'A dinner party? How big?' demanded her husband.

Marina shrugged elegantly. 'I thought twenty to twenty-four. It's been such a long time since we entertained properly.'

'That's because you said you hated all my friends!' James pointed out.

Marina smiled absent-mindedly at him. 'Nonsense, I'm sure I never said that. Anyway, they won't all be your friends this time. Annabel will be here, and we can invite Matthew again; he was an excellent guest, very entertaining.'

'I noticed you liked him,' Tania said casually.

Marina turned her head sharply towards her daughter. 'Is there anything wrong in that?'

'No, it's unusual, that's all.'

'Saw him when I was out riding,' announced James. 'He said you'd been down to look at those puppies of his. Find one you wanted?'

'Well, no,' admitted Marina, 'but I'm going to have another look in a few days. It will be easier to choose when they're a bit older.'

'I didn't think you liked dogs,' said Tania.

'I don't like the dogs we've got because they're all badly behaved and noisy. If I have one I shall train it myself.'

'You'll be exhausted if this goes on,' muttered her husband. 'Riding lessons, dog training and interior decorating; I hope there are enough hours in the day for you.'

Tania giggled; Marina looked irritated and Annabel sat in awkward silence, wondering exactly what was going on. A tap at the door interrupted them.

'Come in,' called Lord Corbett-Wynne.

Susan, the maid, entered. 'Mr Jerry's waiting for you in your study, sir. He was told you wanted a word with him,' she explained.

Marina's eyes widened. 'Don't tell me you're psychic, James! Did you know I wanted to ride again?'

'Of course not; I want to see him about another groom.'

'Haven't you got enough?' asked Tania in apparent innocence.

'Well, please mention my riding lessons to him at the same time,' said Marina. She put down her cup and swept out of the room, to be followed a few seconds later by her husband.

'I wonder what they're both up to,' mused Tania, 'clearly Step-papa's on the lookout for new excitement, but I can't imagine what's got into Mother. She hasn't been near a horse for years, neither does she like dogs. I can only assume she likes Sir Matthew, but as she hasn't shown any interest in a man for years it's a bit surprising. What do you think, Annabel?'

Annabel, who was quite certain that Lady Corbett-Wynne liked Sir Matthew, decided to keep quiet. 'I've really no idea,' she said firmly.

'Well, I thought he was a bit of a dish, far too experienced for Mother. What did you think of him?'

'He's very attractive,' admitted Annabel. 'Handsome and extremely masculine. I'm not too keen on delicate types.'

'He mentioned wanting you to go and look at his place,

didn't he?' asked Tania. 'I'd go if I were you. Who knows what he might show you!'

Annabel, who felt that she'd like nothing better than to have Sir Matthew show her a thing or two inside the Mill House, tried to look disinterested. 'I might not have time,' she said.

'I'd find time if I were you. You are going to join Crispian and me again tonight, aren't you? We've got such a good idea, it would be a shame to waste it.'

Annabel flushed. 'I'm not sure. I don't usually . . .'

'Come on, you loved it last night. I'm an expert; I can tell when someone's faking and when they're not, and you most definitely were not. We really turned you on, so why not enjoy yourself again? Crispian and I enjoy threesomes.'

'We enjoy what?' demanded Crispian, walking silently into the room as his sister spoke.

'Threesomes! I was inviting Annabel to join us tonight. Remember what you suggested?'

Crispian smiled. 'I certainly do. If you decide to join us, Annabel, come along to my room after dinner. We'll be there, and we'll wait until ten o'clock. If you're not there by then we'll start without you!'

Annabel felt tendrils of excitement deep within her stomach and found herself gripping her thighs together tightly to increase the pleasurable sensations.

'How was Amanda?' asked Tania, pouring her step-brother a cup of half-cold tea.

He groaned, pushing his long fair hair back off his face. 'Exactly how I'd imagined – ghastly! We spent most of the afternoon looking at her latest litter of pigs. Well, not *her* litter, although nothing would surprise me with that family, but her favourite sow's latest litter. It made the romance and sweet talk a bit tricky. Still, Pa will be delighted; she's agreed to come to the Winterbrooks' summer ball with me. She said it would be "a bit of a lark"!'

'Mother wants to learn to ride again,' said Tania, suddenly anxious to change the subject.

'Ride? Good lord, what brought that on?'

'I've no idea, although I suspect that a visit to Sir Matthew Stevens' place this morning might have something to do with it.'

'Really?' Crispian glanced at Annabel. 'Looks as though you've got competition there, Annie!'

'My name's Annabel and I'm not particularly interested in Sir Matthew,' said Annabel. She got quickly to her feet. 'If you'll excuse me I must get back to my room. I need to bring my notes up to date.'

'She fancies him like mad,' said Crispian after Annabel had gone. 'I think we ought to make sure they have a chance to get to know each other better, don't you, Tania?'

His stepsister smiled at him. 'That sounds like fun. Perhaps we could arrange something after the dinner party.'

'What dinner party?'

'I forgot, you missed that bombshell as well. Mother wants to have a large dinner party on Saturday week, with Sir Matthew as one of the guests.'

'In that case,' Crispian said slowly, 'we must certainly make the most of the opportunity, for Annabel's sake.'

'And if we get some pleasure from it too?' queried Tania.

'Well, that's just a bonus, for being such helpful people!' he replied.

They both laughed.

Chapter Six

Dinner that evening was once again formal, with the men in dinner jackets. Annabel wore a calf-length blue and grey sleeveless silk dress with a matching jacket, while Tania opted for a bright, multicoloured strapless, knee-length dress that clung to her curves like a second skin.

'Aren't you a little cold, dear?' asked Marina, her voice sharp.

Tania laughed. 'Not me, I'm naturally hot-blooded!'

Her stepfather cleared his throat and let his gaze linger appreciatively on Annabel. 'Fancy a ride while you're here, young lady? Some of our horses are very well behaved.'

'Unlike the children!' joked Crispian, winking at Annabel.

Before she could reply, Lady Corbett-Wynne interrupted. 'Did you speak to that man of yours about my riding lessons, James?'

He nodded. 'Jerry said he'd be delighted to start lessons any time you liked, but he couldn't say much else. If you ask me . . .'

'I am not asking you,' his wife said firmly, and Tania kicked her stepbrother under the table. They exchanged amused glances.

'How was Sir Matthew?' asked Crispian. His tone was casual.

To his surprise his stepmother smiled dreamily. 'Most helpful; in fact, he was the one who suggested I learnt to ride again.'

'Interfering idiot,' muttered her husband.

'Annabel rather fancies him, don't you, Annie?' said Crispian.

Lady Corbett-Wynne turned her head sharply towards Annabel. 'I'd have thought he was a little old for you.'

Annabel, furious with Crispian, tried to look amused by his remark. 'Your stepson's talking nonsense, Lady Corbett-Wynne. I've scarcely spoken to Sir Matthew.'

'Nor will you have time to in the future,' her employer pointed out decisively. 'So far you seem to have accomplished very little during your stay here.'

This unfair criticism brought a flush to Annabel's cheeks but she lowered her eyes and resumed eating her saddle of lamb, well aware that the older woman felt threatened by what Crispian had said. If she felt threatened, reasoned Annabel, then Crispian had clearly been right about his stepmother and Sir Matthew. Whether the attraction was mutual or not she had no way of knowing, but she had to admit to herself that he'd seemed interested in her hostess the previous evening.

After the meal, when coffee was served in the library, Tania and Crispian disappeared. Lady Corbett-Wynne discussed her ideas for the dining room with Annabel, but in a somewhat desultory fashion, and after half an hour she too made her excuses and retired to her rooms.

Alone with Annabel, Lord Corbett-Wynne became more animated. 'No steady boyfriend, then?' he mused, his right hand touching Annabel's thigh as she sat next to him on the sofa.

Annabel moved her legs. 'Not at this moment, no.'

'Sex is good for you; it keeps you fit and active. Marina

would be a far happier, healthier woman if she understood that.'

'She seemed happy last night,' murmured Annabel.

His lordship nodded. 'Damned odd that! If I didn't know her better I'd have thought she was smitten by Sir Matthew, but men don't interest her in that way any more, as I know to my cost.'

Thinking of Sir Matthew made Annabel remember the previous night, and also the fact that Crispian and Tania were at this moment waiting for her in Crispian's room. She glanced at her watch and saw that it was nine-fifty. In ten minutes' time they'd begin their evening's entertainment without her, and suddenly she knew that she didn't want that. She wanted to join them, to wallow in sheer physical pleasure again, letting her sensuality take over.

'I'm sorry,' she said abruptly, getting to her feet. 'I'm really tired and there's a lot to be done tomorrow. If you'll excuse me, Lord Corbett-Wynne, I think I'll go to bed now. Good night.'

Her sudden movement scarcely registered with James. After drinking a great deal of wine with his meal, he'd worked his way through a bottle of whisky since coffee. His thoughts had returned to Sandra, or, more precisely, the prospect of Sandra accompanied by her sister. When consulted, Jerry had protested, claiming they didn't need another groom, but he'd overruled him and with any luck the girl would be with them within a week. Despite his strenuous activities in the copse his penis stirred at the prospect.

'Good night,' repeated Annabel.

Lord Corbett-Wynne glanced up, his eyes vague. 'Good night, Sandra,' he murmured, and Annabel left him to his thoughts.

In Crispian's room the stepbrother and sister heard Annabel's footsteps approaching along the corridor and smiled at each other, delighted that she was as keen as they'd thought.

'Lucky I had two costumes,' said Crispian. 'The pair of you will make an interesting contrast.'

Annabel tapped lightly on the door and immediately Crispian let her in. He smiled engagingly, and she was struck anew by how attractive he was with his white, even teeth and clear blue eyes. As he pushed his fair hair back off his forehead she felt a stirring of desire which was reflected in her eyes.

'Time for some fun!' he said. 'I hope you like dressing up.'

'Dressing up?'

'Yes, I'm on a power trip tonight. You and Tania are going to be my maids; the uniforms are on the bed. You both have to obey my every command. Should be exciting, don't you think?'

'What happens if we don't obey you?' asked Annabel, her desire increasing.

'In that case you have to be chastised, but somehow I don't think you'll be difficult. You seem a very well-behaved employee as far as my stepmother's concerned!'

While he was speaking Tania was peeling off her ball-gown and dressing herself in one of the two outfits on the bed. Annabel watched as the auburn-haired girl pulled on a pair of frilly white lace knickers that peeped beneath the hemline of the short black skirt. The tight-fitting, basque-style top was also black, tightly laced and with a trimming of white lace above the breasts. A small white pinafore and black fishnet stockings almost completed the outfit, which was given the finishing touch when Tania fastened a scrap of lace on the top of her head. She then posed provocatively for the other two, pointing her left foot in its stiletto heel so that her buttocks curved out even more below the skirt. She pouted at her stepbrother.

'There's too much work for me, sir. I need help.'

Crispian's eyes gleamed. 'Help is right here! Quickly, Annabel, get changed.'

For a moment she hesitated, but then warm memories

of the previous night's pleasure started to creep into her mind. She remembered the way the two of them had licked and teased her straining body, the tiny metal ring that had encircled her clitoris enabling them to tantalise her almost beyond endurance. At the memory she grew damp between her thighs and without further thought peeled off her evening dress and quickly donned the second costume.

Crispian eyed her approvingly once she was dressed. 'It suits you. Tell me, Annabel, are you used to being in service?'

To her surprise it proved easy for Annabel to slip into the role she'd been allocated. It was as though when she'd pulled on the blatantly erotic outfit she'd become a different person. 'No, sir,' she said demurely, 'but I've always wanted to try my hand at it.'

'Good. Stand in front of me. I want to make sure you're correctly dressed.'

She moved to stand a few inches in front of him and, although she lowered her eyes as he examined her, she pushed her shoulders back to emphasise her breasts, which felt tight in the constricting basque.

Very slowly, Crispian let the fingers of one hand run round the lace edging at the top of the basque, his fingers cool against her hot skin. 'Is this too tight?' he asked with apparent concern.

'No, sir, it's just right,' she responded.

'I think it's a little tight. I'll unlace the top two holes I think,' he murmured, and she felt his hands brush the undersides of her tightly covered breasts for a moment as he unlaced her. The tightness of the basque meant that by releasing the top Crispian had ensured that Annabel's breasts were pushed upwards so that the top halves of the round globes were clearly visible. Bending his head he let his tongue flicker across the newly exposed area for a moment before straightening up again.

A shiver of desire ran through Annabel as she waited in front of him.

'Point your toe, like Tania did,' he said curtly, his eyes suddenly cold. As she obeyed her hip moved closer to his body until they were almost touching and she had a burning desire to grind herself against him. To be instructed on exactly how to move, to have her clothing adjusted and her limbs positioned, was incredibly arousing and her breathing quickened.

'That's fine. Keep that position, don't move an inch until I give you permission,' he said, and as Annabel's limbs went rigid he turned to Tania. 'You, come and join the new girl. Check that her stocking seams are straight at the back.'

Very slowly and lightly Tania let her fingers trace a line up Annabel's legs and Annabel felt the taut muscles of her pointed leg start to tremble.

'Keep still!' Crispian said shortly.

When Tania's hands reached the top of the stockings she let them wander over the soft flesh that was exposed there and Annabel's breath caught in her throat.

'What did you do?' Crispian asked Tania.

'My hand slipped,' she said, her voice almost insolent.

'Then apologise.'

'Why should I, sir? It didn't hurt her. Her seams *are* straight,' she added as an afterthought.

'You'll apologise because I say so,' said Crispian, and now his blue eyes had darkened until they were almost violet.

Behind Annabel, Tania let her hand slip up the other girl's skirt and she gently caressed the rounded cheeks of her bottom. Annabel began to tremble with sexual tension, hoping that these preliminaries weren't going to go on for too long as her body was desperate for further stimulation.

Crispian saw her body quiver and guessed what Tania was doing. 'Annabel, straighten your leg and stand with your feet apart,' he said softly. Gratefully she allowed her cramping muscles to move and then stood with her feet about six inches apart. To her surprise her docility was no longer assumed. She was being aroused by the fact that she had to do as he said, and taking pleasure from every command.

Tania's hand moved and her fingers slipped between Annabel's parted thighs, grazing along the covered vulva. 'She's already damp!' she exclaimed with glee.

Crispian drew in his breath sharply. 'Who invited you to speak?'

Tania tossed her head. 'I thought you'd be interested. She must like being dominated.'

'If you don't keep silent you'll be punished,' said Crispian, and Annabel saw that his cheeks were flushed.

Tania moved round so that she was standing next to Annabel. 'I need unlacing, sir,' she said in a soft, little-girl voice. 'My bodice is much too tight, I can hardly breathe.'

To Annabel's astonishment Crispian's whole face suddenly darkened and reaching out towards his stepsister he ripped at her basque in one abrupt movement that opened it from neckline to waist so that most of her breasts was clearly visible.

'I told you to be silent!' he shouted. 'What kind of an example is this for a new girl? I'm very much afraid, Tania, that you'll have to be punished.'

Tania turned away with a flouncing movement that made sure her breasts swung clear of the torn basque. Apparently enraged, Crispian grabbed her by the shoulders and pulled her back towards him, his hands hard against her skin. Only a moment passed before he turned towards Annabel.

'Annabel, go and sit on the high-backed chair there. Take off your shoes and put your feet flat to the ground with your knees about three inches apart.'

She hurried to do as he'd ordered, but remembered to use small steps that she felt were in keeping with the costume. Once she was seated Crispian pulled a suddenly struggling Tania across the room towards her.

'I'm sorry to have to ask this of you on your first day as a maid, Annabel, but I'm afraid you'll have to punish Tania for me.'

Annabel stared at him. 'Me?'

'Don't forget to call me "sir",' he snapped.

Annabel flushed, beginning to feel that this was more than a game. 'Me, sir?' she repeated.

'Yes, you. Don't tell me you've never spanked another girl before.'

This time it didn't require any acting on Annabel's part for her expression to make clear to Crispian the fact that she hadn't; her eyes widened and she started to rise from the chair.

'Stay there!' he instructed her. 'You'll find it's very simple, and quite exciting as well. Tania, stop struggling.' Tania wriggled and twisted in his grip but he pulled her remorselessly across the room and then forced her face-down across Annabel's knees. Although she could easily have got away, Tania remained where her stepbrother had put her, while continuing to wriggle and make loud sounds of protest.

As she wriggled, her hips ground against the top of one of Annabel's legs and she could feel the soft flesh of Tania's belly against her. The more Tania squirmed the more pressure Annabel felt, and she watched the other girl's skirt rise up so that her rounded buttocks, covered by the white lace frills, were clearly exposed.

Crispian put one hand on his stepsister's head and pushed against the auburn hair, while he tugged the snow-white panties down her legs until Annabel was looking at smooth, pale flesh. 'Smack her,' he said curtly. Annabel hesitated. 'If you disobey me then I can assure you Tania won't hesitate to smack you,' said Crispian smoothly.

Annabel decided that she didn't want to find herself in the same position as the writhing Tania and so she raised

114

her right hand and brought it down lightly against the other girl's flesh. For a moment there was silence. Tania stopped moving and Crispian stared at Annabel in disbelief.

'What do you think you're doing?' he asked in astonishment. 'She probably didn't even feel that. Look, this is how you discipline her.' Raising his own right hand he brought it down sharply against the tight buttocks, and at the moment of impact there was the sound of flesh meeting flesh. When he removed his hand there was a red mark on the curve of one buttock.

'There, that's how it's done. Now do it properly, Annabel, or you'll be in serious trouble.'

She knew it was a game, that both Tania and Crispian were playing with her, and yet Annabel felt a tiny tremor of fear. She hastily brought her hand down as Crispian had shown her, and when she made contact Tania gave a tiny moan and ground her pelvis hard against Annabel.

'That's better.' Crispian sounded friendly again, and Annabel relaxed slightly. 'Carry on,' he added. 'I'll tell you when to stop.'

As she began to rhythmically slap the increasingly red buttocks Annabel began to feel tendrils of delight snaking through her. She was enjoying the power, and the realisation that Tania was getting pleasure both from the slaps and from her own movements against Annabel's knees.

Tania's breathing became louder, her gasps and moans more pronounced, and soon it was clear to Annabel that the other girl was on the brink of an orgasm. Crispian knew it too and, reaching beneath his stepsister's upper torso, his hands gripped her breasts, his fingers kneading roughly against the swollen globes.

For Tania, the combination of glorious heat from the slaps, the sexual tension in her pelvis from her body movements and the rough handling of her breasts was bliss. Suddenly she felt her whole body go rigid and her

115

toes tensed as the first delicious tremors of a climax began to invade her.

'Stop!' shouted Crispian, and Annabel, her hand in mid-air, obeyed him instantly. At the same time he released Tania's breasts and pulled her sharply to her feet, ignoring her screams of fury as all the sources of stimulation, all the things that had brought her to the very peak of satisfaction, were removed, leaving her body painfully swollen and her belly aching with frustration.

'Right, that will do for now,' said Crispian smoothly. 'After all, it was meant to be a punishment.'

'Let me go!' shrieked Tania. 'That's not fair. I was just about to come.'

Looking at her, Annabel could tell exactly how the other girl was feeling. Tania's lips were moist and full, her breasts heaving beneath the basque, and the sexual flush of arousal covered her chest and lower neck.

'Isn't she beautiful like that?' Crispian said softly, grip-ping Tania from behind and lowering his head so that his tongue could lightly lick at the delicate skin covering the top of her spine. Tania groaned and thrust herself back-wards but Crispian kept her away from him. 'How do you feel, Annabel? Did arousing Tania arouse you too?'

His piercing blue eyes defied her to lie and Annabel nodded. 'Yes,' she said hoarsely.

Crispian smiled. 'That's good; I thought you and I would enjoy ourselves while Tania watched. That will be your reward for doing such a good job on her. What do you think, Tania? Is that fair?'

Tania was really angry now, kicking out at Crispian with her high-heeled shoes and trying desperately to find some means of stimulating her body. But it was hopeless and within minutes she found herself tied to the very chair that Annabel had sat on to punish her. Her arms were fastened behind the back of the chair with a silk scarf, a black leather belt went round her waist and the chair and finally each of her legs was fastened to a chair leg with strong cords. The chair was then turned so that it faced Crispian's bed.

'There, doesn't she look nice!' laughed Crispian. Annabel regarded the scowling Tania and at the look of urgent sexual need in Tania's eyes her own belly tightened and she felt the dampness between her thighs increase.

Very slowly Crispian turned Annabel so that she was facing him and then he gently unlaced the front of her basque, peeling it back as he went so that the flesh was slowly exposed to the relatively cool air of the bedroom.

Shivers of excitement ran through her and when he finally freed her breasts entirely and cupped them carefully in his hands, his long fingers stroking delicately at the undersides, her whole body shook with excited expectation.

'See how greedy she is!' said Crispian, laughing and turning to his silent and fastened stepsister. 'Who'd have imagined she'd be so anxious for pleasure!' Annabel wanted to feel his mouth on her breasts, to savour the sensation of his tongue flicking across her already hardening nipples, but Crispian was busy removing her skirt and apron, letting them fall to the ground so that she was left in the opened basque, white lace knickers, black stockings and high-heeled shoes.

He moved her to face the imprisoned Tania and then stood behind her, his hands roaming over her hips and down her upper thighs while he pressed his body against her so that she could feel his excitement through his trousers.

Very tenderly his hands unfastened the suspenders that held up the black fishnet stockings, and then he was easing them down Annabel's slim legs, his fingers touching her lightly like feathers as the stockings were peeled away leaving the skin bare.

Annabel could feel herself shaking. She wanted more, wanted him to take her fiercely and urgently, to touch her on the hard moist nub of pleasure that was pressing

117

against the crotch of her panties, but Crispian was determined to take his time. This was all part of Tania's punishment.

As Tania watched helplessly, Crispian proceeded to remove Annabel's panties and when he stroked the softly rounded buttocks Tania whimpered with frustration. Her own bottom was still hot and aching from the spanking it had received, and she longed for the same caress that Annabel was now receiving.

To Annabel's shame, the sound of Tania's jealousy only increased her own need and she let out a soft sigh of pleasure as Crispian's hands tightened on the cheeks of her bottom, squeezing and releasing them in a steady rhythm that pulled on the flesh surrounding her clitoris, easing it backwards and then letting it slip back into place again, insidiously stimulated.

Finally, leaving her in just the opened basque, Crispian pressed Annabel back onto the bed and Tania watched furiously as he separated her legs and then drew on his most recent sex toy, a soft latex massage mitten that was covered in tiny probes.

Carefully he eased Annabel's legs apart and spread scented massage lotion over the insides of her thighs and her lower abdomen. Annabel's body jumped slightly at the coolness, but then he began to move the massage glove over her and with a groan of delight she felt him moving across her lower body. It felt as though masses of tongues were gently licking at her flesh. When he applied more pressure, she arched her hips up towards him, loving the coiling, aching sensations that were coming from deep inside her.

Crispian turned Annabel so that Tania could see them both more clearly and then he allowed his tongue to flick sharply against her tight, pointed nipples. When her hands went round his neck and pulled him harder against her, he let his teeth nip at the soft, pale-brown skin of the

118

areolae. Annabel gasped and bucked, feeling the heavy pulse of an orgasm beginning to build between her thighs.

Crispian's right hand encircled her left breast, forcing it upwards so that he could lick and suck the whole of the surface area and all the time his other hand, covered by the massage mitten, continued to arouse her lower body until she was squirming against the bed cover just as Tania had squirmed against her knees.

'Would you like me to use a clitoral ring again?' he whispered against her ear, and Annabel cried out with excitement. It was easy for him to slip a copper circle over her nub, standing proudly erect from the swollen tissue, and once that was in place it was all that Annabel could think about.

She was frantic for his tongue, still working on her breasts, to caress it, to travel along her inner lips and dart into her sex, but he ignored the most vital spot and instead concentrated on continuing to massage her inner thighs and the very base of her belly, pressing firmly over the pubic bone until the ache of need became almost unbearable.

Annabel began to twist and turn, trying to find some way of forcing him into touching the now enclosed clitoris. At last, with a soft laugh, he slid down her body, removed the mitten and after applying more of the lotion to his fingers began to rub in circles just beneath her nub of pleasure.

Annabel could hear her own cries of excitement. She was swollen and open to him, and his clever, practised movements were increasing the rate of the pulse deep inside her while searing shards of pleasure kept shooting through her whole body like slivers of glass.

Crispian turned his head towards his stepsister. 'I think I'll let her come now,' he said quietly, and Tania glared at him, her eyes dark with fury and sexual desire. 'She'll probably be quite noisy; I hope that doesn't bother you,' he added, and then turned back to the frantic figure on the bed.

At last Annabel felt his tongue circling the opening to her sex, drawing out her secretions and spreading them upwards along her inner channel until he reached the imprisoned clitoris. He blew very lightly on it and if it hadn't been trapped in the ring it would have retracted but he knew that no matter what he did it would stay in place, waiting for the final trigger that would release all of Annabel's pent-up excitement.

'Ready?' he teased her.

'Hurry, please!' cried Annabel, her whole body now so tight and needy that she felt she'd explode if he didn't let her come. Carefully he used his hands to part her sex lips even more fully and for a moment he studied her swollen damp tissue as Annabel bucked and jerked in an effort to reach his tongue. Then, at last, he lowered his head and let his tongue drift in lazy circles around the metal ring. This simply increased Annabel's excitement until she was almost delirious with pleasure. When he judged that the moment was right, Crispian slipped off the tiny constriction and quickly drew the now free clitoris into his mouth, letting his tongue roll round and round it as he kept it between his lips.

For Annabel the movement provided the most exquisite sensation she could ever remember and at last her whole body exploded into its long-awaited climax. She screamed aloud at the intensity of the searing pleasure that tore through her, sending tingles of excitement to the tips of her fingers and toes.

When her body was still again, Crispian gently inserted two fingers into her sex until he reached her cervix. Very slowly he started to play with it, and Annabel's breathing began to grow more rapid again, as she started to utter tiny mewing sounds of pleasure. He carefully moved the cervix about, using rotating movements of his fingers. No one had ever done that to Annabel before and the pleasure was so deep and intense that she could hardly bear it.

Imprisoned on her chair, Tania knew only too well what Crispian was doing and she grew frantic. It was one of the things that she liked best, something that only Crispian had ever done to her, and to watch him doing it to another woman, particularly one as attractive and responsive as Annabel, was torture for her. She cried out in protest, but Crispian ignored her, concentrating solely on Annabel.

'I can't stand that any more,' whispered Annabel as the deep aching pleasure continued. He smiled at her, and moved his hand slightly so that he could rub against her G-spot. Within seconds Annabel was once more bucking beneath him as her body was engulfed in another climax and this time he decided that he couldn't wait any longer. Before her contractions had died away, Crispian had positioned himself on top of her, pushing his slacks and pants down to his ankles before slipping on a condom and then sliding into the tight warmth of her vagina.

As her vaginal walls contracted around him with the final spasm of her climax, he felt his testicles growing tight. His hips moved swiftly and urgently until the familiar pricking sensation began at the tip of his penis, and then with startling speed he was caught up in his own climax.

Tania saw her beloved stepbrother's head go back in ecstasy and she watched the frantic thrusting of his hips with increasing fury, a fury that wasn't helped by her own body's growing excitement. When he slumped down on top of Annabel, his head resting against her shoulder, Tania felt like screaming at him to get up. The position was too intimate, too affectionate. She didn't mind sharing him with other women, in fact it always increased her pleasure and they enjoyed comparing notes about the second woman afterwards, but this was different. He wasn't meant to lie with them as though they were lovers rather than sexual partners.

After a few minutes Crispian raised his head and turned to look at Tania. He was surprised by the expression in her eyes; there was jealousy there, and he could never remember seeing Tania jealous before. He wondered briefly why she should be jealous of Annabel, but it wasn't a problem that occupied his mind for long. For Crispian there would never be anyone like Tania, and he assumed that she was as aware of this as he was. Just the same, he had to admit that Annabel was a very attractive and stimulating partner and he was delighted that she'd be staying with them for another two weeks. He grinned at his stepsister. 'Did that sound good to you?'

Tania shrugged. 'I wasn't listening.'

'Did it look good then?'

'I closed my eyes.'

He laughed aloud. 'Fibber! You couldn't close your eyes if you were paid to; I know all about your curiosity. Come on, Annabel. We mustn't be totally selfish. Tania's been punished enough now. I think we should reward her for her patience, don't you?'

Annabel stretched sensuously. Her whole body felt more alive than ever before, and if she'd have preferred it to be Sir Matthew rather than Crispian who'd brought her to such heights of ecstasy that was a small quibble. The pleasure couldn't have been greater and even now she sensed that she was capable of further enjoyment.

'Help me untie Tania,' said Crispian, climbing off the bed and at last removing his clothes so that his slender, well-muscled body was revealed to the two young women. 'We'll untie her legs first.'

Naked, Annabel too rose from the bed, and as she removed the cord from around Tania's left ankle she amazed herself by letting her hand roam up the other woman's leg until it reached the patch of bare flesh above the stocking top. Here she let her fingers stroke lightly and she heard Tania's swift intake of breath.

Crispian laughed. 'That's right, make sure she's still

aroused. I've got some special things planned for her, but she has to be ready first.'

'I'm ready now!' said Tania angrily, hardly able to bear the soft caress that Annabel was inflicting on her.

When both her legs were free Crispian lifted Tania's buttocks up from the seat and pulled her panties down, tossing them across the room so that they landed in a frilly heap by the bed. Ordering Annabel to move away for a moment, he moved his right hand upwards and pressed the heel of his hand against Tania's sex. His fingers tangled in her pubic hair, tugging gently and moving the skin beneath up and down until the first darting streaks of desire began to travel from Tania's clitoris up into her pelvis, and all the time there was the steady heavy pressure of the heel of his hand to accentuate the sensation.

Tania swallowed hard, her hips shaking despite the restraints of the thick leather belt round her waist, and now Crispian signalled for Annabel to crouch in front of his stepsister. 'Open her up for me,' he muttered hoarsely.

Annabel's fingers were hesitant and as she carefully parted Tania's outer sex lips, the very gentleness of the touch and the almost awkward way in which she carefully prised the lips apart caused a surge of excitement in Tania. She loved to see people doing things for the first time, expanding their sexual horizons while she watched, and she knew that Annabel had never done anything like this before.

When she was fully opened to him, Crispian brought out a vibrator, inserted it into his mouth until it was damp with his saliva and then eased the head into her vagina, at the same time switching it on to its lowest setting. As it started to throb, Tania tried to push herself lower down the chair so that the vibrator plunged deeper inside her, but her movement was restricted by the belt and she had to allow Crispian to dictate what would happen and when.

Her buttocks tightened against the seat of the chair and when Crispian withdrew the head and let it play against the sensitive band of flesh that ran between her front and rear openings she almost screamed. Although the feelings were delicious they were still delicate, like butterflies fluttering against her, and she wanted something firmer and harder.

'Unlace her basque,' Crispian told Annabel. 'When her breasts are free, use this pleasure whip on them.' Tania moaned with delight and Crispian frowned at her. 'Keep quiet or you won't be allowed it.'

She bit on her lip. The soft latex pleasure whip was one of her favourite playthings. The feel of it when it fell across her flesh, firm enough to sting and yet soft enough to caress, could bring her to orgasm within seconds if applied correctly. Crispian saw a slight seepage from her opening and smiled. Playing games with Tania was so rewarding.

Annabel quickly unlaced the basque and then her hands were grasping Tania's full breasts. She let her fingertips dig into them, massaging them in the way that she herself liked, which brought a quick gasp of surprise from Tania. Then she took the band of black latex with its tiny wooden handle from Crispian and with her eyes locked onto Tania's, flicked it firmly across the tops of each of the swelling globes.

Tania's whole body jerked against its constraints and her breasts – already thrusting out more than usual because her arms were pinned behind her – thrust forward still more and she had to bite on her lip to stop another moan of ecstasy from escaping.

As Annabel continued to ply the pleasure whip, Crispian reinserted the vibrator into his stepsister's vagina, but deeper this time, and when he moved it round in circles, stimulating each of her vaginal walls in turn, Annabel increased the force of her blows. Suddenly and unexpectedly, Tania's body arched as far as its bonds would allow and with a hastily muffled gasp she was engulfed by her first orgasm.

While she was still in the throes of the muscular contractions Crispian unfastened her from the chair and carried her to the bed. Here he laid her face down on the bed, a pillow thrust hastily beneath her stomach. Sitting astride the backs of her thighs, he inserted one finger inside her rectum so that the dying embers of the orgasm were fanned back into life and even more intense contractions swept over her.

Annabel watched in silence, ashamed to realise that despite her own pleasuring she was ready for more now. Without thinking what she was doing her hands went to her own breasts and she manipulated her nipples until they were standing out tight and hard. Crispian looked at her and smiled. 'Rub your nipples over Tania's back while I fetch something else she likes. Use some lubricating jelly as well, that should give you both pleasure.'

Quickly Annabel did as he'd suggested. As he moved off the bed she took his place, and within seconds she was moving her tight breasts smoothly down Tania's spine, their pathway made easier by the application of jelly, and soon both women were uttering sighs of delight.

As Tania moved her hips restlessly against the mattress, Crispian returned, climbed on the bed and positioned Annabel so that she was sitting by the other girl's side. Then he squeezed some transparent gel onto his hand and signalled for Annabel to open his stepsister's buttocks. Carefully she separated the softly rounded crescents, revealing the dark, puckered opening between. Tania gave a squeal of excitement and Crispian tapped her on the base of her spine with a finger. 'Sshh!' he cautioned her and she buried her head deeper in the bed to muffle her sounds.

Wide-eyed, Annabel watched as Crispian held up four round balls suspended on a slim piece of cord. She pulled Tania's buttocks as wide apart as she could and then Crispian spread the gel around the opening that twitched and shrank from the invading coolness.

Now Tania was uttering cries of excitement that even the mattress couldn't muffle, and as Crispian eased the first ball inside her back passage she gave a loud squeal and her head turned from side to side. 'Yes! Oh, yes!' she shouted, and Annabel felt excitement sliding through her belly at the scene.

Crispian took his time, but eventually all four balls were inserted, and then he handed a remote power control to Annabel. 'There are three settings. Start on the lowest. I'll tell you when I want it increased. All right?' Speechless, Annabel nodded. 'They're incredibly arousing, you must try them some time,' he continued. 'Once they start throbbing it drives you wild, as you'll see from Tania!'

Annabel could imagine it only too well. Suddenly she wished that she was the one lying naked, face down on the bed, awaiting this delicious thrill, and at the prospect her nipples hardened. Crispian ran a hand lightly over her breasts. 'I see you're enjoying yourself! You mustn't be greedy, though; it's Tania's turn.'

With Annabel clutching the remote control, Crispian was free to turn Tania onto her back and at last she was looking up at him, her eyes glazed at the prospect of the sensations that awaited her. Crispian's hands gripped her hips and he pressed her down slightly, just at the moment that he signalled for Annabel to start the balls pulsating. Tania felt them throbbing within her, felt them stimulating the highly sensitive nerve endings of the thin rectal walls. The vibrations began to travel through her, moving from back to front until she was gyrating desperately within Crispian's grip, her breasts and abdomen covered in a thin sheen of perspiration as the tension within her grew.

Carefully Crispian raised Tania's knees, which moved the deliciously throbbing balls, and then he positioned himself at an angle of ninety degrees beneath her legs with his lower leg under her buttocks and his top leg supporting her calves.

For a moment he stared down at her, watching her rapid eye movements and the way her body was rippling beneath the skin. 'You're ready to come, aren't you?' he whispered. 'Do you want me inside you when you do?'

'Yes! Yes!' shouted Tania as the warm glow of the throbbing balls spread further up her belly and through her entire pubic area.

'Increase the power to two,' Crispian said to Annabel, and Tania's whole body began to shake with the sensations that were swamping it. As Crispian's right hand caressed her left leg, she parted her thighs as much as possible and felt him slide into her, staring down with his bright-blue eyes, watching her every response.

He used his legs to give his thrusts impetus and once he was into an established rhythm he gave Annabel another nod. Now she moved the balls into the highest speed and suddenly Tania's shoulders pressed down on the bed as she arched her ribcage in the build-up to orgasm.

Crispian knew that she was right on the edge, and Annabel knew it too. She could imagine the delicious sensations the other woman must be experiencing and her whole body ached with a desperate desire for similar stimulation.

Tania had now passed the point of no return. Every nerve in her body was screaming for release and suddenly the insistent throbbing between her thighs began to dissolve into a white-hot, liquid sensation. At that precise moment Crispian's free hand slipped between her thighs and he carefully massaged the shaft of her clitoris with a firm circular movement.

Unable to control herself a moment longer, Tania's hips were lifted off the bed by the force of the contractions that tore through her whole body while her hands clutched desperately at the covering beneath her.

For what seemed to Annabel to be an eternity the auburn-haired girl's body continued to twist and arch and all the time the balls throbbed within her rectum and Crispian's finger continued its remorseless manipulation of her most sensitive tissue.

127

It was one of the fiercest orgasms Tania had experienced for a long time and when it slowly started to ebb away her body still jerked and jumped at intervals. She could have cried as the glorious feelings slowly dissipated and then vanished.

Only when she closed her eyes and slumped limply against the mattress did Crispian's hand move from between her thighs and at the same time he signalled for Annabel to turn off the power. Then he turned the unprotesting Tania over and withdrew the balls. As each of them was forced out of the tiny opening his stepsister gave a muted gasp that was half-pleasure and half-protest.

'I told you it would be a good evening!' said Crispian, smiling at Annabel.

She stared at him, her lips slightly parted and her breasts jutting out proudly, the nipples still erect. 'Is that it?' she asked softly.

'Afraid so,' he said briskly. 'Time for us all to sleep. Step-mama will be very annoyed if you're not fit for work tomorrow!' Tania gave a tiny sound of contentment and curled up into a ball by his side.

'But . . .' began Annabel.

'What a greedy girl you're becoming,' he said mockingly. 'Don't tell me you wanted more?'

She felt her cheeks turn pink, and with as much dignity as she could muster got off the bed and started to dress. 'No,' she said shortly.

'Now you're the fibber! Never mind, I like responsive women. I expect your Matthew does as well.'

'Sir Matthew is nothing to me,' Annabel threw back, struggling back into her evening dress.

'Well, I think I'll see if I can change that. I'm sure he'd be as fascinated by you as I am, Annie. And I am fascinated you know, very fascinated indeed.'

Half-asleep, Tania heard the words and a sense of unease began to worry away at her. She forced herself upright and put a possessive arm round her naked stepbrother's shoulders. 'Not gone yet, Annabel? You'd better hurry. If Mother gets annoyed with you she'll send you away, and you don't want that, do you?'

'I'm just going,' said Annabel. 'If you remember, you did invite me here.'

'Yes; well, now we're asking you to leave. There are some things we prefer to do in private.'

'Good night, Annie!' called Crispian when she closed the door behind her.

As she walked back to her room Annabel tried to imagine what the pair of them could possibly do that even they considered required privacy.

Chapter Seven

The following morning a rather tired Annabel found herself breakfasting alone. It seemed that no one else in the house was up and about, apart from Lord Corbett-Wynne, whose day it was to go to London and take his seat in the House of Lords.

While she was drinking a final cup of coffee the maid, Mary, came in and told her that Lady Corbett-Wynne would like to see her in her rooms as soon as possible. With an inward sigh, Annabel managed to smile and swallowed the last of the strong liquid. She had a feeling that she was set on a collision course with her employer over the dining room.

Considering that it was only nine-thirty she'd quite expected to find the older woman in a robe, but to her surprise Marina was already dressed in a blue and lilac striped skirt and overshirt, beneath which she wore a dark-blue camisole top with an attractive embroidered neckline. Her hair was loose, making her look younger, and her face was carefully but lightly made up to accentuate her fine bone structure. She looked, thought Annabel, like a woman who had taken pains to look her best without wanting to appear over-dressed.

Marina smiled at Annabel. 'I have to go out this morning and thought we'd better have a little talk about the dining room before I go. Last night I had the feeling that you weren't in agreement with me over the alterations there.'

Annabel took a deep breath. 'I know it's a very dark room, but it does have wonderful character. It's everything that people expect from a stately home in England. I really think that to try and turn it into something foreign by using the Italian influence would be a disaster.'

'Indeed?' Lady Corbett-Wynne's eyebrows rose. 'And what precisely do you have in mind then?'

'I think that the wood could be re-stained in slightly lighter tones, and that soft, concealed lighting would be better than the somewhat harsh glare that's over the table at the moment. A different carpet would also make a considerable improvement. If you chose something that used grey as the predominant colour but had traces of gold and red in the pattern it would still fit in with the general ambience of the room but –'

'I don't like the "general ambience" of the room; that's precisely why you're here, Annabel,' responded Marina, her cheeks flushed. 'Even walking in there is enough to take away my appetite. I want it light; white woodwork, cream walls and perhaps impressionist paintings instead of those terrible portraits of people who've been dead for centuries.'

'White woodwork?' Annabel couldn't believe she was hearing correctly.

'While I'm out,' her employer said firmly, 'I would like you to draw up a design based on the lines I've suggested. If that's beyond you then perhaps you'd better return to London and I'll find another interior designer.'

Annabel looked down at the floor, considering her position. The proposals were sacrilege; the dining room would be ruined, but to her shame she realised that she didn't want to leave Leyton Hall. She was enjoying her sexual adventures there too much to want to return to her previous existence of all work and no play, and she desperately wanted a chance to get to know Sir Matthew Stevens better. If that meant ruining the dining room, well, so be it, she thought suddenly. After all, she'd never have to sit there and look at the end result.

'If you're certain about this then I'm sure I can come up with something that will suit you, Lady Corbett-Wynne,' she said politely. 'I'll spend the morning making some rough sketches and perhaps we could go through colours and fabrics later this evening.'

Marina nodded graciously. 'I look forward to that. Fabrics are quite a passion with me, you know. Now I really must be going. I'm hoping to choose my puppy today. I've never had a dog of my own, not since I was a child.'

'There are plenty of dogs in the house!' said Annabel. She was puzzled.

'All badly behaved and owned by other members of the family. This one will be mine.'

Annabel nodded, but as she left she thought to herself that it was far more likely Lady Corbett-Wynne had really been thinking of Sir Matthew Stevens when she spoke. She tried to picture the pair of them together, but failed. Her employer was so cool and self-contained. She gave the impression of a woman who would never lose control of herself, while Sir Matthew seemed the type of man who'd take his pleasure lustily and without too much regard for dignity.

'You're jealous!' she said to herself, making her way to her room to collect her notebooks.

'Jealous of whom?' enquired Crispian, emerging from his room as she walked past.

'You lying in bed while I'm working!' said Annabel with a light laugh.

'All you do is look round rooms and scribble notes and sketches. I don't call that work.'

'Believe me, when dealing with your stepmother, it is,'

said Annabel with feeling. Crispian grinned at her retreating back. He could well imagine that it was, but he hoped Annabel wouldn't give up and leave. He and Tania were having too much fun with her. They'd spent most of the previous night working out how they could get Annabel and Sir Matthew together. Having solved the problem he didn't want her disappearing before they'd seen the results of their plotting.

As Annabel began work, Marina walked swiftly towards the Old Mill. As she approached her pulse began to quicken and she felt her heart beating erratically against her ribs, while the palms of her hands were damp with nervous excitement.

Matthew saw her approaching through the window of his study and felt a flicker of surprise that she was back so soon. Somehow he'd expected her to play harder to get, and her arrival today took some of the excitement out of the chase, although he was still captivated by her ice-cool exterior and clear lack of pleasurable sexual experience. All the same, he hoped she wasn't going to call too often. He didn't intend to become a one-woman man just yet, and highly strung women like Marina could become rather clingy.

Striding out of his front door he stopped in apparent surprise when he saw her coming up the path. 'Marina, this is an unexpected pleasure. You should have telephoned me. I'd hate you to walk down here only to find me out, and I frequently am out during the day.'

Marina smiled happily, already aroused by the sight of him in cord trousers and open-necked shirt, his curly hair tousled by the slight breeze. 'That's all right. The walk's good for me. I wanted you to know that I've arranged to start riding lessons again, as you suggested.'

Matthew, remembering the scene he'd come upon in the copse, wondered what her husband thought about that. 'Excellent!' he said enthusiastically. 'Who'll teach you?'

'Jerry, he's worked for James nearly ten years now and

he's the one who's responsible for Tania coming on so well.'

'You'll be in safe hands, then,' he said more softly, moving closer to her and taking one of her hands gently in his. 'I expect you've come for another look at the pups, am I right?'

Marina would have liked to tell him that he was totally wrong, what she'd really come for was another look at him, but she nodded and smiled that once again she was doing what was expected of her rather than what she wanted.

Matthew knew very well what she wanted, but this time he thought that it would be exciting to do it somewhere more adventurous than in his drawing room. He was also aroused at the prospect of seeing the immaculate Marina reaching a sexual climax in the less than immaculate surroundings he had in mind. 'I've just got to check the stable,' he said, grasping her firmly by the hand and drawing her along with him. 'I'm not sure that the boy who comes in to muck out does a really thorough job. Once I've checked we'll look at the pups, they're right next door to the stable.'

'James says that our grooms are very good,' murmured Marina, wishing that she hadn't worn white, open-toed sandals if she was expected to walk into a hay-strewn stable.

'I'm sure they are!' laughed Matthew. 'More attractive than my lad as well.'

'James chooses them for their looks, but I think that Jerry makes sure they're good at their job as well. The estate can't afford to carry passengers.'

'But it can afford the services of David Crosbie?' queried Matthew.

Marina smiled at him. 'No, I can afford the services of David Crosbie, or in this case David Crosbie's protegée, who I have to say is turning out to be something of a disappointment.'

'Why's that?' murmured Matthew, pushing open the stable door and feeling his excitement increasing.

'She isn't as modern as I'd hoped.'

'What a shame,' he murmured soothingly, privately thinking that she looked exceedingly modern to him, and highly attractive as well. He realised that Marina was hanging back, loosening her grip on his hand. 'It's all right, the horse isn't here,' he assured her. 'He's out in the field.'

With a sigh of relief Marina followed Matthew inside the stable, but felt a flicker of unease when he closed the door behind them, plunging them into darkness. She could smell the straw, the unmistakable odour of horses and the strong scent of saddle leather, a combination that held no attraction for her. Before she could turn to leave, she felt Matthew's arms slip round her waist and then he was pulling her against his chest and his mouth was on hers, his kiss deep and passionate.

It took Marina a few seconds to respond. She wasn't feeling relaxed – the surroundings weren't to her liking – and she could tell by the way Matthew's hands were roaming down her back and over her hips that he intended to do more than kiss her in this unhygienic and highly unromantic setting.

He felt her tense against him but ignored it, certain that once he could arouse her more she'd forget her inhibitions. His hands eased their way under the back of her short-sleeved jacket and the camisole beneath until he was able to stroke her soft warm skin, the tips of his fingers travelling up and down her spine while he thrust one leg forward so that his thigh was between hers.

Almost without thinking Marina pressed her pubic area against this welcome hardness and when Matthew removed her jacket, throwing it carelessly across the stable, she didn't even protest. Her body was coming to life again, remembering how it had felt the last time they'd been together and hungry for more.

Swiftly and deftly Matthew unbuttoned her skirt, and at

135

the same time as he removed it he managed to remove her French knickers as well. It wasn't easy, as even now their eyes had adjusted they were still in semidarkness, and he was grateful her legs were bare.

When his mouth returned to hers, Marina responded more enthusiastically, her tongue slipping between his teeth in tiny thrusting movements while her hips rocked back and forth in the same rhythm. Slowly Matthew edged her back towards the stone wall until finally she felt her bare flesh against the cold rough surface. She gave a tiny gasp of protest, but he was already removing her front-fastening bra and as that fell away she was left totally naked, except for her sandals.

Matthew knew exactly what he wanted, but he had to get her into the right frame of mind and so he gripped both her wrists and spread her arms out against the wall on either side of her. 'Stay like that while I undress,' he said hoarsely. 'I like looking at you.'

Marina didn't want to stay there. She didn't like the position and hated losing her dignity, but at the same time she'd never felt such an overwhelming desire for anyone as she was experiencing now. Once he was naked and his muscular body with its rigid, erect penis was moving back against her, all her doubts fled. Whatever he wanted, she'd do, because her body was throbbing with arousal as the blood coursed through her veins.

Matthew's hands returned to Marina's wrists and, keeping her firmly fastened against the wall, he proceeded to rub his body over hers. She felt his hardening nipples move across her own tight peaks. When he lifted his thigh between her legs slightly and she felt the pressure against her vulva, her knees almost buckled with excitement.

Slowly Matthew rotated his hips, and his swollen glans moved against the base of her stomach, its touch as soft as silk. Marina's body was shaking, and when he released one of her wrists she failed to notice and kept her arms outspread. Matthew moved the free hand urgently down her body until it was between her thighs. There his fingers kneaded lightly against her sex-lips, massaging and stimulating the tissue beneath until he felt her opening to him, the outer labia parting as her level of desire grew.

Now he was able to feel her moist inner lips, and he slid his hand lower so that he could insert two fingers into her opening, moving them rapidly in and out while she moaned softly, deep in her throat. He spread her secretions up her inner channel until he reached the spot that was driving Marina insane with desire and, to her astonishment, the moment he caressed her there she climaxed, the spasms abrupt and fierce.

Matthew was breathing heavily now, excited as much by her unexpectedly powerful response as by her body, and without any further preliminaries he moved her away from the wall and turned her sideways. 'Lift your right leg,' he said abruptly. 'There's a mounting block there; I want you to rest your foot on it.'

Still dazed from her first climax Marina scarcely knew what was happening but she did as he said and he guided her foot forward until she felt the solid top of a mounting block beneath her foot. Her leg was raised uncomfortably high and balance was difficult, but Matthew seemed unaware of this as he approached her from behind, and she felt his penis moving between the cheeks of her bottom searching for her front opening. As he slid into her she reached backwards and rested one hand against the top of his thigh while his upper torso provided support for the rest of her body.

He moved very slowly at first, with long gaps between each stroke so that she wasn't certain when the next thrilling sensation would come. Then, moving his fingers as slowly as he was moving his hips, he began to caress her upraised inner thigh with the pads of his fingers, gradually inching his way towards the centre of her, where a heavy ache was deepening all the time.

This time he avoided the clitoris, and instead massaged

137

the surrounding tissue, moving with extraordinary light-ness around the opening to her urethra. This caused her abdominal muscles to jerk and sent bittersweet tingles shooting upwards through her body as she felt her breasts swell even more.

Now Matthew increased the pace of his thrusting and as his own arousal grew he licked and sucked at Marina's bare shoulder, occasionally allowing his teeth to graze against the flesh. Suddenly Marina's upper torso went rigid and her head flew back as his skilful fingers swept unexpectedly upwards and caressed the stem of her clitoris.

She felt a hot, liquid sensation between her thighs and then the shockwaves, small at first but rapidly increasing in power, gripped her body and once more the carefully built up sexual tension exploded into release.

This time it took her longer to recover and for a few minutes she slumped back against her lover. He continued to lightly caress and stimulate her, his hand moving around on her pubic mound and across the surface of her lower abdomen.

Marina was certain that she was totally satisfied; every muscle felt limp and replete, but he continued to use his hand on her and then his hips started to move again until suddenly she felt the first flicker of renewed desire and made a sound that was a mixture of excitement and despair.

'Just one more,' he murmured. 'I want us to come together.' As he spoke he withdrew from her, leaving her temporarily bereft, and then with what she later realised seemed to be practised ease he moved her away from the mounting block and sat on it himself, quickly pulling her onto his lap so that she was staring into his eyes which seemed to gleam brightly in the semidarkness.

Carefully, he eased his rigid penis into her. She heard him tell her to lift her legs and rest the soles of her feet against the stable wall. As she obeyed, his hands went behind her and slowly she leant back, supported by his hands, until finally she was lying along the top of his thighs.

'Grip the tops of my arms, Marina,' he said huskily. 'Move yourself up and down by pulling against me. I'm going to sit quite still and let you make me come.'

She was totally overwhelmed by the whole experience, half-ashamed and half-proud of her behaviour, but these words were almost as arousing to her as his touch. She began to pull against his strength and once she'd mastered the technique she found that with every movement the area around her clitoris was indirectly aroused and once more the heat started to increase between her thighs and the delicious tightness gripped her body.

Looking down at her, Matthew could see exactly what was happening. The sight of her head thrown back in wild abandon, and the feel of her long, blonde hair rubbing against the thin skin of his shins, made his own climax start on its remorseless climb to satisfaction and he knew that he couldn't last much longer.

'That's perfect!' he exclaimed. 'You're incredible, just move a little faster. I want you to come, too.'

Marina knew that she was very close, and spurred on by his words she managed to increase the tempo. Just as Matthew made a sound of excitement so the first, almost electric darts that heralded her own climax began to shoot through Marina.

All at once Matthew's hands, passive until now, started to help her move and she struggled to keep her feet against the stable wall as he jerked her body roughly against his shaft. There was a flash of white light behind her eyelids and once more her body was consumed by an explosion of pleasure.

Matthew's climax went on for a very long time, and by the end he was uttering tiny guttural groans of satisfaction while his body continued to twitch and jerk.

Marina felt lifeless, as though all the strength had gone

out of her body, and she lay limply against his legs, her feet now dangling down behind him and her eyes closed as she tried to recall the exact feeling of her final orgasm.

At that moment the stable door opened and a stable lad walked in. Despite himself he couldn't suppress a gasp of surprise and Marina shot upright, pressing her naked breasts against Matthew's chest and hiding her face in his shoulder.

Matthew looked at the eighteen-year-old and gave a small smile. 'We're busy, come back later,' he said calmly.

'I'm sorry, Sir Matthew, I didn't ... I mean, I never thought I should knock on a stable door.'

'Certainly not when the horse has bolted!' laughed his employer. 'Rufus is in the field.'

'Yes, sir. I'm very sorry, sir,' the boy was still muttering as he backed out of the stable and slammed the door behind him.

Marina remained where she was, her hands clutching Matthew's body with almost frantic strength, and he could feel her body shaking. To his surprise the interruption had proved something of an aphrodisiac. He wished that he had the time to take Marina again, but he didn't, and in any case he knew that she hadn't been affected in the same way.

'You'd better get dressed,' he said softly.

Marina felt close to tears. 'What if he recognised me?' she wailed. 'I'll be the laughing stock of the county.'

'How could he recognise you? He'd have been half-blind coming in from the light, and anyway all he saw was your back and long hair.'

'How could I have been so stupid!' Marina continued, searching through the grubby hay for her clothes and retrieving her sandals, which had fallen off in the heat of their passion, from a particularly dirty patch. 'My clothes smell horrible!' she exclaimed, pulling on her skirt.

'Well, *you* smell delicious. I love the scent of you when

you're excited,' Matthew said softly, his hands caressing her still naked breasts.

Marina pushed them away. 'Stop it! I can't imagine what I was thinking of, letting you . . .'

'Marina, you didn't "let me", you *wanted* me to do all those things. You loved it, and I loved watching you so lost in sexual pleasure. Don't you think it's more exciting than spending all your time planning how to redecorate a house that isn't even yours?'

She knew that he was right, but suddenly she didn't want to hear it said. She could imagine only too well how she'd looked as she abandoned herself to him, and at this moment all she wanted was to look like Lady Corbett-Wynne again, rather than one of her husband's stable girls.

'Let me go!' she said crossly when his fingers remained on her breasts, pulling softly at the nipples until they came erect beneath his hands.

'You could go on doing it, couldn't you?' he teased, kissing the side of her neck where a pulse was throbbing violently.

'No! Please, Matthew, I must go. That boy might come back.'

'First, tell me that you enjoyed doing it like this.'

She looked at him and her eyes were dazed. 'Yes, I did, but I can't imagine why. It isn't like me at all.'

'It's just a part of you that's been hidden for far too long,' he said easily. 'Once you've learnt to ride we can take the horses out and then make love out-of-doors beneath some trees or in a copse. Wouldn't you enjoy that?'

'No! Yes, perhaps; I don't know!' she wailed, totally confused by the contradiction between what her body wanted and what she believed to be the proper way to behave. Sex, even good sex, was for the bedroom, or at the most on a sofa or comfortable armchair. And yet she knew that today she had had the most exciting sex of her life so far.

Matthew helped her on with the rest of her clothes and kissed her on the corner of the mouth. 'You'll get used to it,' he promised her. 'I thought it was wonderful, and you were absolutely incredible.'

'I'll start my riding lessons today,' she said firmly, knowing that this would please him and wanting to please him because he'd given her so much pleasure and self-confidence.

'Good,' he murmured against her mouth, and then he was kissing her more thoroughly until in the end she had to break away. 'Matthew, I must go. When will I see you again?'

He frowned. 'Unfortunately I've got to spend a few days in London this week. I leave this afternoon and won't be back until Friday lunchtime; perhaps on Friday afternoon?'

It seemed a long way away to Marina, but she knew that she was being ridiculous. He was a busy man, probably with a wide circle of friends; she just hoped that not too many of them were women. 'I'll walk down about three,' she said slowly.

'Excellent; then you can tell me all about your first riding lesson.'

Marina shuddered. 'I don't know how I'm going to manage. My nerve's completely gone, and James says that once that happens it's better to give up.'

'James would say that,' responded Matthew, his eyes darkening.

'Why?'

'Because he doesn't want you venturing out of the home. I suspect that he rather enjoys keeping his beautiful wife all to himself at Leyton Hall.'

'He certainly isn't interested in me,' retorted Marina. 'Neither am I interested in him. The marriage is nothing more than one of convenience.'

'That doesn't prevent your husband from finding plenty of things to enjoy though, does it? I think it's time you did the same. At least we've made a start over the past few days!'

Marina felt herself blushing. 'You don't think I'm too forward, do you?' she asked hesitantly.

Matthew nearly smiled at the thought, but knowing how important this was to Marina he kept his expression neutral. 'No, Marina, I don't. I like my women to take as much pleasure from everything as I do. That's what most men want.'

'Really? Someone should tell James.'

'I'm not sure James is typical but, then, I haven't known him long,' said Matthew, remembering the expression on Marina's husband's face when he'd come across him in the copse.

'I've decided to have a dinner party on Saturday week,' continued Marina, suddenly worried that her most important guest wouldn't be free. 'There should be twenty or so people; you will come, won't you?'

'I'd be delighted. Is it your birthday?'

She smiled mischievously. 'No, but perhaps it's my coming-out party!'

'Then I most definitely won't miss it. I'm sorry, Marina, but I think I can hear the phone. I must go now. I'll see you Friday afternoon.'

As he strode away from her, Marina strained to see if she could hear the phone, but she couldn't and for a moment she wondered if he'd been trying to get rid of her. Dismissing her fears as paranoia she began to walk slowly up the hill to Leyton Hall, brushing hay from her skirt as she went.

Back inside the Old Mill, Sir Matthew picked up his phone and dialled Leyton Hall. He'd begun to think that Marina was never going to leave. Crispian answered.

'You're lucky you caught me, I'm on my way to see the dreaded Amanda!' he laughed.

'Sorry, had a surprise visitor. What did you want to speak to me about?'

'The thing is, my stepmother's having a dinner party Saturday week, I expect she'll tell you about it soon, and Tania and I were wondering if you'd be interested in some late-night party games, once the proper evening's officially over that is.'

Matthew hesitated. 'What kind of party games?'

'Pretty original ones. I promise you won't be bored.'

'Will there only be the three of us?'

'Good lord, no! Annabel will certainly join us, and my friend Luke could probably be persuaded to bring his girlfriend too. She's amazing, really athletic.'

It was the mention of Annabel's name that decided things for Matthew. He was enjoying himself with Marina Corbett-Wynne, but knew that once he'd persuaded her to lose all her inhibitions and she was totally enslaved then he'd get bored. He wasn't proud of the fact, but it was the way he was. Annabel had seemed to him at their only meeting so far to be an altogether more experienced young woman who would be a partner rather than a pupil.

'Sounds like fun. Does your father take part?'

Crispian was clearly amused. 'Not in our games; he has plenty of his own, but they're for people with very special-ised tastes.'

'Why did you decide to invite me to your private party?' asked Matthew.

'Two reasons, really. One is that if my stepmother finds you attractive, and you might be surprised to know that she does, then you must have something special, and two, Annabel likes you.'

'How do you know?'

'How does a man ever know? If you hadn't been busy with Step-mama you'd have seen for yourself the other evening. Not that she's been pining away here in your absence.'

Matthew's mouth went dry at the thought of what Annabel and Crispian might be doing at Leyton Hall. 'I'm not sure you're right about your stepmother,' he said

144

carefully, 'but hopefully you are about Annabel. Now I have to go, bye.'

Putting the receiver down carefully he stared out of the window. He'd been afraid that life in Wiltshire might be boring. It seemed his fears had been unfounded.

Chapter Eight

That afternoon, freshly bathed and wearing tan jodhpurs and a white silk blouse, Lady Corbett-Wynne made her way to the stable block looking for her riding instructor. She stopped a passing girl groom. 'Where's Jerry?' she demanded, her voice more imperious than usual because of her tension.

'I'll fetch him, your ladyship,' said the girl, walking away with a pronounced wriggle of her rounded hips. She returned a few minutes later with a man in his mid-thirties whose blue-black hair was far too long and whose dark blue eyes swept over Marina's body in what she considered to be a highly insolent manner.

'I believe my husband spoke to you about riding lessons for me,' she said shortly.

He smiled, showing very white but slightly uneven teeth. His skin was so dark Marina wondered if he had gypsy blood in him. 'He did.'

'Well, I'd like a lesson now.'

'I'm busy now,' he responded curtly.

'Doing what?' enquired Marina.

He shrugged. 'This and that.'

'Well, this and that can wait; I cannot.'

It looked as though he was about to argue, but then he seemed to change his mind and with a small sigh he nodded. 'As you like. How long since you rode?'

'Twelve years.'

'Why did you stop?'

'I had a bad fall.'

He pulled a face. 'You should have got back on straight away.'

'I'd broken my collarbone.'

'I've ridden with a broken collarbone before now,' he said in a bored voice.

'I didn't come here for a lecture,' said Marina, her voice chilly. 'A lesson is all that I require from you.'

Jerry's initial annoyance was beginning to ebb away as he realised exactly how nervous Lady Corbett-Wynne was. Although her voice was steady and controlled her hands were clenched into tight fists and her skin was pale despite the light covering of make-up.

'As it's so long since you rode, I think you'd be better off just leading one of the horses round today, getting used to being near one again,' he said casually, walking towards Betsy's stall. She was easily the most placid animal Lord Corbett-Wynne owned, and so lazy that she was affronted when asked to break into anything faster than an easy trot.

She was also one of the smallest horses, and Marina gave an inward sigh of relief as the fair-haired girl she'd spoken to earlier brought her out of her stall. 'Thanks, Sandra,' said Jerry, and the girl gave him a knowing smile from beneath lowered lids.

'She loves apples,' said Jerry as Marina stood rooted to the spot looking at the animal. 'Here, put this on the palm of your hand and feed her. She'll follow you anywhere after that.'

'Perhaps you should try blowing in her ear,' called a light, clear voice from the other side of the stable yard.

147

Marina spun round on her heel to see her daughter advancing towards them.

'Blow in her ear?' she said in bewilderment.

'That's what Jerry does to the girl grooms, and then they follow him anywhere. Isn't that right, Jerry?'

He looked at her challenging expression, recalled the feel of her velvet skin beneath his hands and the amazing collection of sex toys she'd used during their one and only encounter and decided to play dumb. 'I wouldn't know,' he said coldly.

'Surely all those stories about you aren't exaggerated?'

'It depends on what the stories say. If you'll mind the way now, I'm giving your mother a lesson.'

'Well, that should certainly be interesting!' drawled Tania. 'My stepfather likes the grooms, so my mother goes to the stable manager for lessons!'

Jerry took hold of Betsy's reins and walked the horse so close to Tania that she had to step backwards. 'Look where you're going!' she said furiously. He caught the scent of her distinctive perfume and had a fleeting vision of the way her legs had wrapped themselves around his waist when he'd taken her standing up against the foot of her bed, but then a small sound from Lady Corbett-Wynne brought him back to the present.

'Do you really want spectators?' he asked her softly.

Marina bit her bottom lip. 'I most certainly do not. Tania, please go away.'

'Why are you bothering to learn?' asked her daughter, intrigued at the sight of her mother, clearly apprehensive but apparently determined to go through with it all, even the humiliation of leading a horse that any child could ride.

'Because I want to,' her mother said firmly.

'I suppose it's all Sir Matthew's doing,' laughed Tania. 'He must have something special if he can get you out here. You used to say that you'd rather die than get on a horse.'

'I've changed my mind. Now go away,' said her mother, anger beginning to take the edge off her nerves.

'I only came over to tell you that Annabel's gone off with Crispian into town,' said Tania. 'I hope you're not being taken for a ride by her.'

'No one will get taken for a ride if you don't leave,' said Jerry, irritated beyond his limit by the auburn-haired girl's presence.

'I'm going,' Tania assured him, and with the lightest of touches on his arm she walked away.

After a good ten minutes walking Betsy, Marina found that she was no longer stiff with terror; in fact she actually wanted to get on the horse's back. 'I think I could try and sit on her now,' she told the impassive Jerry, who seemed to have no small talk at all.

Jerry, who took in a great deal more than people realised, had been watching his new pupil closely and had come to the same conclusion. 'Fine,' he agreed amicably. 'I'll help you up.' Lacing his hands together he waited for her to use this to help her mount.

As she slipped her foot into his hands Marina remembered the way her sandals had fallen off her feet that morning and the memory of her behaviour then brought the colour into her cheeks. 'Don't worry, it's easy,' Jerry assured her, thinking it was fear causing her to flush. Once she was in the saddle he adjusted the stirrups and pressed the back of her spine to make her sit straighter. 'You need to keep your weight well balanced, makes life easier for the horse and you!' he said with a smile.

Marina sat straight, her thighs gripping the sides of the horse, and when Jerry came round to the horse's head and started to adjust her over-tight grip on the reins she couldn't help noticing how gentle he was, and yet there was a tightly controlled strength about him that was highly arousing.

Shocked at her thoughts she tried to concentrate on the lesson. It was bad enough to be obsessed with Matthew

Stevens, but to find herself lusting after her husband's stable manager was more than she could stomach. She wondered if she was going mad.

The rest of the lesson went well, but to her horror Marina found that she was becoming more and more aware of Jerry. When he praised her and his dark-blue eyes smiled into hers she felt a flutter in her stomach, and every time he ran his fingers through his mop of dark hair her throat went dry as she pictured herself running her own fingers through it in passion.

By the time he helped her down, his hands firm around her waist, she was exhausted, but more by her thoughts than by the actual ride. 'Thank you,' she muttered, her voice far less assured than when they'd begun. 'Perhaps we could continue another day?'

'Tomorrow afternoon, same time?' he suggested.

'That will be excellent,' replied Marina, who walked away at a leisurely pace until she was out of sight.

After that she almost ran into the house and up to her rooms where, to the astonishment of her maid, she took another bath and then lay on her bed trying to rest. Images of herself and Matthew together fought with images of herself doing the same things, but this time with the younger man's brown, work-roughened hands on her body.

Jerry handed the horse back to Sandra and went into his office. He'd been strangely disturbed by the lesson. From all that he'd heard he'd expected Lady Corbett-Wynne to be a sharp-tongued, dried-up stick of a woman but in reality he'd found her slender fine-boned beauty very desirable, more so than her over-ripe daughter, with her obvious charms.

'Not for you, Jerry,' he told himself firmly as he settled down to the accounts. 'Keep your mind on your work and you'll stay out of trouble.'

Crispian had taken Annabel into town so that she could look at the fabrics in one of the large department stores, hoping for inspiration to strike. Clearly she had to lighten the dining room, but white wood still seemed a heavy price to pay for three weeks' sexual pleasure and she was trying hard to discover a compromise. When she rejoined Crispian for the drive back he looked unusually dispirited.

'Something wrong?' she asked curiously.

'I invited Amanda to this dinner we're having and she accepted,' he said gloomily.

'Did you expect her to refuse?'

'Yes, I damned well did! She never goes anywhere at night except out to the piggery. What a mess. Now I'll have to entertain her all through dinner and play the attentive suitor.'

'If you're not serious about her, isn't it all rather a waste of time?' asked Annabel.

Crispian scowled. 'Yes, but it's the only way I can keep Papa happy.'

'He's not going to stay happy for long. Surely in the end you'll either have to ask this Amanda to marry you, or give her up.'

'No, in the end she'll get tired of waiting for me to ask her and that will be the end of it. I'll then feign a broken heart, which should be good for a few months. After that I'll start again with someone else.'

'Aren't you ever going to marry?' asked Annabel.

Crispian shot a sideways glance at her. 'How can I? I'm obsessed with Tania. She's the only woman I really want but because she hasn't any money, and our parents imagine we should think of each other as brother and sister, I can't have her.'

'How could your father stop you?'

'He wouldn't *stop* me, Annie; the point is that without a fresh injection of money my marriage to Tania would effectively lose us Leyton Hall.'

'Does that worry you?'

He thought for a moment. 'I suppose it does. After all,

some of my ancestors worked damned hard to get it. I'd be letting the side down if I threw it away.'

'Then you'll have to hope you meet someone you like as much as you like Tania,' said Annabel.

'You've no idea what you're saying,' Crispian retorted coldly. 'We're perfect together; no other woman would enjoy the things we enjoy doing. Even if I wanted to break free I couldn't. She's like a sorceress and I'm caught in her spell!'

Annabel understood what he was saying. She could imagine only too well the long, erotic hours that the pair of them must have passed together over the years as they explored their sexuality, gradually discovering how well they were matched.

'You never know; Tania can't be unique,' she said, trying to offer him some kind of comfort because she didn't like seeing him so depressed.

Crispian braked hard as they approached a sharp bend in the road and Annabel was thrown against his arm. 'No,' he said thoughtfully. 'I used to think she was, but since I've met you I'm not so sure. How would you fancy being Lady of the Manor, Annabel? Think what fun the three of us could have.'

'No thanks,' laughed Annabel. 'My dreams have never involved marrying a man and his stepsister!'

'Perhaps you should start considering it,' said Crispian. 'It could be the perfect solution.'

'For you, but not for me, and most definitely not for Tania,' Annabel said firmly.

Crispian decided to change the subject, satisfied that he'd at least planted the idea in Annabel's mind. It was strange but what he'd said had been true. Annabel excited him more than any other woman he'd met, apart, of course, from Tania.

'Amanda will hate the dinner party,' he said suddenly.

'Why?' asked Annabel.

'Well, after we've eaten and when everyone's had plenty

152

to drink we usually have a game or two to liven things up. Everyone takes part, except for my stepmother who always withdraws gracefully to her rooms before she's forced to see anything undignified!'

'What kind of games?' Annabel was intrigued.

'You'll see. Oh yes, and after the official evening ends I'm having some of my friends up to my rooms to continue the entertainment. You will join us, won't you?'

'I'm not sure.'

'But you have to!' he exclaimed, driving the car through the gates of Leyton Hall at breakneck speed. 'I've told Sir Matthew that you'll be there.'

Despite herself Annabel felt a moment's excitement. 'All right then,' she promised. 'I'll be there.'

'You won't regret it,' Crispian assured her.

As they got out of the car, Tania came down the front steps. Dressed in green trousers, a white open-necked shirt and a long red and green waistcoat with brass buttons down the front she looked very attractive and very annoyed.

'Where the hell have you been?' she asked Crispian, totally ignoring Annabel.

'I had to see Amanda; I told you that earlier.'

'And did Annabel come with you?'

'No, Annabel went into town looking for fabrics and then we met up so that I could give her a lift back.'

'Forgotten how to drive, Annabel?' enquired Tania.

'There's something wrong with my gearbox. Someone's coming out from the local garage to look at it.'

Tania's top lip curled. 'How convenient. You could always have borrowed my car.'

'Don't be silly, Tania,' said Crispian, clearly irritated. 'I was going into town anyway and offered Annabel a lift.'

'I was bored,' Tania said sulkily. 'My horse threw a shoe and when I went to the stables to talk to Jerry he was giving Mother a riding lesson. Can you believe it! She was walking round leading that plodding Betsy by the reins and looking petrified. God knows how Jerry put up with it.'

'He's paid to put up with it. Besides, perhaps he was grateful he didn't have to keep you amused.'

'I need a couple of lessons before the gymkhana,' said Tania. She looked cross. 'I hope Mother isn't planning to monopolise him.'

'I'm sure he'll find time to fit you in!' laughed Crispian, slipping his hand through her arm. 'Come on, I'm back now so you won't be bored any longer!'

A few days later, Annabel was surprised to find herself summoned to Lord Corbett-Wynne's rooms. Lady Corbett-Wynne had seemed lethargic and uninterested in everything Annabel had suggested of late, and as she made her way up the stairs she wondered if she was going to be asked to leave. She hoped not, particularly with the dinner and its attendant entertainment only two days away.

She tapped on the door and waited. There were a few scuffling sounds and then Lord Corbett-Wynne's voice boomed out for her to come in. Taking a deep breath she pushed open the door.

At first she couldn't see the master of Leyton Hall, but what she couldn't fail to see was the curvaceous blonde-haired girl standing in front of his dressing-room mirror. Her outfit was astonishing. The full breasts were contained by a shiny black leather lace-up bustier; her midriff was bare and her full hips were covered by a matching lace-up suspender belt which held up sheer black stockings. Her light-brown pubic hair peeped out from beneath the bottom of the suspender belt, and to add to the eroticism of the outfit she was wearing long black gloves that laced down the outsides of her arms and ended halfway over her hands, leaving her fingers free. In her right hand she was holding a riding crop.

Annabel thought the girl looked vaguely familiar, and suddenly she remembered seeing her walking away from

Lord Corbett-Wynne's room soon after her arrival at Leyton Hall. She looked around the spacious dressing room, searching for his lordship, and realised that he was sitting quietly in the far corner, perched on a high stool. He was naked to his waist, where a heavy buckled belt secured a pair of very tight-fitting black leather trousers.

'Sit down, sit down,' he said sharply, apparently expecting Annabel to ignore the incongruous scene. He waved his hands in the direction of a chair and she realised then that he was wearing handcuffs.

'I'm sorry, I'll come back another time,' stammered Annabel, rapidly becoming unnerved by the whole scenario. 'I thought that you wanted to see me.'

'I do! Sandra wanted to see you as well; she's heard a lot about you, isn't that right, Sandra?'

'Yes, your lordship,' said the girl. Her eyes were bright with suppressed amusement.

As Annabel stood motionless, Sandra moved across the room and turned the key in the door lock, slipping it inside her bustier and then walking back to her original position. Annabel felt a flicker of fear.

'It's about my wife,' continued Lord Corbett-Wynne. 'She doesn't seem right to me, much too quiet and agreeable these days. What's it all about, that's what I'd like to know. Confided in you, has she?'

'Lady Corbett-Wynne and I only ever discuss work,' said Annabel, hoping her voice didn't betray her increasing anxiety. 'She seems perfectly normal to me.'

'Does she argue with you? Make a lot of fuss about nothing?'

'No, she's been very co-operative.'

He nodded. 'There you are then, there's something wrong with her. That woman's never been co-operative with anyone from the day I married her. She won't even let me in her bedroom any more, but luckily I've got other girls happy to take her place. Isn't that right, Sandra?' The girl nodded, her eyes scanning Annabel's face, testing her reaction.

'How about you?' continued Lord Corbett-Wynne. 'You're a pretty filly; there are plenty of costumes here that would fit you.'

Annabel backed against the door. 'It's very kind of you, but this really isn't my kind of thing,' she said feebly, wondering if any of the inhabitants of Leyton Hall led what she'd always considered to be a normal sex life.

'Ever tried it?' She shook her head. 'How do you know then? Tell you what, we'll let you watch.'

'I'd rather not,' said Annabel quickly.

For a moment Lord Corbett-Wynne's face lost some of its good humour. 'I'd rather you didn't encourage my son and my stepdaughter in their games, but I'll keep my dissatisfaction to myself as long as you do as I ask.'

'Who told you about that?' she asked in amazement.

He smiled. 'No secrets here, my dear. We're a very united family, in our own peculiar way.'

'Be quiet!' said Sandra, her voice hard and commanding. Immediately the man on the stool fell silent. 'How dare you keep me waiting like this!' she continued. 'Don't you know that I've got work to do? I can't spend all my time here with you.'

Annabel watched and listened, and her eyes strayed to the increasingly obvious bulge in Lord Corbett-Wynne's crotch. Sandra walked round and round the stool as she talked, and every now and then she'd let her whip trail over his back or down his chest until it came to rest against his belt. Each time the whip touched him he would draw in his breath sharply, and all the time his erection pressed hard against the tight leather trousers.

Now Sandra reached down and her right hand played idly with the bulge. 'Can't you control yourself better than that?' she demanded. He hung his head. 'Very well, I'm going to blindfold you. Perhaps then you'll manage not to get excited so quickly.'

156

'No!' he protested, seemingly genuinely put out. 'I like to watch you.'

'Be quiet!' snapped Sandra. 'If you speak once more without permission I'll leave.'

Annabel realised that her own breathing was quickening as she watched Sandra at work, and when the heavily padded blindfold was placed round the seated man's head she took a half-step forward, fascinated by his helpless vulnerability.

Sandra glanced at her and smiled knowingly. She could tell that, despite her reservations, Annabel was becoming excited, just as Sandra's arousal was increasing. Having a third person present had certainly added an extra dimension to the pleasure.

Very slowly she unzipped Lord Corbett-Wynne's trousers and then eased his straining penis out of the opening. It was thick and dark, the veins throbbing. Already some pre-ejaculatory fluid had leaked out of the tiny slit at the tip of the glans. With great delicacy Sandra ran the end of her whip along the top of the shaft and then round the head but when he thrust his hips upward she removed it and struck him a stinging blow over his shoulders.

Without realising it Annabel had moved closer now and she stared down at the massive erection in fascination. She'd never seen a man fettered and blindfolded before, but suddenly she could understand how exciting it was to be the woman and have total control.

'Touch yourself,' Sandra ordered him. 'Make yourself bigger, but don't come.'

Annabel didn't think it could be possible – he looked ready to burst already – but with a muffled groan he held out his fastened hands and Sandra carefully poured a little oil into his palms.

As soon as he let his slippery fingers touch the base of his shaft Lord Corbett-Wynne's pelvis jerked and he thrust his hips towards the watching women but then fell back on the stool again, straining to keep himself under control.

Sandra watched as he worked his fingers up and down the lower half of his stem, but after a few seconds she lost patience. 'Move higher, I know that's what you prefer,' she instructed him. Reluctantly he obeyed, and now the glans turned an even darker shade of red and the angle of his erection increased until it was pointing up to his stomach.

'He's very near,' whispered Sandra to the silent Annabel. 'Why don't you take him in your mouth? When I speak he'll realise what we've done and that will really finish him off.'

Annabel was shocked to realise that this was something she wanted to do. The intensity of Lord Corbett-Wynne's sexual arousal, the whole atmosphere in the room as his leather-clad mistress stalked around him, everything about the scene seemed to call to Annabel to take part, to experience yet another new sensation.

Sandra ran her fingertips down his lordship's heaving chest, stopping at his waist to trail them from side to side until a gasp of anguish from him made her stop. 'Where's your famous self-control?' she asked with a sneer in her voice, but the words only increased his excitement and yet more clear fluid seeped out of his slit.

'Now I'll have to lick you clean,' Sandra said irritably, but she motioned towards Annabel with her head. Annabel knew that an opportunity like this wouldn't come again, and suddenly she found herself down on her knees, her mouth opening to take the large, velvet-skinned glans between her lips.

'You have to last for three minutes,' said Sandra, knowing full well that he wouldn't. Then, much to her delight, Annabel took the throbbing penis into her mouth and began to caress the sensitive ridge beneath the glans with her tongue.

As she worked she felt her own desire growing, not for

the man in front of her, but for Sir Matthew Stevens. She wished that he was there watching, and that once Lord Corbett-Wynne had taken his pleasure Sir Matthew would take her in his arms, carry her to the nearest bed and then take her swiftly and without any preliminaries.

Inflamed by her own thoughts, Annabel increased her attentions to the now audibly gasping man on the stool. After teasing him lightly with her tongue she suddenly changed rhythm and began to suck on the bursting rod and at the same time she grabbed hold of the chain of his handcuff and pulled his hands to the base of his shaft.

Sandra smiled to herself. It was the best thing Annabel could have done and she hadn't needed any prompting. As Lord Corbett-Wynne's hands brushed against the base of his erection Sandra spoke.

'Use your fingers again; work them up and down to add to your pleasure.'

James couldn't believe his ears. He'd been picturing Sandra's mouth closed about him, enjoyed the feel of her lips encasing his manhood in the way he liked best and yet now, even as the delicious suction continued, she was speaking to him. His brain raced for a few seconds and then he realised what must be happening. At the moment of realisation Annabel's hands grasped his and he was forced to obey Sandra's final instruction.

It was too much for him to bear and with a loud shout of triumph he felt his sperm rushing upwards and then gushing out of him into Annabel's greedily receptive mouth, a mouth that continued to milk him remorselessly until his spasming flesh was exhausted.

Sandra touched the other young woman on the shoulder. 'He's finished.' Slightly dazed, Annabel released him and stared up at the stable girl. 'I never meant . . .'

'I know, but it's exciting, isn't it?' Annabel nodded, wishing that there was some way her own excitement could be appeased.

Sandra looked down on the masked man. 'You didn't

last three minutes; you only lasted two. Annabel can choose your forfeit.'

Suddenly Annabel knew what she wanted. Unbelievably, she found that she didn't care about the other girl watching, or even what Lord Corbett-Wynne wanted; all she cared about was her own satisfaction. Swiftly she slipped off her skirt and panties and sat down across his lordship's legs, unfastening the front of her blouse as she faced him.

Sandra pushed firmly on the back of his head and as he moved it forward his mouth encountered Annabel's naked breasts. Immediately his tongue flicked over one of the throbbing nipples and she felt it grow tight and hard. Between her thighs there was a hot ache and she rocked herself to and fro on his leather-covered thighs until Sandra, realising what was needed, released his hands from the cuffs, enabling him to run his right hand down from the valley between Annabel's breasts to the valley hidden between her thighs.

As he parted her sex-lips and searched for the little bud that she knew would trigger her climax, Annabel felt him drawing her nipple and the surrounding tissue deeply into his mouth, sucking and licking frantically at her.

Already aroused by all that had gone before, Annabel's clitoris quickly responded to the skilful manipulations of his fingers and within seconds she was balanced on the edge of her climax. She loved that moment, the moment when all the tension and heat gathered together into a focal point. She wanted to savour it, but Lord Corbett-Wynne suddenly slipped two fingers up around her clitoris in a V-shape, softly squeezing the fingers closer together until she could feel the pressure, at which point he stopped and the fingers remained quite still so that the pressure was maintained and all the time his mouth was tugging and suckling at her breast.

Annabel closed her eyes, still trying to delay that final moment of gratification a few seconds longer, but she couldn't. Small shock waves travelled from where his fingers held her, up to her nipples, and as his teeth grazed the very tip of one she finally gave up the battle and allowed her body the release it craved.

Sandra watched as Annabel shook and trembled on Lord Corbett-Wynne's lap, her mouth slightly open and her eyes closed as she revelled in the sheer sensuality of it all. The girl groom had an urgent desire to join in, to tease the free breast with the tip of her whip or replace his lordship's fingers with her own, but she knew that wasn't part of her role and had to content herself with watching.

When the last tremors of her orgasm had died away Annabel's eyes opened and she shook her head, trying to work out how she'd ever allowed herself to take part, but her replete body was all the answer she really needed.

Climbing off the masked man's lap she pulled on her discarded clothing and walked over to Sandra. 'The key, please,' she said calmly. Sandra retrieved it from her bustier and handed it over without a word.

As she unlocked the door to let herself out, Annabel glanced back for one final look. Sandra was unfastening his lordship's blindfold and his hands were already reaching for her tightly laced breasts. Silently, Annabel left them. Martin had been right, she thought, once she regained the privacy of her own room. She was learning a lot about life at Leyton Hall.

For a time she sat on the side of her bed and considered what had been happening to her since her arrival. Quite apart from the work, which for some strange reason no longer seemed to be of much interest to Lady Corbett-Wynne, she'd become involved with Crispian and Tania in the kind of sexual games that she'd never in her wildest dreams imagined existed. Now, as though that wasn't enough, she'd allowed Lord Corbett-Wynne to demonstrate his own particular fetish in front of her very eyes. The old Annabel would have been shocked, she thought to herself, but the new Annabel hadn't just stayed – she'd stayed and taken part.

Wide-eyed she studied herself in the dressing-table mirror. She looked the same; her eyes were still wide and guileless, her face softly feminine but not overtly sexual, yet she didn't feel the same. All the time now she was aware of her body; her skin felt sensitive, all the nerve endings nearer the surface, and her breasts would swell and the nipples harden at the slightest provocation. Worst of all, despite everything that she'd done with such enjoyment, she was being consumed with desire for Matthew Stevens.

The old Annabel would never have been so stupid. In the pre-Leyton Hall days if Annabel saw a man that she liked and nothing came of it then she quickly forgot him. This time she couldn't get Sir Matthew out of her thoughts. In the daytime she'd imagine meeting him by chance in one of the large, deserted rooms and at night her dreams were of the pair of them locked together in a darkly erotic embrace, driving each other to fever pitch so that she woke drenched in perspiration and with a deep ache between her thighs.

'I'm going to have him,' she said softly to her reflection. 'I know we're meant for one another and I want him. I'm not going back to London until I've had a chance to find out if sex with him is as good as I think it will be.'

The reflection didn't answer, but it smiled and Annabel realised that she was smiling in anticipation. The only problem was Lady Corbett-Wynne, whose lack of interest in Leyton Hall was, Annabel thought, almost definitely due to an affair with Matthew. He and Marina were close in age and lived similar lives, especially now she was taking riding lessons. All Annabel could do was wait for the night of the dinner party and trust that Crispian had been telling her the truth.

Giving herself a mental shake, she at last got out her plans for the house. She was very pleased with her ideas for the entrance lobby, and her employer had seemed delighted. She'd used an arched trellis screen and numerous plants to provide cover for the rubbish that would always be deposited there, and replaced the narrow marble table with a round, pedestal-style one in tan and cream, round which she planned to have three green lacquer chairs, while the floor would be pale-green Italian tiles. The music room too had met with approval, but still the dining room was a major stumbling block.

Reluctantly she went downstairs to have yet another look at what was rapidly becoming a nightmare room. Carefully, she consulted her colour charts and checked the design of the room itself. It was far too large for Lady Corbett-Wynne's ideas to work. If it was all white with light furniture, it would look like a cross between an operating theatre and a French café, thought Annabel with a laugh. No, somehow she had to come up with more than her original suggestion of using green and pink fabrics combined with a new lighting system.

'Red!' she exclaimed suddenly as she gazed at the wall at the farthest end. 'That's it. If that wall were to be red and the woodwork stained just a shade lighter, then the other walls could be a neutral colour and lighten everything, but the room wouldn't lose its richness.'

Excited that at last inspiration had struck she began to jot down all the changes that would be necessary, including some *trompe l'oeil* niches where Lord Corbett-Wynne's plaster maquette horses by George Stubbs could be shown to good advantage.

Unnoticed by Annabel, Crispian and Tania had been watching her from the doorway for some time. In her crisp, striped multicoloured dress with its elbow-length sleeves and side slits she looked slim, cool and infinitely desirable.

'Lunch!' Crispian called softly when she next glanced up.

Annabel jumped. 'How long have you been there?'

'Just arrived,' he lied. 'Tania and I are lunching alone today. We thought you might like to join us.'

'Where are your parents?' asked Annabel as the three of them sat down together.

'Step-mama's probably "choosing a puppy" for the sixth time. Pa's gone out for a ride on – sorry, with – Sandra!'

Annabel flushed and he looked at her in surprise. 'Don't tell me you didn't know about my father and the stable girls?'

'Yes, I knew,' she muttered, seeing the morning scene again all too vividly.

Crispian's eyes gleamed. 'You've been peeking, haven't you? I can tell, you're looking guilty.'

'I have not been peeking. Your father sent for me and when I arrived he already had one of the girls with him.'

'I thought he'd soon be after you,' laughed Crispian. 'Did he ask you to join in?'

'Of course not!'

Tania watched the other girl closely. 'You mean you didn't even stay and watch?'

Annabel shifted uncomfortably on her chair. 'The girl locked the door. I couldn't get out straight away.'

'How deliciously decadent!' said Crispian. 'Did it excite you?'

'Not much. Do you think we could change the subject?'

'It excites me,' Tania said slowly. 'I often watch him when he goes out for rides with one of his grooms. They always tie up at this copse and it's easy to get there first and hide in the trees. Once he gets going he's far too wrapped up in the sensations to worry about the odd bit of leaf rustling. By the end I'm usually frantic for them to go so that I can pleasure myself. The other day Matthew came along just as they were leaving. I nearly called for him to stay and help me out!'

'Naughty!' reproved her stepbrother. 'You know Matthew's for Annabel.'

'All I know is that I need two jars of maraschino cherries

164

and a large sheet for the party games next Saturday,' said Tania. 'I wonder what kind of explanation the housekeeper will need when I ask for them!'

Crispian and Tania started to giggle, and Tania perched on her stepbrother's knees with her arms round his neck at the exact moment that Susan brought in their lunch. She remained there being fed by him for the whole of the first course, and Annabel was left wondering exactly what the games were going to be.

Chapter Nine

The day before a dinner party, Lady Corbett-Wynne would normally have been driving the staff at the Hall mad with incessant instructions and queries. To their astonishment, after spending forty-five minutes with her housekeeper checking arrangements and a brief half-hour with her social secretary, she left them all alone to get on with their work.

The housekeeper watched from the kitchen window as her ladyship walked briskly towards the stables, dressed in very tight black jodhpurs and a smart, open-necked check shirt, riding hat dangling from her right hand. 'She's going for a ride!' she exclaimed to Richard, the footman.

He smiled. 'Makes a change!'

The housekeeper swung round to face him. 'Mind what you say, Richard. At least her ladyship understands how things should be done, unlike her husband.'

'If she doesn't, she soon will,' he muttered, tales of her riding lessons having come back to him via one of the lads who helped Jerry.

Marina felt an unaccustomed spring in her step as she approached the cobbled yard. Since her last meeting with Matthew, which had consisted mainly of a lesson in the skills required to provide good oral sex, she'd stayed away from the Old Mill. It wasn't that she didn't find Matthew attractive any more; she did, but somehow it wasn't working out the way she'd hoped. Technically everything was fine. She always came away physically satisfied, but she sensed that Matthew's feelings for her weren't the same as hers were for him. Sometimes he seemed to regard her as a fascinating experiment rather than a person, and she didn't like that any better than being expected to dress up in leather harnesses for her husband. She wanted to be able to be herself and have a satisfying sexual relationship at the same time, but was starting to wonder if this was possible with any of the men in their social circle.

She was keeping up with her riding lessons because, much to her surprise, she was enjoying them. Jerry had proved to be a very sensitive teacher, never attempting to hurry her but always willing to go at her pace. She wondered if he'd be the same where sex was concerned.

At that moment he strolled over the cobblestones towards her, lifting a hand in lazy greeting. He was undeniably very handsome in an unkempt way and she'd grown used to his offhand manner and habitual silences. Whenever his hands touched her, adjusting her grip, moving her legs into position or helping her on and off her horse, she'd feel a frisson of pleasure and her heart had lately taken to pounding fiercely in her chest. Having despised James for years for his liaisons with the girls from the stables it was disquieting to discover that she herself was attracted to the man in charge of them.

'Good morning,' he said briskly. He never used her title, and she no longer wanted him to. It placed too much distance between them, a distance that she was now anxious to dispel.

'Today's my big day then,' she exclaimed with a nervous laugh.

'That's right; we won't be going far. There's a nice little bridle path once you cross the road that runs past the south wall; we'll take that. We won't be gone more than an hour.'

'You mean I've got to ride Betsy on a public road!' Marina said in horror.

'Betsy could cross on her own,' he laughed. 'Come on, time to mount.'

Marina knew that she was now perfectly capable of getting into the saddle on her own, but she waited with one foot in the stirrup until Jerry came round and helped her on. His hands moved slightly from her waist and she felt them travel down over her hips where they lingered for a moment before he removed them.

'Right, let's go,' he called, swinging himself onto his own horse, and with a click of his tongue he started them off on their ride.

At first Marina was petrified. She wondered now why she'd ever worried about organising dinner parties and mixing at large social gatherings; this was far worse. Her hands gripped the reins tightly and she kept her thighs glued to the horse's sides.

'Just relax,' said Jerry after they'd negotiated the road and were on the bridle path. 'That's not the way you've been riding her back on the estate. You've lost all your rhythm; the poor horse must feel as though she's got a ton weight on her back. Rise and fall like we practised.'

Marina tried; she tried very hard, but her legs had gone solid with fear and when she tried to rise and fall she ended up banging against the saddle like a sack of potatoes.

As they approached a clearing – a clearing that, unknown to Marina, was more used to visits from her husband – Jerry called a halt. 'I think you'd better get off for a moment, stretch your legs and try to relax,' he said shortly. 'I've never seen Betsy get in a state before, but you've managed to rattle her out of her habitual lethargy!'

Marina half-fell out of the saddle and stood on the grass, her thighs trembling after gripping the horse so tightly.

168

'I'm sorry,' she said quietly. 'I know I did everything wrong, but I'm still petrified of falling off.'

He tied the horses to a tree and leant against the trunk. 'Why should you? You've never fallen off yet with me.'

'Betsy might bolt.'

He laughed. 'She couldn't bolt, she hasn't got the energy!'

To Marina's horror she felt tears welling in her eyes. 'That's right,' she said haughtily. 'Laugh while you can. You seem to forget that I can always ask my husband to dismiss you for insolence.'

Jerry moved closer and took her hands in his. When he spoke his voice was softer than she'd ever heard it. 'Why would you want me dismissed?' he said. His voice was gentle. 'I wasn't laughing at you, I was laughing at the thought of Betsy moving fast. I'd never laugh at you; I admire you too much.'

'Admire me?'

He nodded. 'I know how hard this is for you, but you've stuck at it, and you were doing well until today. It's my fault. I thought you were ready but you weren't. We'll go back a bit and then try again some time next week when you've had more practice.'

'I don't know why I'm learning,' she murmured, staring into his blue eyes and very aware of the sharp tang of his aftershave.

'I thought you wanted to be able to go out riding again. Didn't your new neighbour suggest it?'

'Yes, but he suggests a lot of things that I'm not certain I really want to do,' she said softly.

Jerry released his grip and put the palms of his hands on each side of her face. 'I'd like to suggest something right now,' he whispered. 'How can I be sure you'll want to do that?'

Marina stared at him. She didn't reply but her eyes told him all that he'd been hoping to hear and very slowly he lifted her right hand and tenderly kissed the inside of her wrist. Marina shivered and moved towards him. 'Keep still,' he whispered, his eyes bright with admiration and desire, 'I want you to stay right there while I kiss you properly.'

She closed her eyes and remained quite still, waiting for the touch of his hard mouth on hers, but instead he continued to kiss her wrist and inner arm until he reached the inside of her elbow. Here his tongue traced a lazy circle across the fine blue veins beneath the pale skin and Marina trembled even more.

His other hand was stroking her left arm and shoulder. He gentled her as he would a horse, murmuring softly as he moved his mouth to her tender collarbone where his lips grazed against the slight bones while his hands ope-ned her shirt a little wider to allow him easier access.

She longed for him to unbutton her blouse and kiss her breasts, but it seemed that he was in no hurry, preferring to linger at her neck where his mouth roamed up and down the slim column, his teeth just skimming the surface of the flesh beneath her ear until her whole body was quivering with anticipation.

She longed to move, to take his head between her hands and move his mouth against hers, but at the same time she didn't want the delicious sensations to cease and so she stayed motionless while he continued to softly tease some of her most erogenous zones.

Just when she thought that she couldn't stand it any longer he stopped and she felt his mouth against her ear. 'I want to cover your whole body with kisses,' he said softly. 'I want to kiss every inch of you, but not here, not out in the open where people might see us.'

Marina's eyes flew open, and she knew that he must be able to see the look of desire on her face. 'I don't want you to stop,' she moaned, unable to disguise her need.

'Nor do I. Don't worry, I live in a cottage at the other end of the track. Do you think you can bear to get on Betsy's back once more?'

She'd have done anything to ensure that her tingling, swollen flesh was satisfied, and without another word she let Jerry help her back into the saddle and then they were moving slowly along the pathway until a few minutes later they arrived at his cottage.

It was small and the brickwork was in need of repair, but Marina didn't care. She wanted to feel his hands on her, wanted him so badly that she was already moist with excitement; she scarcely took in the disarray of the rooms as he led her up the narrow stairs and straight into his bathroom.

Marina had been expecting the bedroom, and for a moment she drew herself up in a manner more fitting to the wife of Lord Corbett-Wynne than the would-be mistress of his riding manager. Jerry put his arms round her. 'I thought it would be nice if we took a shower together after our ride.'

Marina didn't reply, but as he started to take off his clothes she slowly began to unbutton her check shirt. Her excitement increased when he kept his eyes on her all the time she stripped, and she saw nothing but admiration in his face.

'You're lovely,' he whispered when she was finally naked. He ran a finger lightly round each of her breasts. 'Don't worry; if I do anything you don't like just say and I'll stop. I want to make you happy, that's all.'

She followed him into the shower, and as the warm spray beat down on them he got her to place her feet on the raised sides of the base, so that her legs were parted and her body lifted and their heights became equal.

His arms went around her, reaching down for her buttocks which he squeezed softly, and then he reached for the shower gel, poured some into his hands and began to lather each of her breasts in turn. His hands moved slowly and sensuously around each areola before massaging the nipples themselves and Marina uttered soft cries of pleasure, as at long last the aching globes received the touch she'd been imagining ever since he'd first kissed her wrist.

As he massaged, he bit softly at her earlobes, sending a sharp tugging sensation down through her body, and then he lightly inserted the tip of his tongue inside her left ear, flicking it rapidly until her hips began to shake with desire.

Her breasts had never felt so hard and when he took each of her nipples in turn between his right thumb and index finger and rolled them gently she was certain she'd explode as all her muscles started to tense and her feet nearly slipped from the narrow edges of the shower.

'You look wonderful,' he murmured as he started to soap her across her ribs and stomach, and then he applied gentle pressure at the base of her belly just above her pubic hair, keeping his hand still until a warm glow began to spread down between her thighs and a sweet ache suffused her entire sex.

Once she was covered in soap, Jerry moved closer and rubbed himself against her slippery flesh, stimulating them both until Marina was crying out with desire, thrusting her hips towards him in frantic movements as the sweetness of the ache became unbearable.

Jerry's hands returned to her buttocks and at last he pulled her firmly towards him, sliding into her swollen vagina with a slow steady movement. He then stayed motionless inside her while one of his hands began to fondle her between her parted thighs.

He massaged the whole pubic area, pressing and releasing the flesh then rotating it in tiny circular movements followed by an up and down stroke that soon had her body on fire as her indirectly stimulated clitoris swelled and she felt her internal muscles growing taut and hard.

'Tighten round me,' he whispered. 'Use your muscles on me so that I can feel you grip me.'

She looked deep into his eyes and as she obeyed she pressed her mouth against his, her tongue thrusting between his lips and circling his gums, before flicking between his teeth and moving backwards and forwards as though she were a man performing oral sex on a woman.

Her sudden taking of the initiative, together with the heat that he could feel from her damp body and the tightness of her vaginal walls as she gripped and released him in quick spasmodic movements, drove Jerry wild.

Now he abandoned his slow tender approach and responded to her new needs. His hands tightened on her buttocks and he allowed one finger to ease its way between them. Marina was so caught up in the frantic excitement of the moment that she didn't even notice, and it was only when her body was teetering on the brink of its climax that he allowed the finger to ease its way inside her rear entrance. With a loud cry of ecstasy, Marina gave herself over to her orgasm, an orgasm that went on and on as his fingers stimulated her from both sides until she was finally still.

'Now it's my turn,' he murmured, and at last he began to move inside her.

He moved in long, leisurely thrusts, allowing the full length of his erection to glide in and out, and at every outward movement Marina clutched desperately at his shoulders, terrified that he was going to withdraw completely and leave her achingly empty. Jerry was too experienced for that, and enjoying himself far too much to break the carefully built-up rhythm; all he was doing was prolonging his moment of pleasure and, he hoped, enabling Marina to achieve another climax.

Slowly she felt her body tightening once more and she writhed against him, pressing her erect nipples against his chest and her stomach hard against his to give herself the feeling of pressure that she'd enjoyed earlier.

After a few minutes Jerry's tempo quickened as his own climax grew closer. He felt his testicles pull upwards against his body and the tip of his penis was filled with light tingling sensations. He knew that he was about to come, and sensed that Marina was close too. Quickly he moved the heels of his hands until they were resting on her hip bones and then, just as the tingles spread lower down his shaft, he started to knead her pelvis with firm fingers.

Marina's whole belly rippled in a delirium of excitement and she kept her eyes locked onto Jerry's as they were both shaken by a simultaneous climax of shattering intensity. By the time hers was over, Marina was almost collapsing against him, and she found that she was crying tears of joy while the soft caress of the shower continued to fall on her naked body.

For a moment he held her against him, running his fingers through her wet hair and smoothing the damp strands off her forehead, but then he turned off the water and stepped slowly away. 'We've got to get dried,' he said reluctantly. 'I don't think we can make your first ride last too long or someone might get suspicious.'

'I don't care if they do,' murmured Marina, letting him wrap her in a large, if somewhat coarse, towel and then rub her briskly all over. 'I've never been so happy before.'

'That's what I like to hear,' he said with a smile.

Marina glanced at him, his jet black hair plastered to his head and his teeth gleaming white against his tanned skin. 'I imagine all your women say the same,' she teased.

The laughter went out of his eyes. 'I don't usually have women. Girls, yes, I've had a lot of girls, but not women. Now I know what I've been missing.'

She wondered if he'd slept with the fair-haired girl she'd seen in the stables, or even Tania, but then she pushed the thought away. What did it matter if he had? He'd just made love to her, and done it more skilfully and with more feeling than anyone had before, even Matthew, so what did his past matter?

'When can I see you again?' he asked and she felt like laughing aloud with happiness.

'Not until Sunday,' she said regretfully. 'I've got a

174

dinner party tomorrow night and simply can't get away then, but Sunday morning will be all right.'

'We'll take the horses out,' he said, his eyes bright at the prospect. 'Do you mind coming back here again? We'll use the bedroom next time.'

'I don't mind where we go,' she said truthfully.

They rode back slowly and in comparative silence, but it was a friendly silence and Marina realised that Jerry was continually glancing at her, as though proud to be in her company.

'Is Sir Matthew Stevens coming on Saturday night?' he asked casually when he was helping her dismount in the stable yard.

Marina touched the back of his right hand. 'Yes, he is, but he isn't important to me any more. I don't really think we've got a lot in common.'

'Sometimes it takes a long time to get to know someone,' he said slowly, 'but at other times you have this feeling, a kind of instinct if you like, that it's right. Do you know what I mean?'

Marina nodded. She knew it was ridiculous, that he was younger than her, worked for her husband and had spent most of his adult life bedding nubile young girls, yet she was quite certain that he was going to be a very special person in her life.

'I'll see you on Sunday,' she promised.

Jerry watched her go and wondered if she'd regret it once she was back inside her luxurious house. He hoped not. Already, after this one time together, she meant more to him than any other woman had done, and no one could have been more surprised by that than he was.

'We'll have to wait and see, Betsy,' he told the docile mare, leading her back into her stable. 'I must be mad, but the way I feel at the moment I want to spend the rest of my life with that woman. She's made for pleasure, and I intend to be the man who gives it to her.'

When Marina arrived at the front door of the house she

found Matthew Stevens waiting for her on the steps. He smiled, and she noticed with surprise that his smile didn't have its usual effect on her. Only a week or so ago it would have made her legs tremble and there would have been a nervous fluttering in her stomach, but now there was nothing.

'I gather from your outfit you've been riding,' he said softly, his eyes bright with appreciation. 'Even if you never become highly proficient, the clothes look incredible on you, very erotic indeed.'

She smiled, but in an absent-minded way and Matthew realised this. He wondered if she wasn't enjoying being on horseback again. 'If you're not happy riding, then give it up,' he said with another quick smile. 'I'm sure we can find other ways to meet.'

'I am enjoying it,' Marina assured him, pushing open the door and preceding him into the entrance lobby. 'In fact, I can't remember when I've been happier.'

'That's good. I can't remember when I've been happier either,' he added, his voice suddenly low and caressing.

Marina realised that she was comparing him unfavourably with Jerry. Jerry was always sincere; when he paid her compliments she knew that they were genuine. With Matthew Stevens she wasn't certain, and his recent insistence on honing her sexual skills in the way that he wished, rather than following her desires, had done nothing to help his cause.

'I'm afraid I'm rather busy today,' she said politely. 'Was there something special you wanted to see me about? I've got about half an hour to spare, but after that all my time will be taken up getting ready for tomorrow's dinner party.'

Matthew both looked and felt taken aback. 'I'd hoped we might have some time alone together,' he said. 'I've only just returned from town and . . .'

'Out of the question, I'm afraid,' Marina informed him, her tone unusually crisp.

Matthew moved closer to her and took hold of her left elbow. 'What's the matter? Have I done something to offend you?'

She managed a smile, but it wasn't the usual adoring one he'd become used to. 'Of course not. What could you possibly have done?'

That was what he was trying to work out, because despite her denial he knew that something had changed. He had a suspicion that it might be connected with their last meeting, when he'd tried to teach her the best way to go down on him. He'd known she wasn't keen, had sensed her dislike even as she went through the motions, but because it was something he loved he'd wanted her to love it too. Now he realised that might have been a mistake and he cursed inwardly. He hadn't expected their affair to last very long, but he preferred to be the one to end a relationship. He'd also been enjoying tutoring her, despite the fact that she lacked the robust, extreme sexuality he really preferred.

He had a sudden image of her bent on her knees in front of him, her long hair falling over her face as she'd closed her soft, tentative mouth around his erection, and suddenly he wanted her with an almost painful urgency.

'Is your husband here?' he asked, his grip on her elbow tightening.

Marina shook her head. 'He's in London; why?'

'Then we could spend the half-hour alone together here. No one would know, and even if they guessed they wouldn't say anything, would they?'

She removed her arm from his grip and raised her eyebrows, suddenly very much Lady Corbett-Wynne, rather than his mistress, Marina. 'I wouldn't dream of compromising myself in my own home,' she said icily. 'Really, Matthew, I find it hard to believe you'd expect me to.'

'Isn't it a little late to play the lady of the manor?' he asked shortly.

Marina felt herself flush and turned away, furious with him for making her feel cheap. Jerry would never make such a mistake, she thought to herself. Despite his so-called lack of breeding he knew instinctively how to talk to her, how to make her feel wanted as a person and not just as a sex object. 'I think I'll ignore that remark, Matthew,' she retorted. 'You really should go now. If you happen to see Annabel in the grounds would you ask her to come and see me, as there are some things I want to discuss with her.'

Furious with himself for making such a stupid mistake, Matthew nodded. 'Of course, and I'm sorry, Marina. It's just that I wanted you so badly, I lost control for a moment. You surely can't blame me for that. It's your fault for being so desirable,' he added.

Normally that would have flattered her, boosted her gradually increasing sexual confidence and encouraged her to move towards him again, but her eyes remained calm and aloof and she turned and left him without another word.

Angry and puzzled, Matthew left the house, crossing the drive towards his car. As he did so, Annabel came towards him, the golden streaks in her hair shining in the bright sun. She glanced sideways at him, giving him a half-smile that held in it a world of sexual knowledge. Matthew wondered what was happening to the women at Leyton Hall; they were changing out of all recognition.

He still couldn't fathom Marina's change of attitude, but the new sexual awareness in Annabel's eyes was, he suspected, the direct result of close contact with Crispian and Tania. This thought re-aroused his desire and he felt himself growing hard as Annabel walked over to stand opposite him.

'Were you looking for Lady Corbett-Wynne?' she asked politely. 'I think she's out riding, but she should be back soon.'

'I've seen her,' he explained, his eyes assessing her slim

but extremely feminine shape appreciatively. 'In fact, she asked me to look out for you on my way back home. She'd like a word with you.'

Annabel sighed, brushing her hair back behind her ears as she did so. 'I'm afraid she and I aren't getting on too well at the moment,' she confessed. 'I think perhaps I'm the wrong person for this job.'

He frowned. 'I hope you won't leave before the weekend's out. I'm looking forward to seeing more of you at the dinner party.'

Standing so close to him, Annabel was struck once more by the powerful physical attraction that he held for her. She wondered what it was that she found so compelling. He had to be nearly twenty years older than her, and, although attractive, wasn't breathtakingly handsome. But there was something about his eyes and the way he moved that suggested an exciting sexuality honed by years of experience. She felt literally weak with desire but was determined not to let him see the effect he had on her.

'Don't worry,' she said quickly, with another sideways smile as she turned towards the house. 'I couldn't possibly leave yet; I've promised Crispian and Tania I'll be there for the games.'

Matthew's mouth went dry as he realised that he was right. Since her arrival at Leyton Hall, this girl had become involved with Crispian and Tania, which could only mean that she must be sexually adventurous as well as highly attractive.

'Games?' he asked with a questioning look.

Annabel turned to face him full on. 'That's right; Tania's been gathering all kinds of weird objects together for the after-dinner games, and I think there's a small private party afterwards in Crispian's room, although presumably Lady Corbett-Wynne won't be joining her stepson for that!'

'I'm sure you're right, but that doesn't mean that I can't,' he said softly.

'I thought you and Lady Corbett-Wynne were close friends?'

Matthew shrugged. 'We were, but I have a feeling the friendship's cooled. When I spoke to her a few minutes earlier she seemed a little distracted to say the least.'

'How disappointing for you,' Annabel said lightly.

Matthew touched her gently on the face, letting his fingers trail softly down her left cheek and round her jaw bone, sending shivers of desire through her. 'Not really; the friendship had probably run its natural course.'

'Your friends don't last very long then,' remarked Annabel with a smile.

At once his fingers touched the upturned corner of her mouth, and she had a desperate longing to draw them into her mouth.

'Some do,' he said softly. 'It's always difficult to work out how much two people have in common. Sometimes it's less than you expected, but sometimes it's more.'

He drew his forefinger round the outline of her mouth, his touch feather-light, and Annabel had to make a conscious effort not to move towards him. Then he leant forward, kissed her lightly on the tip of her nose and climbed into his car. 'Until tomorrow night.'

She watched him drive away and desire stirred deep in her belly as she imagined what it would be like to have those fingers touching her more intimately.

When his car was out of sight she hurried indoors, remembering that she was wanted by her employer. To her surprise, Lady Corbett-Wynne seemed to be in a good mood and she smiled at Annabel with far more warmth than she'd been displaying lately.

'Annabel, my dear, I wanted to ask you about tomorrow night.'

'Tomorrow night?' asked Annabel in surprise.

'The decoration of the dinner table. You see, I'd originally thought predominantly blue, but now I'm not so sure. Would that be too heavy, do you think?'

'Perhaps a little,' said Annabel, shuddering inwardly at the thought of a blue table arrangement in such a dark room. 'Why not dusky pink? It's such a lovely warm colour, particularly in candlelight.'

'Candles too, you think?' Marina wandered around her sitting room, picking up objects and putting them down again in a thoroughly distracted manner. 'Well, perhaps you're right. To be honest with you, Annabel, I simply don't have my heart in this, nor in the house any more, as I'm sure you've noticed.'

'It seemed to me that it was more a question of us not being on quite the same wavelength,' Annabel said tactfully. 'I had wondered if you'd like me to leave, so that you could try someone else who was more in tune with your ideas. After all, no matter what I may think, you're the one who has to live here. I'll be gone within a week!'

Marina's eyes widened and she stared thoughtfully at Annabel. 'Who knows what the future holds,' she said quietly. 'Life can be so unpredictable, don't you think?'

For the first time since their original meeting, Annabel felt flustered. She couldn't imagine what Marina meant. Even if she'd had some kind of a fling with Matthew Stevens, that seemed to be over, and yet here she was talking as though her own future was uncertain. She'd always seemed to Annabel to be firmly settled into her role as the third Lady Corbett-Wynne.

'I agree that none of us knows what's going to happen in the future,' she said at last, 'but there are certain fixed points, as it were.'

'But are there?' asked her employer, her eyes suddenly bright. 'Is that the way we're meant to live? Or should we be more open to change?'

'As I'm single, my life's permanently open to change!' laughed Annabel. 'But I think it's bound to be different once you're married, and with responsibilities such as yours.'

'Do you think my husband's worried about his responsibilities?' Marina asked fiercely. 'It doesn't seem so to me.

Look at the way he behaves with the stable girls, flaunting them in my face the way he does. Is that the behaviour of a mature man with responsibilities? No, it isn't. And if he doesn't care what people say, then why should I?'

Annabel knew that the distraught woman wasn't really asking for answers: she was talking to herself and Annabel was simply unlucky enough to be the recipient of the voicing of all her doubts and frustrations. She only hoped Marina didn't regret it within the hour and send her packing.

'Well?' continued Marina, fixing Annabel with her gaze. 'Answer me.'

'I don't suppose there's any reason why you should feel answerable to anyone but yourself,' replied Annabel, hoping this was what her employer wanted to hear.

To her relief it seemed that it was because the fierce light went out of Lady Corbett-Wynne's eyes and she nodded in agreement. 'How sensible you are. I felt sure you'd understand, after all you've become closely involved with our family since your arrival, haven't you?'

It was a statement, not a question, and Annabel shifted uncomfortably from one foot to the other as she wondered how much this woman really knew about the things that went on at Leyton Hall.

'I hope you're not falling in love with my stepson,' continued Marina, her voice back to its usual gracious tone. 'You see, he's in love with my daughter but has to marry money, which rather excludes you from the contest.'

'I'm not in love with Crispian,' said Annabel quickly. 'He's very handsome but . . .'

Marina smiled. 'Exactly, there's always a very large *but* hanging over anything to do with Crispian!'

'I hardly know either of them,' protested Annabel.

Marina sighed. 'You must think me very stupid, Annabel, if you imagine that I don't know everything that goes on in this house. I'm well aware of my daughter's pointless obsession with Crispian, and equally well aware of the fact that they've involved you in their games. Don't look so surprised; the fact of the matter is they involve everyone who comes here, providing of course that they consider them beautiful enough and suitable for their requirements. I hope I'm not disillusioning you,' she added politely. Annabel shook her head. 'Good. No doubt my husband too has attempted some kind of familiarity, although I rather doubt that his particular kind of sexuality would hold any great attraction for you, although I may be wrong.'

Annabel hoped that her face wasn't giving anything away.

'Normally I'd never mention any of this to you,' continued Marina, 'but you see I'm not certain exactly where I fit in any more, and so I feel more free to speak out. My advice to you is, stay away from my daughter and my stepson. This dark obsession they have for each other is hopeless and, once they accept that, they'll turn on anyone and everyone within reach. They both have a very self-destructive streak, I'm afraid, which coupled with their twisted desires makes them dangerous company.'

'I don't see why they can't marry,' said Annabel, emboldened by her employer's astonishing frankness. 'It isn't as though they're related.'

'Tania has no money of her own, and having wasted years of my life on Crispian's father I have no intention of giving her money so that she can waste years of hers on his son. And without money, Tania is quite useless as a prospective bride for Crispian. This house eats money like a moth eats wool.'

'Crispian will never be happy with anyone else,' said Annabel.

Marina frowned. 'Happiness is not always found where we expect it. Besides, I have no doubt that he will marry someone suitable – Amanda Fitzwilliam perhaps – and then keep my daughter as his mistress. That way he will probably attain a higher degree of happiness than most of us manage, don't you think?'

Annabel shook her head. 'It wouldn't be fair on Amanda.'

'Like me, Amanda has been brought up in a tradition of duty. She would know better than to expect happiness from Crispian – at least he'd save her from living at home with her parents all her life.'

'I really don't know why you're telling me this,' protested Annabel.

Marina put her head on one side and considered the younger woman. 'I'm not certain either. Perhaps because I have the feeling that, like me, you will soon have to make some kind of decision, and I don't want you to make the wrong one.'

'Why not? What do I mean to you?'

'Despite your experiences since you arrived here, Annabel, you seem to me to be intrinsically pure. I don't think it can have escaped your notice that everyone who lives in Leyton Hall is corrupt, morally and sexually. I'd hate to see you succumb to this malaise.'

'Perhaps I'm not what you think,' murmured Annabel.

'None of us are what we think, but there is a difference between being adventurous and being depraved. Remember that when you have to make your choice.'

'I really don't . . .'

'Crispian and Tania are depraved. Believe me, I know this to be true. They enjoy destroying people; don't let them destroy you. Now, was it dusky pink you suggested?'

Totally confused, Annabel nodded, hardly able to remember the original reason for her presence in the room.

Marina smiled. 'I believe you're right. A good choice, Annabel. You can run along now. I have a lot to do.'

'I've finished the plans for the whole of the ground floor,' Annabel said hesitantly. 'Shall I leave them with you?'

'If you wish.'

Disconcerted, Annabel placed her sheaf of notes and drawings on the small French table and left. She was still going over the extraordinary conversation in her head when she came face to face with Crispian at the entrance to his stepmother's quarters.

'Hard at work?' he asked cheerfully.

'In a way,' muttered Annabel.

'I've been on the phone to Sir Matthew. He sounded very keen to join our exclusive little party on Saturday night.'

She stared into his bright blue eyes and saw the almost feverish glitter of excitement in them. His stepmother's warning came back to her, but she knew that she would still follow him. Not because she was in love with him but because he was showing her a new and exciting way of life, revealing an entirely unexpected side of her, a side that she'd never suspected existed. It was proving addictive.

'Aren't you pleased?' he asked with a grin.

'Of course I am. He seems very nice.'

Crispian laughed. 'He's a lot of things but very nice isn't one of them! God, I can't wait for the boring part of tomorrow evening to be over. Think what fun we'll all have then.'

'These games,' said Annabel. 'Are they part of the private party?'

'Heavens, no! They're traditional at Pa's dinners. Most of the guests would be extremely disappointed if they weren't allowed to take part.'

'Surely not your stepmother?'

'She'll withdraw after the coffee's served, unless Matthew's wrought a drastic change in her outlook.'

'He seemed to think he may no longer be quite so much in favour,' Annabel said slowly.

Crispian looked pleased at the news. 'All the better for us then! I've got some wonderful things lined up for you,

Annabel. You'll be out of your mind with pleasure before we've finished with you.'

Her whole body tightened and she trembled slightly at his words. They conjured up such glorious images, and already in her imagination her flesh was straining for the wonderful flooding sweetness that every sexual peak released in her.

'Imagination's a wonderful thing!' said Crispian, watching her pupils dilate. 'Anticipation should add an even keener edge to your appetite. I know it will to mine.'

'And Amanda?' asked Annabel.

The laughter faded from his face. 'She'll be gone as soon as I can decently take her home, although the party games might send her packing without my assistance!'

'Poor Amanda,' said Annabel.

'Yes, but lucky us,' he whispered, his mouth against her ear, and as his warm breath teased her flesh she shuddered with excitement.

Chapter Ten

*A*t six o'clock on the evening of the dinner party, Annabel began her preparations. She wanted everything to be perfect; her clothes, her perfume, the way she wore her hair, every tiny detail, because knowing that she looked her best would help give her the confidence that she felt she'd need to cope with whatever Crispian and Tania had in store for her.

All day she'd felt on edge, her senses keenly alert as she thought about the evening and Matthew Stevens. She'd dreamt about him the previous night, and although the details had been blurred she'd awoken in a state of aching arousal, with a tell-tale dampness between her thighs and her nipples hard. She couldn't remember ever having wanted a man so much.

At the same time as Annabel was taking a long, scented bath and washing her hair in banana shampoo, Crispian was perching on the edge of his stepsister's bath and watching her lazy soaping of her full breasts and slender ribcage. 'Want any help?' he asked.

Tania shook her head. 'If you start helping me I'll never be ready on time. You're sure you've made all the arrangements?'

'Of course. Luke and Sheba will join us upstairs, and so will Sir Matthew, along with the delectable Annabel, naturally!'

Tania raised a tightly muscled leg and pointed her toes as she rubbed the suds over her calf. 'You like Annabel, don't you?'

'She's very sexy,' agreed Crispian, letting one hand trail in the bath water, his fingers searching for and finally locating Tania's triangle of curly auburn hair.

Tania lifted her hips slightly, sighing softly as the pleasurable sensations stirred within her. 'If your father wanted you to marry Annabel, you would, wouldn't you?'

He tugged at the curls, letting one finger slip into the cleft between her sex-lips and massaging in tiny circular movements as he went. 'I might,' he agreed cautiously.

Tania's eyes glittered. 'Lucky for me she isn't rich, then.'

'She isn't like you!' exclaimed Crispian. 'I'd soon get tired of her. It's only that she does have something about her, something more interesting than the Amandas of this world.'

Tania lowered her leg and crossed it over the other one, trapping Crispian's hand. 'I think you'd give me up for Annabel,' she said slowly.

'That's nonsense,' said Crispian, astonishment clear in his voice. But when Tania looked up at him his eyes held the innocent expression of a small boy trying to bluff his way out of an awkward situation.

'She isn't what you think, you know,' continued Tania, moving herself against the trapped finger and letting the tendrils of arousal start to build. 'Annabel has limits.'

Crispian knew that Tania was close to an orgasm. Her eyes were shining and her mouth had opened slightly as her breathing grew more rapid. With some difficulty he withdrew his hand and saw a flash of anger cross his stepsister's face. 'Naughty! You said you hadn't got time for me, remember,' he laughed.

'Did you hear what I said?' Tania asked tightly.

'About Annabel having limits? Sure.'

'Don't you believe me?'

Crispian shrugged. 'I don't know; but after tonight we'll find out, won't we?'

At last Tania smiled again, and the slight tension in the air vanished. 'Yes,' she said softly, 'I rather think we will.'

In blissful ignorance, Annabel continued her evening's preparations. When it came to choosing a dress she hesitated for a long time. She wanted something sexy and yet glamorous and was about to put on the same gown she'd worn before when her eye was caught by a paprika-coloured silk dress. It had a sleeveless bodice that crossed over to one side and then dropped in a waterfall drape to the hem. She'd bought it the previous year and never worn it, but she could still remember the sensuous feel of it when she'd first tried it on. Somehow both the design and the colour fitted the image she wanted to project that night.

Once she'd put it on she knew that she was right. Worn with sheer black stockings and high-heeled, black Italian shoes the effect was dramatic and flattering. In the end the only jewellery she wore were tiny gold earrings and a slender gold bracelet on her right wrist.

Finally she brushed her hair behind her left ear, leaving it forward on the right side, and then, after spraying herself with Shalimar perfume, she looked in the mirror and knew that she was ready. Tonight was quite definitely going to be memorable, and she could scarcely wait for the dinner to begin.

At eight forty-five the guests started arriving and five minutes later Annabel went down to join them. Tania, who had been listening for the sound of Annabel's door opening, immediately slipped out into the corridor as well.

'Shall we go down together?' she called. Annabel turned to look at her. Suddenly her confidence drained away and she wondered if she'd made a terrible mistake. Tania was wearing a severely cut three-piece man's suit with a white satin shirt and black bow tie. Her auburn hair had been streaked with plum-coloured highlights and then sleeked back like seal's fur, emphasising the wonderful shape of her head and her high cheekbones. Because the suit was tight her voluptuous breasts seemed even more noticeable, and Annabel knew that by dressing like a man Tania had drawn attention to her almost overwhelming sexuality.

'Like it?' asked Tania.

'You look incredible,' Annabel responded truthfully. 'You'll drive the men mad.'

'Good, that's the whole idea! You look nice,' she added. 'The dress looks as though it comes off easily.'

'Well, yes but . . .'

'Very sensible of you. It's just a pity we've got this boring dinner to sit through before the fun really begins. Never mind, hopefully I'll be next to someone interesting. I've changed the place names around: you were next to some ghastly friend of my stepfather's, but now you're next to Matthew.'

Annabel's stomach did a strange somersault and the palms of her hands went moist. 'Won't your mother mind?'

'She won't notice; her head's full of Jerry at the moment.'

'Jerry?' Annabel was confused.

'Sure, he's her latest paramour. Quite funny, isn't it? For years she wouldn't even have sex with her husband and now she's hopping from one bed to another like a sex-crazed teenager! At least it might stop her criticising me.'

'I don't think I know anyone called Jerry,' said Annabel.

At the door to the music room Tania paused. 'You probably don't; he's in charge of the stables,' she said with a grin, and then she was opening the door and the pair of them walked into the room.

For a moment all conversation stopped. Annabel was acutely aware of numerous pairs of eyes turning towards them. Although some of them lingered on her, it was Tania who held everyone's attention and eventually it was

Lord Corbett-Wynne himself who broke the silence by crossing the room with two glasses of sherry in his hands.

'Here you are, ladies, just as you both like it, I believe.'

Tania's lips curled upwards. 'I didn't know you knew how I liked it,' she murmured provocatively and he swallowed hard. Dressed like that he found his stepdaughter disturbingly appealing; she looked so aggressively sexual and dominant that he could clearly picture her standing in front of him, whip in hand as he waited for her commands.

'Aren't you going to introduce me to your friend, Tania?' asked a male voice, and Sir James turned away, grateful for the interruption.

Tania gave a smile of genuine warmth. 'Luke! How nice to see you again. This is Annabel. She's an interior designer down from London to help Mama redesign Leyton Hall.'

Luke's light-brown eyes were merry as he smiled at Annabel. 'I've heard about you from Crispian. He and I were at school together; now we only manage to meet up a few times a year, so we try and make the meetings memorable. I'm sure tonight will more than meet the required standard!'

'Luke's coming to our private party afterwards,' Tania whispered in Annabel's ear.

Annabel nodded, smiled back at Luke and then glanced around the room looking for Sir Matthew Stevens. At first she thought he hadn't arrived, but then she realised that he was standing talking to his hostess. Dressed in an evening suit and with his dark curly hair more tidy than usual he looked even more attractive than at their last meeting, and once more Annabel's body tightened with longing for him.

For a few seconds she studied him without his knowledge, and as she did so she realised that Tania had been right. Marina Corbett-Wynne was no longer captivated by her neighbour. As he talked her eyes were vague and although she smiled once or twice it was a social smile that failed to register anywhere apart from her mouth.

Dressed in a powder-blue dress with a pleated skirt of mid-calf length and a pleated bodice with wide shoulder straps, she looked once more remote and elegant. Her long gold chain had a huge pearl tear-drop at the end and there were matching earrings hanging from the lobes of her ears.

At that moment Sir Matthew looked around and caught Annabel staring at him. Before she had a chance to look away he was smiling warmly at her, and with a murmured excuse to Marina he moved to Annabel's side.

'You look fantastic!' he said warmly. 'Every woman in the room's envious.'

'Not of me!' responded Annabel, taking a sip of her sherry. 'I think it's Tania who's caught their attention, and I'm not surprised. Don't you think she looks incredible?'

'Dramatic certainly, but then that's Tania's forte, making outrageous statements, either verbally or by her behaviour.'

'I still think she looks amazing,' said Annabel.

'She's an amazing girl, or so I've been told. I haven't heard very much about you, which suits me very well as I prefer to find out for myself.'

A shiver ran through Annabel as she looked directly into his eyes and saw tiny flecks of gold in their depths. 'That should be exciting,' she said softly.

At that moment they were joined by a coffee-skinned young woman who was nearly six feet tall and whose jet-black hair, piled on her head, only added to her height. 'I'm Sheba, Luke's girlfriend,' she said with a smile. 'He told me to come over and introduce myself since we're all going to Crispian's little private party later tonight.'

With both Tania and Sheba at the party Annabel was beginning to think she was going to look extremely conventional. She smiled at Sheba, and as the other woman talked she admired her burnt-orange crepe dress with its spaghetti straps and thigh-high slash on the left-hand side of the skirt. As a designer she could only admire the other woman's fashion flair.

'Who's Luke?' asked Matthew when Sheba finally moved on.

'An old school friend of Crispian's, I think.'

'Should be fun then. Are you nervous?' he added in an undertone.

Annabel glanced at him. 'Should I be nervous?'

He smiled, his teeth very white against his tanned skin. 'Definitely not; excited, yes, but nervous, no.'

'That's lucky, because I have to admit to being excited.'

He put a warm hand on her bare arm. 'I'm sure you're not as excited as I am,' he murmured. 'I think that was the gong I heard then; I hope you'll allow me to take you in to dinner?'

Annabel nodded; even the touch of his fingers had set her skin on fire. When they entered the dining room and he pulled out her chair for her, his chin grazed the top of her hair as he bent over her to move the chair back in again. It felt as though an electric current had passed straight down her spine. When he took his seat next to her he gave her a quick smile and she knew that he was as aroused by her closeness as she was by his.

The food was excellent, although Annabel thought afterwards that it had all been wasted on her because the only thing she was thinking about was the moment when Matthew would finally start to make love to her. Just the same, she knew that the entrée of baked aubergines with goat's cheese was superb, the rib of beef perfect and the dessert of chestnut purée and whipped cream on a meringue base something she'd never forget.

The wines were some of Lord Corbett-Wynne's finest, ranging from the crisp Chardonnay served with the aubergines to the incredible Petrus 1990 which accompanied the beef.

At last the spectacular meal was over, coffee and mints were brought to the table and the servants withdrew. With

193

a quick glance round the table Lady Corbett-Wynne rose to her feet. 'For those of you who don't care for party games, more coffee will be served in the drawing room,' she announced. She and one or two other ladies then withdrew, but most of the guests remained, including Amanda, who had been seated next to Crispian at dinner.

James Corbett-Wynne looked at the remaining guests and smiled expansively. 'There, that's cleared away the dead wood. Now we can really have some fun. I suggest we start with the cherry game. Have you got some, Tania?'

'Of course!' laughed his stepdaughter, leaving the room for a moment.

'What's the cherry game?' Annabel asked Matthew, but he only smiled at her.

'Wait and see,' he replied.

When Tania returned she was carrying a large plate which she placed in the middle of the table. Annabel saw that the plate was covered in long-stemmed maraschino cherries and the guests quickly began to take one each, placing it on the small side plates that had been left behind when the table was cleared.

At the end of the table Lord Corbett-Wynne smiled at his guests. 'Anyone not know the rules?' he asked.

Several people raised their hands, including Annabel and Amanda. 'Quite simple,' their host assured them. 'Each of you has to hold the cherry level with your mouth and then tie a knot in the stem using only your tongue. The ladies have a go first, then the gentlemen. The winners from each of the two groups are allowed to choose their own prize!'

Everyone laughed, and Annabel turned to look at Matthew. He looked quizzically at her. 'Think you can do it?'

'I doubt it, but I'll enjoy trying! What about you?'

His eyes gleamed. 'Let's put it this way, I'll be very disappointed if I can't do it!'

'That sounds promising,' said Annabel.

'I won't be the only one,' retorted Matthew. 'Crispian's said to be an expert at this.'

Remembering the way Crispian's tongue had played over the aroused and taut tissue between her thighs as he traced the letters of the alphabet for her to guess, Annabel knew that Matthew was telling the truth and her pulse beat faster as she started to anticipate the games that would take place later, in the privacy of Crispian's rooms.

Matthew saw the change of colour in her cheeks. 'I take it you know something of his skills?' he said softly.

Annabel nodded, but before she could speak Lord Corbett-Wynne was tapping a spoon on the table for silence. 'Any questions? No? Excellent, then off you go, ladies!'

To the cheers and encouragement of the men the ladies picked up their cherries and started to work at the stems with their tongues. It was far more difficult than even Annabel had anticipated. She could quite easily fold her tongue around the tip of the stem, bending it down and around, but when it came to drawing it through the loop she'd created her control was nowhere near good enough.

She had no idea how the others were doing because all her concentration was focused on her own efforts. Every time she came near to drawing the tiny stem through the loop and the edges of her tongue curled upwards while the tip contorted into the necessary position, Sir Matthew watched her closely, whispering advice in her ear.

'You're nearly there!' he said suddenly as she manoeuvred the stem towards her goal. 'Come on, Annabel, I know you can do it.'

She concentrated as hard as she'd ever concentrated on anything, and was just about to draw the end through when Matthew whispered, 'I can't wait to feel your tongue on me,' and she lost it. The stem slipped out of her control and was suddenly upright again, leaving her to start from the beginning once more.

'Oh no!' she wailed, but Matthew simply laughed.

'Don't worry, I've seen enough to know you're very accomplished,' he said.

Annabel turned to him. 'I was just about to tie the knot then!'

'Tania's already won,' he said lightly. 'You were so lost in what you were doing you didn't hear the announcement. Clearly you enjoy this kind of thing!'

Flushed and strangely excited, Annabel glanced down the table and saw Tania holding her maraschino cherry triumphantly aloft while Crispian kissed the nape of her neck and all the men round her clapped and shouted approval.

Tania laughed. 'I shouldn't take part really, I get so much practice it isn't fair!'

'What do you practise on? Or should that be who?' asked Luke, and there was a burst of laughter from almost everyone except Amanda, who was sitting staring down at her plate on which the cherry sat, apparently untouched.

'Didn't Amanda try?' Annabel asked Matthew.

'Not that I saw. She sat and watched Crispian watching Tania. Bizarre, don't you think?'

'At least she might realise there's no point in continuing to see him,' said Annabel.

'Her parents are very keen and so is James. I'm not sure she's going to have much say in it.'

'Crispian will never marry her,' Annabel said firmly.

'You may be right. It's the men's turn now; I hope you'll encourage me as much as I encouraged you?'

'You distracted me!' exclaimed Annabel. 'And that's what I intend to do to you.'

'You do it just by sitting there,' he said lightly, and then he was picking up his cherry and Tania started the men off.

Watching them was even more erotic than trying to tie the knot herself, thought Annabel. Crispian's tongue was certainly skilful, and he was the only man who trapped the stem firmly between the curled sides of his tongue, but

196

Matthew seemed to have the edge when it came to suppleness of movement. As she sat next to him, watching the stem being drawn inexorably through the loop, Annabel imagined what it would be like to have the same tongue playing around her already swollen clitoris.

She pictured it swirling around the circumference, then lazily snaking down between her inner lips, before plunging deep inside her, drumming against the sides of her sex in firm but sensitive movements that would drive her insane with pleasure.

So real were her thoughts that her stomach began to tense and between her thighs she could feel her clitoris pressing against the tight silk of her briefs.

She looked again at Crispian and saw that he was now behind Matthew, failing to draw the end of the slender stalk through the loop while next to her Matthew was very close to completing the task.

Annabel leant nearer to him. 'I want to feel your tongue inside me,' she murmured against his ear. 'I want you to use it like that for my pleasure. You will, won't you?'

As she'd guessed, her words made him lose his concentration just as he'd made her lose hers and suddenly the stem sprang free from his encircling tongue while at the same time Crispian gave a shout of triumph. 'I win!' he cried gleefully.

Matthew turned to Annabel and his eyes were bright with anticipation. 'Don't worry, Annabel. I shall certainly use all my expertise on you tonight,' he promised, and she shuddered with desire.

'What about the prize?' called Luke, and all around the table people fell silent as Tania and Crispian looked at each other across the damask tablecloth.

Their eyes locked and the sexual tension between them was so great that Annabel wondered how anyone could possibly miss it. Lord Corbett-Wynne started to flush a deep purple, but seemed incapable of breaking the silence. At last Crispian smiled his most winning smile, at the same time putting one hand on the downcast Amanda's bare arm.

'I want Amanda and Tania to get to know each other better,' he announced. 'If Tania's agreeable, Amanda can join us younger ones at our own party later on tonight. What do you say, Tania?'

Annabel glanced at Matthew. 'Is he serious?' she whispered.

He shrugged. 'It looks like it. I wonder what Tania will have to say?'

Tania seemed thrown for a moment, but then she rallied, and there was a look in her eye which made Annabel feel a brief pang of pity for Amanda. 'I think that's a wonderful idea! I'm sure Amanda's as anxious as I am to get to know all of our family better, not just Crispian. You *can* stay overnight, can't you, Amanda?'

The rather plump and unflatteringly dressed Amanda was obviously uncertain, but when Crispian put an arm round her shoulders and murmured something in her ear her face lightened and she nodded. 'Of course. I'd love to get to know Tania better. Crispian's told me so much about you,' she added brightly.

Matthew smothered a laugh. 'Not everything, I imagine!' he said softly to Annabel. 'Well, this should be interesting, don't you think?'

Annabel wasn't certain. 'It could spoil the whole evening, quite apart from damaging Amanda for life,' she protested.

'Nonsense, she's a red-blooded country girl; she might surprise us all! Anyway, it's cheered James up. I thought he was going to have a fit when those two wouldn't stop devouring each other with their eyes.'

Lord Corbett-Wynne was indeed looking more cheerful and his colour had returned to a safer ruddy hue. 'Sounds an excellent idea,' he said gruffly. 'What about the sheet game to round the evening off before we join the others?'

Tania jumped up and left the room again, returning this

time with two footmen who were carrying a large piece of thick sheeting with circular rings all along the top edge.

'What on earth's that for?' asked Annabel.

'No idea,' confessed Matthew. 'We'll have to wait and see.'

'The ladies all have to leave the room,' said Tania as the footmen started to hook the rings over a long wooden pole. 'You wait outside, in the study. I have to stay here and I'll call you when everything's ready.'

'Don't you take part?' asked Sheba, gracefully unfolding her long legs as she left the table.

'No, I'm not allowed to any more because I always win. Anyway, a spare woman's needed to set the scene properly.'

As they all waited in the study Amanda came up to Annabel, her face paler than at dinner. 'I'm not very good at games,' she confessed. 'I didn't even try that one with the cherry. I felt too uncomfortable. I mean, everyone looked so . . .'

'So what?' asked Annabel gently.

'Sexual!' blurted out Amanda. 'I don't suppose you realised if you were taking part but it was terribly disconcerting to watch.'

'I think that was the idea!' laughed Annabel. 'These are adult party games. There isn't going to be any "pass the parcel", you know!'

Amanda stared at her. 'I'm not stupid, but I do think there are some things that should be kept private, don't you?'

Annabel thought for a moment. 'I used to think that,' she said at last. 'Now I'm not so sure. I certainly don't think there's any harm in things like the cherry game.'

'Perhaps you don't have as many inhibitions as I do,' said Amanda, her voice low.

'I'm sure I don't. You know, Amanda, Crispian's a very –'

'He's gorgeous, isn't he?' interrupted Amanda, her voice

suddenly full of feeling. 'I'm just so lucky that he's interested in me. Are you going to the second party tonight?'

'Yes, but . . .'

The dining-room door opened and Tania emerged, looking as incredible as ever in her tailored suit. 'Right, the scene is set and, as they say in all those old detective stories, I'd like everyone to come into the dining room!'

'I think it's usually the drawing room,' said Annabel with a smile.

'Well, even if the room's different, this is still a kind of detective puzzle,' retorted Tania. 'Come in quietly, ladies; the men don't want to be distracted.'

When she entered the room Annabel could hardly believe her eyes. The sheet had been suspended from the pole which was now fastened to one of the beams at the far end of the room. It hung down to the ground but whereas before it had looked like an ordinary sheet it was now clear that it had been specially adapted for this particular purpose.

A series of circular holes had been cut out of the sheet and through these holes there now emerged a long row of penises. They were all fully erect, testimony to Tania's skill, Annabel assumed, and were fully exposed in their respective glories. Some were circumcised, some not; the tips of some were purple, others merely a dark red and a few had drops of transparent moisture in the slit at the tip.

'Here's a piece of paper and a pencil each,' announced Tania. 'All you have to do is match what you see with the names on the paper. The first penis on the left is penis A, the second B and so on. The winner is the lady who matches the most penises to the correct owners!'

Behind Annabel a woman laughed. 'I know one of them very well,' she whispered to a friend. 'I only hope I get my husband's right too!'

Annabel, who knew she didn't have a chance of winning since most of the men at the dinner were strangers to her, was astonished by the air of excitement among the women.

Even those who had baulked at the cherry game seemed to want to take part this time.

'You've got ten minutes starting from now,' said Tania.

'Are we allowed to touch?' asked one woman.

'Only if you need to re-arouse,' explained Tania. 'The actual judging has to be done using your eyes only.'

Annabel turned to Amanda, ready to commiserate with her, but to her astonishment the other girl had already walked over to the sheeting and begun writing on her paper.

Annabel walked up and down the line, studying the phalluses with increasing interest. It was easy to pick out Lord Corbett-Wynne; his massive erection, thick and dark with the throbbing veins, brought back vivid memories of the scene she'd witnessed in his bedroom and she quickly noted his letter against his name on the paper.

The man next to him had a far less impressive erection; it was short and slim and already starting to droop. Remembering Tania's words, Annabel reached out and ran the tip of her fingernails along the underside. Immediately it sprang upright again and she heard a quick intake of breath from behind the sheeting. A feeling of power swept over her, and she couldn't resist one final touch before moving on. As her encircling fingers gripped the unknown man just beneath the rim of his glans a drop of fluid appeared in the opening and she knew that if she was allowed to continue he would quickly reach orgasm.

'Move on, Annabel,' said Tania, trying to suppress her amusement. 'Either you recognise him by now or you don't!'

Annabel smiled and reluctantly released the man, who gave another sigh, but this time of relief. She had no idea who he was, and didn't really care, but his helplessness and her position of power had aroused her even more and she longed for the moment when she joined the others upstairs.

Next in line was Crispian. There was no mistaking his

long, circumcised penis which, although not thick, was impressive due to its length.

The next two were unknown to her, but she hesitated by the third because, despite never having seen it before, she was convinced that this was Sir Matthew Stevens. The erection was rock hard, standing proudly upright, with the swollen glans a dark purple. It wasn't as long as Crispian's, but it was far thicker and Annabel could imagine it inside her, filling her as it moved rhythmically in and out. There was no reason for her to touch it, no hint that re-arousal was needed, but she found it impossible to resist and quickly caressed the swollen sensitive tip between her thumb and first finger. The veins throbbed and the outline of the heavy testicles was clear behind the sheet. Annabel longed to drop to her knees and take it in her mouth, to lick and suck at it until Matthew was driven to the edge of ecstasy, but behind her another woman was trying to push her away and she realised that she was holding everyone up. Quickly she scribbled the letter against Matthew's name, then wandered down to the end of the line and back again. She made a haphazard guess as to which one might be Luke before finally handing her paper over to Tania, who glanced at it and smiled.

'Was Sir Matthew a good guess or have you had a private viewing already?' she enquired.

'A good guess,' responded Annabel.

'Well, you won't win the prize but I'm sure you're more interested in what comes later anyway.'

'I can't wait,' Annabel assured her.

'You're not nervous?' queried Tania.

'Only that it might be cancelled!'

'You know, I'm beginning to understand why Crispian's so taken with you,' Tania murmured, turning away to take a paper from another woman. 'I think you might be rather a dangerous opponent.'

'We're not after the same prize,' retorted Annabel.

202

'Just the same, I'd hate to think Crispian would have chosen you if you'd been interested.'

'I think Amanda's the only competition you have to face,' said Annabel, losing interest in the conversation.

'Amanda doesn't worry me,' said Tania beneath her breath, her eyes cold as she watched Annabel walking away. 'But you do. I shall have to make quite sure that before tonight's over Crispian understands that I'm the only woman who'll ever keep him totally satisfied.

Finally all the papers were in and the women left the room again while the men got dressed and Tania checked the papers. When she called them back to announce the winner she had a strange expression in her eyes, an expression that Annabel couldn't quite analyse. The men were all sitting round the table again, chatting and joking as they drank the port. They only fell quiet when Tania tapped on the table for silence.

'I'm sure you're all anxious to know who the winning lady is,' she said slowly. There were shouted suggestions, names that meant nothing to Annabel, and Crispian and Luke continued whispering together despite Tania's glare.

'The winner,' she said loudly, 'and the only lady to correctly identify every single gentleman in the room, is Amanda.'

Annabel couldn't believe that she'd heard Tania correctly, but when she looked at the men she saw that they were all averting their eyes from each other and there was a lot of throat clearing and low muttering from the older guests.

'She couldn't have known everyone!' exclaimed Crispian, who looked totally shell-shocked.

Annabel turned to look at Amanda, who was slightly pink in the face but otherwise looked exactly the same innocent, out-of-place girl she'd looked earlier. 'I was lucky,' she said in an apologetic manner. 'I made inspired guesses a lot of the time.'

'You might think things should be done in private but

clearly you don't mind variety,' murmured Annabel, remembering Amanda's earlier comment.

Amanda's eyes were guileless. 'That's right! All I meant was, what goes on between two people should be done in privacy.'

Tania looked almost as stunned as her stepbrother, and suddenly the light-hearted tone of the game seemed to have died away and there was an air of awkwardness in the room, an awkwardness shared by everyone except Amanda, who smiled happily at Tania.

'Is there a prize?' she asked brightly.

'I can't think of anything you haven't had,' Tania responded.

Before Amanda could think of a reply the men had risen from their seats and were once again mingling with the women so that the moment passed without further embarrassment.

Matthew joined Annabel. 'Couldn't you wait?' he teased softly, one arm going round her waist.

'I don't know what you mean!' she protested in mock-innocence.

'You broke the rules; you touched when there was no reason.'

'How do you know it was me?' challenged Annabel.

'Let's just say that I sensed it. After all, how did you know it was me?'

'Intuition,' she admitted.

'It seems we're well in tune with each other,' he murmured. 'How much longer is this damned dinner going to go on?' he added irritably.

'I think some of them are leaving,' said Annabel, noting with relief that the women who'd left with Lady Corbett-Wynne had now returned to reclaim their husbands and were putting on evening wraps over their dresses as they prepared to leave.

She'd expected Marina to look annoyed or disapproving, but surprisingly she seemed quite tranquil, even managing a smile for her husband as she stood with her arm through his bidding their guests goodnight. However, as soon as the last guest had gone she removed her arm and the smile faded. 'I take it the games were a success,' she said coolly.

Her husband nodded. 'As usual a great success. It's a pity you haven't more sense of fun, my dear. If you'd only learn to loosen up a little you might be surprised at the result.'

A slight smile played about Marina's mouth. 'I'm sure you're right, James. However, your idea of fun and mine are not the same. Did you invite that girl, what's her name, Sandra? Yes, Sandra, to join you?'

'A groom?' Lord Corbett-Wynne looked suitably affronted. 'Good Lord, no! What would the others have thought?'

'Much the same as they think now, knowing that you spend every possible spare moment with the grooms, I imagine. Why should it be any different at the dinner table? You've never baulked at inviting them into your bedroom, which is after all a more intimate setting.'

Crispian and Tania looked at each other in astonishment as their respective parents argued in front of everyone. 'What's got into your mother?' asked Crispian, turning to Tania in amazement.

She sighed. 'I think it's more a question of who!'

Next to Annabel, Sir Matthew Stevens stiffened slightly as he strained to hear the reply. He hoped that the wretched girl wasn't going to go and name him as her mother's lover just as he was about to start making love to the deliciously exciting and sensual Annabel.

'Well, who then?' hissed Crispian as his father marched out of the room looking thoroughly discomfited while his stepmother also returned to her own part of the Hall, but looking a great deal more cheerful than her husband.

'She's having a fling with her riding instructor,' said Tania.

'Jerry?'

'Yes, he seems to be teaching her more than how to mount a horse! Amazing, isn't it? I find it rather hard to imagine the pair of them together, but obviously opposites do attract.'

Matthew didn't know whether to be annoyed or relieved to hear who'd replaced him in Marina's affections. Aware that for him she'd only ever been a challenge, he decided that he should be relieved. She was clearly the kind of woman who needed a man as part of her life rather than simply as a lover, and he had never intended to become deeply involved. He wondered if Jerry was willing to make such a commitment either, but then put the thought aside. It was nothing to do with him, and right now all he wanted was to join Annabel and the others in Crispian's rooms.

Crispian looked around him. Only Luke, Sheba, Annabel, Matthew and Amanda remained apart from Tania, and that was exactly the way he'd envisaged it, except for the presence of Amanda. However, having seen her win the sheet game earlier he was beginning to think that there must be more to Amanda than met the eye. She might well add a little something to the night's proceedings, even if it was only the shock of someone taking part in group sex for the first time.

'Does anyone else want to leave?' he asked slowly, 'or shall we go upstairs now?'

Matthew's arm tightened round Annabel's waist and she found that she could hardly breathe for nervous excitement. 'Let's go up,' he said, his voice husky.

Tania smiled at him. 'I hope it will prove worth the wait, Matthew.'

'I'm sure it will,' he said lightly. 'At the very least I'll find out if all the tales I've heard about you are true!'

'They're true,' Tania assured him. 'What about you, Amanda? Is this really your scene?'

'I want to stay with Crispian. He chose me, remember?' Amanda said doggedly.

'You won't just be with Crispian,' Tania pointed out. 'Everyone joins in the fun at Crispian's parties.'

Amanda nodded. 'Of course, I mean that's what parties are for, isn't it, to mix?'

'That's right,' said Luke, taking hold of Amanda with one hand and Sheba with the other. 'And there's nothing I like more than a party with the right mix of people. Come on, I'm sure this is going to be a night we'll never forget.'

Matthew gripped Annabel's left hand tightly in his right. 'Is that what you think?' he said quietly.

'It's what I hope,' replied Annabel, and swiftly the party climbed the staircase and made their way along the corridor to Crispian's rooms.

Chapter Eleven

*A*t the door to his room, Crispian paused. 'I think we'll use Annabel's room,' he announced. 'Tania likes the four-poster bed and I like the ceiling!'

'What's special about your ceiling?' asked Matthew, his hand on Annabel's elbow.

'It's got an unusual mural on it,' she replied, remembering the thrusting bare breasts of the women riders in the colourful hunt scene.

'Fascinating,' he murmured.

'I think I left it in a bit of a mess,' she protested as they all started to follow Crispian to her room.

'Don't worry,' he said with a slight smile. 'Luke and I got it ready a few minutes ago.'

'Ready?' asked Annabel.

'Well, you know the kind of things we like to use, Annabel! And don't worry, we've laid in a plentiful supply of little metal rings.' Annabel felt herself going hot and she trembled beneath Matthew's hand.

When they entered the room she saw that Crispian had been telling the truth. All her things had been tidied away and the room looked immaculate. The door into the bathroom was open and the glow from the candles around the basin and mirrored shelf threw shadows on the rich wood panels, adding a gleam to the copper bath.

'What a lovely bathroom!' exclaimed Amanda.

Tania narrowed her eyes. 'I'm glad you like it; we're going in there later on.'

'But . . .'

Behind them, Luke turned the key in the door and at the sound of the click Amanda's eyes widened. 'Did you lock us in?' she asked anxiously.

'Of course not, I was simply locking everyone else out!' drawled Luke. 'Don't worry, you can go any time you like. I've left the key in the lock, see.'

This seemed to calm Amanda a little, but Annabel was surprised to see that the other girl was moving closer to Crispian, apparently for protection. Of all the men in the room, he was the least likely to come to her aid, she thought, and felt a moment's pity for her.

'Right, first of all, you gentlemen have to undress the ladies,' said Tania, standing in the middle of the room. 'Annabel, you can go in the alcove by the window, Amanda can stand by one of the posts at the foot of the bed, and Sheba can be in the doorway through to the bathroom. Now, who wants to undress who? Or whom, as the case may be. I'm never certain which is correct. Do you know, Crispian?'

'No, and I bloody well don't care,' he muttered thickly.

'You do realise we're a man short,' said Sheba.

'Not for long,' Tania replied. 'I've told one of the footmen to come up and join us as soon as he's free. He'll do exactly as he's told because if he doesn't he'll find himself out of a job. He knows me rather too well, if you know what I mean, and my stepfather would never approve. He can mix with the hired help, but he doesn't expect me to and naturally he'd blame the man!'

At that precise moment there was a hesitant tap on the door and when Luke unlocked it a tall young man in his early twenties was standing there, still dressed in the dark trousers and jacket that he'd worn when serving at dinner.

'I was just talking about you, Michael!' laughed Tania. 'Come in quickly, we don't want anyone else seeing us.'

He came in awkwardly; his expression apprehensive. 'Was there something special you wanted?' he asked.

'Actually, yes. I want you to undress Sheba. She's the tall girl standing in the bathroom doorway. You can see her, I take it?'

He nodded, moistening suddenly dry lips with his tongue.

Tania laughed. 'There, and you thought you were going to be in trouble. Don't you think I'm kind to you?'

'Very kind, Miss,' he mumbled.

'There's only one thing you have to remember,' said Crispian, his face cold. 'If one word of what goes on here tonight gets out, you'll never work in Wiltshire again, understand?'

'Don't worry, sir. I wouldn't dream of discussing anything about the family's private affairs,' Michael assured him, already taking his first steps towards the sensuous Sheba.

'Private affairs,' mused Crispian. 'That's really rather a good way of putting it. By the way, Sheba's a film star, or at least she stars in a certain kind of film, so you'll find she's used to quite a high standard of service!'

Sheba smiled at the footman. 'Ignore Crispian,' she said softly. 'I like shy young men.'

'Right,' said Crispian. 'How will the rest of you pair up?

'Matthew can undress you, Tania; I'll do Annabel and Luke can have Amanda. Though once the clothes are off we'll change round, okay?'

Annabel felt a brief moment of disappointment, but she knew that waiting for Matthew would only make the first moment of contact all the sweeter. Anyway Crispian still had the ability to send the blood coursing through her veins.

He stood in front of her and ran his eyes over the silk dress. 'I like this,' he said slowly. 'In fact, I like it a lot, but I prefer you naked.' Annabel stared at him, her eyes unchanging. 'Let me guess what you're wearing underneath it,' he mused, running one finger around the line of her jaw. 'A strapless bra perhaps? A flesh-coloured body? No, I think the strapless bra. Let's see if I'm right.'

Very slowly he peeled the straps of the dress off her shoulders, easing them down her arms until they reached her elbows. She went to draw her arms out but he stopped her. 'No, you mustn't move. That's one of the rules. I see I was wrong,' he added, his eyes now shining. 'You didn't bother with anything beneath it. How daring!'

He licked the middle finger of his right hand and slowly drew a circle around each of her exposed nipples. They sprang to life, the tips pink and hard in the cool air of the bedroom.

'Shall I lick them?' Crispian asked thoughtfully. 'I'd like to, but I'm not sure that's allowed at this stage. Would you like me to lick them, Annabel?'

She wanted to say no, to make it clear to him that she was in total control of her body. But to her surprise she found herself nodding and a tiny pleading sound issued from her mouth. Crispian moved his mouth lower but at the last minute he simply blew gently, causing the peaks to harden even more. 'Better not, I think,' he said reluctantly. 'Plenty of time for that later.'

Annabel stood in the tiny alcove, her breasts jutting out proudly as Crispian dropped to his knees and slid his hands up the sides of her legs. Her arms were still fixed to her sides by the straps of her dress. When she felt his fingers teasing her flesh beneath the edge of her silk panties her whole body felt hot and feverish and there was an ache low in her abdomen.

Very carefully, he caught hold of the lace-edged sides

and eased them down her legs. As he did so, his fingers brushed against the silk of her stockings, pausing halfway down to play lightly with the paper-thin skin at the backs of her knees.

Now she was quivering with arousal and her breasts started to swell, the veins gradually becoming more prominent as blood began to engorge the area. She lifted each leg in turn until the panties were removed.

Next he moved on to the stockings, which were held up by lace-covered elastic tops. He took great delight in rolling each stocking down as slowly as possible, and this time he allowed his fingers to splay across her pubic hair, teasing lightly at the curls but without anywhere near enough pressure to do more than increase her excitement with the intimacy of the caress.

'Only the dress left,' he said after that, straightening up to stare into Annabel's eyes again. They were no longer impassive but bright with need, the pupils dilated. 'You look delicious,' he whispered, lifting each of her arms in turn and releasing them from their captivity. 'What fun we're going to have tonight.'

His words inflamed her as much as his actions. He drew the dress upwards over her head, and finally she was standing naked in front of him, her legs parted and her breasts thrusting forward. 'Annabel's ready!' he called, and at his words the others in the room turned to stare at her as well.

Matthew, who had been busy removing the complex suit and shirt from Tania, looked at Annabel in her resplendent nakedness and felt himself growing hard with desire. He'd already been aroused by the sight of Tania's breasts when they'd finally sprung free from the confines of the underwired bra she'd worn beneath her white shirt, but there was something about Annabel's sensuality that appealed to him more.

Luke, who was still trying to remove Amanda's tights, turned to look at Annabel and uttered an unmistakable sound of pleasure, while Amanda remained silent. Her rather heavy breasts were exposed now and the red marks of her bra still remained beneath them. Her dress lay in a heap around her feet and a strange, sick excitement was creeping over her as the tights were drawn down. Now, looking at Annabel standing so confidently, her almost perfect figure accentuated by the pose, Amanda felt uncomfortably aware of her own physical shortcomings.

Crispian, though, seemed pleased by what he saw.

'Good tits, Amanda!' he said enthusiastically. 'Can't wait to get round to those. What do you think, Matthew?'

Matthew glanced at the red-faced Amanda, and he smiled. 'Most inviting,' he agreed.

'Can I touch or is it just the undressing at the moment?' asked Luke.

'No touching yet,' reminded Crispian. 'I've already had to restrain myself, despite Annabel begging me to suck her nipples.'

Sheba, who was as naked as Annabel, sighed. 'Hurry up, all of you. Isn't it about time you got undressed as well?'

'Once you've completed your woman you can take your own clothes off,' said Crispian. In front of Sheba, the young footman Michael began to fumble hastily with his clothes. He could hardly believe his luck and kept expecting to be sent out of the room before the action really began; it was the kind of trick he knew Tania was quite capable of playing on him.

Finally everyone was naked and the women were invited to gather together in the middle of the room. The men were all fully aroused, and Michael seemed to be having trouble controlling himself as drops of clear fluid spilled from the end of his glans.

'Now for the first game,' said Crispian with a half-smile. 'Luke, you have to hold Annabel from behind while Matthew brings her to orgasm, and Michael here will hold Amanda for me while I do the same. We'll tell each other what we're doing as we do it, just to liven things up for those who aren't taking part, and the winner is the last to climax. The loser will be punished, but I haven't quite decided on the punishment yet; it rather depends on who the loser is, of course!'

'How about a drink before we begin?' suggested Tania. 'You did remember to bring some up earlier, didn't you, Crispian?'

'Sure, there's some Bellini in the bathroom. I hope you all like Bellini?' he added as an afterthought.

'What is it?' asked Amanda, her voice tense.

'Half champagne and half peach juice, you'll love it. Actually, as you're in the game I'll give you yours, and perhaps a few nibbles as well!' He laughed to himself. 'Matthew, you can give Annabel hers too, the rest of you had better fill your glasses before the game begins.'

'Why do the women have to be held?' enquired Matthew, taking a sip of his drink while Annabel watched him.

'In case it's all a bit too much for them,' explained Crispian. Annabel heard Tania laugh softly to herself. 'Well, you know how it can be,' he added. 'Sometimes the pleasure's almost too much and we don't want them moving and spoiling it for themselves. Anyway, they might move to stop themselves coming, and that wouldn't be fair. I do like my games to be fair.'

Annabel couldn't imagine how she was going to make herself last any length of time at all. Even before they'd begun her whole body felt tight and swollen and her skin longed for the touch of Matthew's hand.

She knew that Amanda would be far slower to arouse if only because she was totally unused to group sex and from her expression wasn't yet certain that it was an experience that really appealed to her. However skilfully Crispian played her, her inhibitions would certainly delay her orgasm, but Annabel had the feeling that it would be better not to lose. She was acutely aware of the fact that any punishment Crispian devised would be a telling one.

'Time to begin,' announced Crispian, his voice breaking in on her thoughts. Luke caught hold of Annabel's shoulders and then he drew her hands behind her back, holding her wrists together lightly with one hand while his free arm encircled her waist. He stood close to her; if she attempted to step backwards his body would prevent it, and this meant that she was totally exposed to Matthew's undivided attention.

Michael copied Luke and all at once Annabel and Amanda found themselves side by side in the centre of the room. The others sat around on the bed or the floor watching intently as Crispian and Matthew set to work on the naked women waiting in tense anticipation before them.

Tania moved a small table between the two couples, and Annabel saw that there were various gadgets and lubricants arranged there to assist the men. Her breathing quickened as Matthew stood looking into her eyes.

'So you wanted Crispian to lick your nipples,' he said softly, his deep velvet voice seeming to the straining Annabel like a caress in itself. 'Perhaps I'll start by doing that. What do you think?'

She was silent, afraid that if she spoke, if she started to tell him what she wanted, then she'd lose her self-control even quicker. To the side of her she was aware that Crispian was talking to Amanda, but the words were indistinct; all her attention was focused on the man in front of her.

With agonising slowness he reached out and then, at last, his hand was actually touching her, his fingers lifting the undersides of each of her breasts in turn. He pressed them upwards, weighing them on the tips of his fingers before bending his head so that he could bathe the tight nipples with his tongue.

The moment she felt the moist roughness of his tongue's surface moving across the sensitive skin around the nipple, Annabel heard herself give a low moan of pleasure, and then he was sweeping his tongue across the peak itself, going back and forth in leisurely movements that made her try to press forward for greater pressure. It was then that she remembered Luke's presence, because his arm around her waist tightened its hold and she had to remain where she was and allow Matthew to dictate the exact pressure and strength of every movement. Her lack of control over events increased her excitement and between her legs she felt moist and swollen.

'I think I'll use the nipple clippers,' Matthew said quietly, and Tania laughed with pleasure.

'Perhaps I will, too,' responded Crispian, who was fascinated by the heaviness of Amanda's breasts and the length of her now erect nipples. 'I don't suppose Amanda's ever experienced those before, have you, Amanda?'

Annabel wished the two men would stop talking, she just wanted Matthew to get on with what he was doing, but for the others in the room it added to the thrill and Tania's right hand crept between her thighs as she gently massaged her own clitoris.

Matthew picked up two pairs of nipple clippers from the table and pressed the length of them against Annabel's stomach so that she could feel their size. They were as long as normal kitchen scissors but made of plastic and when the handles were pressed together the opposite end opened up with two small insets in which the nipple could be encased.

Annabel felt them against her, and then they were being applied to her breasts and her rigid nipples slid into the openings easily. Matthew then allowed the clippers to close and she felt a tightness around the base of the nipples, a tightness which made them ache in a way that was new and strangely pleasurable.

Once both her nipples were encased Matthew tugged softly on the clippers, extending the nipples as far as they would go, and Annabel gave a muffled gasp of mingled excitement and fear as she felt her breasts being moved by the highly sensitive tips of the nipples.

'Lovely!' exclaimed Matthew, slowly easing the clippers back towards her body. Once they were in their original position he moved the clippers to the sides and again Annabel's breasts moved as the nipples sent flashing sensations of excitement to her brain.

'Do you like it?' whispered Matthew. 'Does it feel good?'

'Yes,' responded Annabel, her hips squirming despite Luke's attempts to keep her still.

He continued to use the clippers, occasionally releasing the nipples for a few seconds to allow her a moment's respite from the intense sensations. Then he would begin again until she heard herself whimpering with increasing need for something different, a more intimate touch than the cool plastic.

As she whimpered she heard Amanda start to protest. Her heavy breasts with the very long nipples were providing entertainment for the onlookers, but her body was fighting against the pleasure that could be gained from the delicious torment. Instead she was trying desperately to forget that the room was full of people and to concentrate on the fact that it was Crispian who was using her and so clearly enjoying her body.

'Enough of that for me, I think,' said Matthew at last, and Annabel's nipples were released. He drew the red, swollen little buds into his mouth and sucked hard on each of them in turn. This time she felt the tight stirrings of desire between her thighs spread upwards towards her breasts and a slight flush began to cover her upper body.

Matthew's strong hands moved to her stomach and he rested one on each side of her waist so that he could knead her abdominal muscles with his thumbs. He pressed hard at first and then very lightly, until it felt as though every muscle in her belly was squirming and wriggling with excitement; her upper thighs trembled violently.

'Where do you want me to touch you now?' he asked.

Annabel didn't answer, she didn't want the others to hear, but instead she moved her hips slightly forward until Luke caught hold of them and forced her to be still.

'On your hips?' queried Matthew, deliberately misunderstanding her, and she could have groaned with disappointment as he picked up a tiny paintbrush. He proceeded to use it to draw tiny circles over the incredibly sensitive skin of her hips until her lower body was jerking and shaking as the spirals of electricity shot through her.

Annabel could feel a climax building deep inside her. The muscles of her belly were twitching and her heart was racing as her excitement increased. Matthew was well aware of her approaching orgasm. Her inner sex-lips were flushed a deep shade of pink, while on her breasts the area around the nipples had darkened and blue veins stood out prominently.

Next to them, Amanda too was becoming aroused. Matthew could hear her quickened breathing, and when he glanced across he saw that, like him, Crispian was using a tiny brush. However, Crispian was using it along the creases of Amanda's thighs and her legs were shaking violently at the delicious sensations he was arousing.

'You mustn't come yet,' Matthew whispered to Annabel. 'You don't want Amanda to be the winner, do you?' Annabel shook her head, but she had no idea how she was going to contain herself if his expert attentions continued for much longer.

'Perhaps the hair dryer,' he said thoughtfully, and as Luke kept Annabel quite still, Matthew picked up a small travelling hair dryer. Once Tania had plugged it in for him he proceeded to play a gentle stream of warm air over Annabel's body.

He started with the breasts, directing it over the whole area before concentrating on the nipples. He then moved it down over her straining stomach until she could feel it against her pubic hair.

The sensation was delicious, a soft warm caress that

both soothed and aroused until the dreaded tingling pulse that preceded her orgasm began to make itself felt behind her clitoris. Now Matthew parted her legs wider and then the warm air was blowing onto the clitoris itself. But before she could fully appreciate the feeling, he'd changed the setting to cold and suddenly the highly sensitive bud was covered by a chill breeze. The abrupt contrast in temperature brought the clitoris erect, and when Matthew inserted a finger into Annabel's sex he could feel her tight moistness close around it. Very gently he moved his finger in and out until she was gasping with pleasure, every muscle rigid with tension and every nerve ending straining for release. Still she struggled to subdue the sensations as next to her Amanda also drew near the point of no return.

For Amanda the whole experience was overwhelming. Not only was Crispian doing the most thrilling things to her body, she was also astonished to find that once she was over the initial shyness her excitement was actually increased by the fact that she was being watched. Every time she gasped or her hips bucked, Tania would utter a tiny sound that added to Amanda's delight, because she knew that it meant Tania was jealous.

By the time Crispian had used the nipple clippers and his tongue and fingers on her, as well as the diabolically clever little brush, she felt as though her body was ready to burst. But like Annabel she didn't want to lose the contest and for the first time in her life she tried to damp down her responses.

Aware of what she was doing, Crispian took a tube of clear lubricant from the table and spread it between her thighs, massaging it into every tiny crevice and working it around the base of her clitoris until the sensitive nub withdrew beneath its protective hood as the intense pleasure grew too great.

With a smile, he placed a hand on the top of her pubic hair and pushed the skin upwards, drawing the hood away until Amanda's clitoris was once more exposed. As

219

soon as it reappeared he deftly slipped one of the clitoral rings that Annabel had found so satisfying over it and then stood up to look into her eyes.

'Do you know what I'm going to do next, Amanda?' he whispered, and she shook her head, her whole body aching with the need for release while her mind fought frantically to oppose her body's needs. 'I'm going to use the brush on your clitoris; use it very softly, brushing round and round over the top until I drive you out of your mind with pleasure.'

Amanda whimpered at his words, longing for the touch of the brush even though she knew it would be fatal because then her orgasm would tear through her and she would be helpless to control it. 'First, though, it's time you had some Bellini,' he said softly, and at a signal from Crispian Michael started to pour some of the ice-cold liquid down over her shoulders. It streamed across her breasts and belly, running in random trickles along her nerve endings so that she found herself wriggling and shuddering and her orgasm grew even closer.

Crispian's questing hand between her thighs found her soaking wet and the clitoris, pushed up by the ring, was very moist with the combination of her own excitement and the lubricant he'd applied. For a few seconds he licked at the champagne drink, trailing his tongue over her rib cage and into her belly button, but then he crouched down and very slowly, just as he'd told her, he began to draw the paintbrush over the tight mass of throbbing tissue.

Annabel, who was now enduring the cool air from the hair dryer on her breasts and across her collarbone, was aware of Amanda's whimpers and then heard her crying, 'Yes! Oh, yes!' Knowing that the other girl was so close to release heightened Annabel's own excitement and she felt her stomach muscles bunching as the insistent drumming increased between her thighs.

Matthew couldn't wait any longer to see her climax. He no longer cared if she won or lost, all he wanted was to see her body quaking and shuddering in the throes of bliss. Abandoning the hair dryer he knelt down on the floor and began to lick around the entrance to her opening, his tongue spreading her milky secretions up towards her clitoris. At the same time he reached behind her and pressed the cheeks of her bottom closely together and slightly forward, tilting her upwards against his tongue and putting delicate pressure on her anus.

Annabel knew that the moment his questing tongue reached her clitoris she would explode and the sexual tension grew so intense that every part of her began to shake in anticipation. Suddenly the others in the room gathered around the two couples, moving in closer to watch the final moments.

'Annabel's going to come first,' said Sheba, watching the way that Annabel's body was trembling. 'You're very near, aren't you, Annabel?'

'So's Amanda,' remarked Tania. 'I'm surprised at you, Amanda. I'd have expected you to have more shame but it seems you're quite an extrovert. Don't you love those clitoral rings, Sheba?' she added, looking at the way Amanda's nub was swollen and trapped as the brush approached it.

Amanda's breathing was fast and audible now, her mouth open and her cheeks flushed while Annabel's eyes were closed and her head thrown back, the tendons of her neck rigid as the final moment of ecstasy approached.

Matthew's hands pressed the cheeks of Annabel's pert little bottom tightly together and his tongue at last circled her clitoris. For a moment it touched it like a feather, but then as the red-hot sensations lanced through her he changed the tempo and began to flick at the tender tip, in a rapid rhythm that ended all hope she'd ever had of controlling her final moment of bliss.

Just as her body responded, just as the straining, despairing tissue finally gave itself over to the shattering moment of climax, Crispian tenderly drew the paintbrush around the stem of Amanda's trapped clitoris, spreading the cool lubricant as it went, and with an ear-splitting scream her body went into a series of violent spasms as her climax tore through her.

Annabel was only seconds behind, but her relief at having won meant that she was able to obtain maximum pleasure from the moment as the heavy pulse seemed to explode deep within her pelvis and a warm rushing sensation of glowing heat suffused every inch of her body. Every muscle went rigid for a few brief seconds before she too was writhing and shuddering in Luke's grip.

Matthew, his penis tight and aching with desire, watched her climax, and when her lips parted in a tiny mewing cry of joy he poured some of the Bellini into her mouth. As it spilled over her chin and down her chest, he pulled her out of Luke's hands and held her close to him so that he could drink it from her even as she orgasmed.

At last both the women were still. The heavy, erotically charged silence in the room was broken, finally, by Luke. 'Which one of them came first?' he asked, his own excitement evident in his husky voice.

'Amanda did,' Tania said with a slow smile.

Amanda opened her eyes and stared at Crispian with an expression that was almost fearful. 'Does that mean I get punished?' she whispered.

'Afraid so. Don't worry, it won't be too awful. You did very well,' he added, pressing his hand upwards between her thighs again and noting the way her body gave a final shudder. 'You'll just be tied up to the bedpost while you watch me with Tania and Luke with Sheba.'

'Why do I have to be tied up?' she asked in bewilderment.

'In case any of the others want to use you while we're busy,' he explained casually. 'They can use you in any way you like. You'll be a sort of sex slave for the next session.'

'I don't want to be a sex slave,' she protested.

'Okay, you can leave then. Hurry up and get dressed. The rest of us are in a hurry.'

Amanda's eyes were huge in her face. 'I don't want to leave either!'

'Well, you have to do one or the other. Which is it to be?'

'I'll be a sex slave,' she said in a low voice.

'That should be interesting,' remarked Matthew as he helped Annabel over to sit on the bed. 'Lucky for you she lost, don't you think?'

All at once everyone in the room became very busy, with the exception of Amanda, who stood passively at the foot of the bed waiting to see what happened. Tania handed a thin muslin nightshirt to Matthew, who pulled Amanda's arms above her head and slipped on the shift. He and Annabel then led their temporary slave into the bathroom where Matthew ordered her into the copper bath. She stood uncertainly in it as he attached a shower head to the taps before indicating to Amanda that she should kneel.

Annabel found the sight of the other girl obeying so meekly highly erotic, and reaching out she pressed on Amanda's shoulders until she was in the right position. Matthew then let cold water from the shower head spray over the short muslin shift and Amanda gasped with shock as icy needles stung her skin. 'Now step out,' he said curtly. 'Annabel, give her a hand, she looks a little wobbly!'

Once Amanda was standing on the crimson rug that covered the floor by the bath Annabel realised that the muslin shift was now totally transparent, and due to the cold water Amanda's full breasts were pushing outwards, the nipples elongated and hard. She tweaked them casually, and heard Amanda's sharp intake of breath.

Matthew laughed. 'Try and restrain yourself, Annabel, there's plenty of time for all that once the others get going.

Bring Amanda back into the bedroom, we'll fasten her to the bedpost.'

Annabel worked swiftly and eagerly. Suddenly she couldn't wait to start arousing the girl herself. She wanted to hear Amanda climax again, climax as she had done earlier when Crispian was working on her.

Once Amanda was securely tethered, Crispian and Tania walked into the centre of the room and stood just in front of her, followed by Luke and Sheba.

Despite her initial fear, Amanda was becoming excited. Her body was starting to warm up again, and the clinging muslin was like a continuous caress against her skin, making her wriggle within her constraints. 'Stand still,' said Matthew sharply, noticing what was happening. 'You're here for our pleasure, not your own.' Amanda immediately stopped moving, and then stared at the two couples in front of her as they began to make love.

Annabel watched closely while Crispian ran his hands all over his stepsister's body, moulding them to her curves and letting his fingers trail delicately into every hollow. Tania closed her eyes and let the feelings wash over her. At the same time Luke was working on Sheba, but in a very different way. He covered her entire body in a jelly-like lubricant which he then proceeded to spread between her thighs, dipping his fingers into her entrance and working it in there with extra care while Sheba squirmed and quivered with rising desire.

Once he was satisfied with what he'd done, Luke produced a pair of soft studded latex balls joined together by a piece of cord, and leading Sheba over to the bed he got her to lie across it width-ways with her legs outspread and feet just touching the floor so that he could insert them into her vagina while Amanda watched.

Sheba gave a soft groan of pleasure as they were inserted and her hips lifted off the bed, twisting slightly to increase the sensations that the studs produced if the pelvis was moved. When they were both inside her, Luke pressed the palm of his hand heavily upwards against Sheba's vulva and this pressure against the encased balls caused a tiny orgasmic ripple to travel through the coffee-skinned girl's long body.

When Sheba stood up she looked directly at Annabel, and Annabel could almost feel the stimulating pressure between her own thighs. She longed for Matthew to do something similar to her, but then remembered that it was Amanda they were to use for their pleasure this time. She glanced at him. 'Do you think Amanda would like that?'

'No, I wouldn't!' protested Amanda, but her voice was uncertain. Her breasts and belly were clearly visible through the clinging muslin and there was no doubting her excitement.

Matthew bent casually down and drew one of her nipples into his mouth through the material. Once it was between his teeth he nipped softly at it until he felt it swell even more and then he expelled his breath so that the nipple and surrounding area were covered in a steady stream of warm air. Amanda moaned and tried to move from side to side so that her aching breasts could receive further stimulation, but she was too tightly bound to move sufficiently and she gave a tiny protest, quickly subdued.

'Yes, I think she'd like it,' Matthew said firmly.

Annabel collected another pair of soft studded balls and then sat down and spread Amanda's legs apart. Very slowly she let her hand creep up the girl's legs until she touched the soft curls of her pubic hair. She was amazed at how heightened her own sexuality had become. If anyone had told her before she came to Leyton Hall that she'd find pleasure in scenes like this she wouldn't have believed them. But now she seemed to have been taken over by a side of her that she'd never known existed and the pressure within her own body grew as Amanda's breath caught in her throat at the touch of the slim, questing fingers.

'Does she need additional lubrication?' asked Matthew.

225

Annabel slid her finger along Amanda's inner channel, feeling the way the tethered girl jerked and almost spasmed at the tender caress. 'A little,' she said with a laugh. 'Although I must say she's doing quite well on her own.'

Now it was Matthew's turn to crouch down in front of their slave, and he smoothed a generous amount of lubricating gel around the entrance to Amanda's sex before pressing the balls inside her with one hand while the other worked with almost cruel lightness around her straining clitoris. For a few brief tantalising seconds Amanda was poised on the edge of an orgasm.

'She nearly came then!' he commented as he inserted the second ball and straightened up. 'Better luck next time, Amanda!'

There were tears of frustration in Amanda's eyes but Annabel and Matthew ignored them. She was theirs to enjoy, and their pleasure was growing with every passing second. Idly Annabel stroked the round breasts, while Matthew ran his hands intermittently over the quivering belly, but at no time did they allow Amanda total satisfaction.

The other two couples were now moving towards each other, both the women breathing swiftly, and there was a sheen of perspiration on Tania's shoulders and breasts. Annabel watched closely as the two women moved slowly and gracefully towards each other, almost as though they were taking part in some kind of erotic dance. When they met they wrapped their arms around each other in an embrace that ended when their entire bodies were touching. Tania then stepped onto a footstool so that she and Sheba were the same height.

The two women rubbed their breasts together sensuously, rotating their upper bodies so that their nipples were directly stimulated. Annabel's own breathing quickened at the sight of the pale cream of Tania's skin against the darker tones of Sheba's, and then she stared as Crispian and Luke went to the table before positioning themselves behind the women. They then proceeded to fondle their buttocks.

'Hurry! Hurry!' Tania urged Crispian, her voice high with excitement, but Crispian took his time. He lifted each of the rounded bottom cheeks in turn and then squeezed them closely together before moving the taut flesh in a circular motion.

At this point Luke and Crispian started to work as one. Clearly each knew exactly what the other was going to do because not a word was spoken and the only sound was the women's rapid breathing, and tiny whimpers from the tethered Amanda, who found herself aroused beyond belief by the scene.

Very gently, almost tenderly, each of the men brushed a finger across the entrance to the women's rear openings, and then Michael handed them large butt plugs, the ends covered in lubricating gel. Tania and Sheba tensed in anticipation, their bodies suddenly still as they waited for the delicious sensations to begin. Moving with incredible slowness the two men eased the wide heads into the sensitive second openings, stretching the flesh so that it would be easier for them to penetrate there themselves later on.

As the plugs were inserted and carefully rotated, Sheba and Tania began to move their breasts more rapidly against each other. Sheba's legs shifted forward so that their hip bones also met and as they writhed their pubic bones touched. Annabel could well imagine the delicious sensations that must be shooting through them.

Matthew's erection was huge. He looked at Amanda, trembling in her captivity. 'I think we should help bring Amanda to a climax now, Annabel,' he said softly.

Annabel really wanted a climax herself. She felt as though she'd burst if her body wasn't given some kind of release from the incredible tension it was experiencing, but this was the game and she knew that she had to play it the way she'd been told.

Reluctantly she nodded and helped Matthew loosen Amanda's bonds. Once she was in position Michael brought a third anal butt plug over to Matthew and for the first time Amanda made a sound of protest.

'Don't be silly,' said Matthew. 'Look how much the other two are enjoying it.'

'But I've never . . .'

'All the more reason to experiment,' said Matthew, and then he was parting the cheeks of her bottom and with a swift turn of the wrist inserted the lubricated end inside her rectum.

Amanda gave an initial gasp at the extraordinary sensation of fullness that it caused, but as he carefully moved it from side to side and the inner walls of her back passage were stimulated she was flooded by intense, piercing darts of pleasure that were totally new to her, and she started to thrust her hips forward just as Tania and Sheba were thrusting.

'Stand in front of her, Annabel,' said Matthew, his voice deep and thick with desire. 'I want you to do the same as the other two, but we'll leave Amanda clothed.'

'No, I want to feel her skin against mine,' protested Amanda.

'And I want Annabel to feel the roughness of the muslin,' said Matthew. 'Remember, this is for our amusement, not yours. You lost the competition earlier, which is why the choice is ours.'

At last Annabel realised that her clamouring flesh was about to receive some kind of direct stimulation and she quickly moved so that her naked breasts were pressed against the muslin that encased Amanda's orbs. The slightly rough feel of the muslin was wonderfully arousing and when Matthew increased the pressure against the anal plug Amanda's pubic bone came into contact with Annabel's. Annabel squirmed and writhed against her, moving herself up and down so that she could feel the glorious indirect stimulation of her throbbing clitoris.

In the middle of the room the other couples were moving on to the final stage of their lovemaking. The anal plugs were carefully withdrawn and then the men drew protective sheaths over their erections before plunging into the now stretched and accommodating tightness of Tania and Sheba's rectums.

Tania gave a scream of excitement, bucking violently as Crispian moved hard and fast against the delicate tissue that was enclosed so snugly about him, but Sheba reacted more slowly and Luke had to work at a different pace until at last she too started to moan with ecstasy as her orgasm approached.

'You mustn't come before they do, Amanda,' Matthew warned her as he removed the anal plug and prepared himself. Amanda bit on her bottom lip, wondering how she could control herself when every inch of her felt so tight and needy.

'Or before me,' added Annabel cruelly, and Matthew smiled, knowing full well that it would be impossible for Amanda, who would be receiving double stimulation, to come after Annabel.

'What if I do?' wailed the hapless girl.

'You'll be punished again,' said Annabel, still rubbing herself against Amanda and feeling the hot, lava-like sensation beginning to spread through her pelvic area.

'Right, Amanda, I'm going to enter you now,' whispered Matthew, and very slowly he inserted the end of his penis inside her secret opening, pausing after a moment to allow her time to get used to the sensation. Amanda lurched forward, certain she couldn't take the thickness of him inside her, but the front of her lower body merely rubbed more fiercely against Annabel.

The sound of Tania's screams of excitement and Sheba's low groans of desire were like an aphrodisiac for Annabel, who twisted and turned this way and that until every inch of her that could be stimulated by Amanda was, and at last the tingling heat started to draw in on itself to a bittersweet centre that she knew would soon explode into a shattering orgasm.

Behind her, Tania was the first to climax and her shouts of excitement made Amanda's body throb while Matthew worked steadily, his hips now thrusting in a harder, faster rhythm as her body grew used to this new intrusion.

'Yes!' shouted Sheba as she climaxed. Suddenly the sensations caused by Annabel's body rushed to join the dark bitter-sweet pleasure that Matthew's movements were producing in her and Amanda felt her entire body grow rigid as her orgasm approached.

'Not yet!' warned Matthew, but he knew that his words would only make it worse for Amanda and smiled to himself as she shook and gasped in her efforts to cling on to the last remnants of control.

Annabel's climax was close now as well, and she arched back from Amanda slightly so that their breasts were no longer touching, but the stimulation of their pubic areas increased, enabling Annabel to trigger the moment of final, blissful release.

Once again, poor Amanda was just ahead of her and with a cry of despair her body was torn by a series of violent spasms that toppled Annabel over the edge so that she too was crying out with delirious excitement as the almost unbearable pressure was finally released in a wrenching explosion of white light.

Matthew withdrew from the shuddering Amanda, rolled a new condom onto his still erect penis and, without a word, picked Annabel up in his arms, threw her on the bed and within seconds was inside her, thrusting fiercely and hungrily so that the dying embers of her first orgasm were rekindled. As the others watched, her hands clutched fiercely at Matthew's shoulders, the nails leaving long scratches against his skin as she once more found herself shuddering with ecstasy as a second powerful orgasm swept over her.

'I said it would be a good party, didn't I!' the watching

Crispian commented with satisfaction, as he tugged on the cord between Amanda's thighs and pulled out the latex balls.

Her moan of ecstatic pleasure told him that even for her it had been a night to remember.

Chapter Twelve

*D*awn was only just breaking as Marina Corbett-Wynne put a few clothes into her leather suitcase and then walked quietly out of Leyton Hall. The events of the dinner party the night before, and the humiliation of making small talk in the music room while her husband and other guests played their lewd games in the dining room, had finally helped her come to a decision.

She was no longer going to subjugate herself to a man who wasn't interested in her needs and desires, but instead spent all his time in pursuit of his own brand of sexual pleasure. For too long now she'd expended her energy on preserving the facade that Leyton Hall had demanded of the family. She'd played the loyal wife and the perfect hostess and she'd channelled her own unused sexual energy into attempting to improve the stately home. But first Matthew and then, more importantly, Jerry had shown her exactly how hollow a life this was.

She no longer cared about appearances. As far as she was concerned, James, Crispian and Tania could do exactly as they wished. If the Hall went to rack and ruin due to neglect it wouldn't worry her because she too was going to be selfish. In Jerry she knew that she'd found a man who understood her, who would not only bring her alive sexually but would also value her as a woman. He wouldn't mock her or make fun of her. He appreciated her, and if possible she intended to spend the rest of her life with him.

He was waiting for her in the stable yard, his dark hair falling untidily over his forehead. When she appeared he hesitated for a moment and then walked quickly towards her. 'I didn't think you'd really come,' he said in a low voice.

'Why not?' asked Marina in surprise.

He shrugged. 'I thought that once you'd had your grand dinner party, spent more time with your friends, you'd realise that I'd simply been a small adventure.'

She shook her head. 'If you'd been at the dinner you'd know why I'm here. Can we go to your cottage now?'

Jerry stared hard at her. 'Are you sure? I'm not in this for fun, you know. You mean something to me.'

At last, Marina gave one of her rare smiles. 'I hoped you'd say that,' she said. Her voice was soft. 'Please, don't make me beg. Let's go to your cottage, and I don't ever intend to come back here. That's why I brought my case.'

Jerry's eyes widened but he didn't say anything. He didn't voice his doubts about her ability to live in the only home he could offer her, or cope with the way she'd be ostracised by all her friends and acquaintances once the affair became known. And the reason for his silence was because he was totally consumed with desire for her. 'Let's go then,' he said quickly. 'I brought my car over. I'll put the case in the boot and we'll drive. That way I don't even have to bring the horses back.'

They were silent on the drive, both lost in a world of erotic fantasies. As soon as they arrived at the cottage, Jerry led Marina up the stairs to the bedroom, which he'd tidied in advance, and there he carefully removed her clothes and laid her face down on the bed.

Once he too was naked he straddled the calves of her

legs, poured some massage oil into the palms of his hands and very lightly ran them across her buttocks. Marina gave a sigh of contentment as she settled into the soft comfort of the bed. Gradually the pressure on her buttocks increased and she gave a quiet moan at the pleasure caused by the way her pubic area was pressed against the mattress.

Now Jerry lightened the pressure again until finally only his fingertips were gliding against the lubricated skin of her softly rounded bottom. Watching the way her hips were moving he knew that her excitement was mounting. Using well-oiled fingers, he stroked up along the inside of each of her thighs in turn, starting at the knee and trailing up to the little dip at the base of her spine. On the downward stroke the pressure was so light she could scarcely feel it and every nerve ending in her body yearned for a heavier touch, but it was the contrast between the upward and downward movement that caused her sexual arousal to increase.

'Turn over,' he whispered as her cries increased in urgency. Half dazed by the glorious sensations she obeyed, and found him looking down at her with an expression of such tenderness that any remaining doubts that might have lingered in her mind were instantly banished.

To her surprise he lifted her right foot in his hands, cradling it behind the ankle and very slowly rotating it. At first it simply felt pleasant and relaxing, but as he persisted she started to feel a stirring in her pelvis and groin, a stirring that increased until the whole area became heavy and engorged with longing. She could hardly bear it when he released the foot only to lift the other and start the whole process again. Now the heaviness overflowed into her vulva and she could feel her outer sex-lips parting as she grew moist and receptive between her thighs.

Jerry could tell how aroused she was by her swollen breasts, her erect nipples and the continual, tiny jerking movements of her hips, but still he prolonged the exquisite torture. Moving his body so that he was sitting beside her on the bed he let his fingers trail over her belly in a sideways movement and then did the same between her hips and across her ribs. There was a throbbing between Marina's thighs that screamed for attention and the more he touched her, the heavier the insistent pulse grew, until without realising what she was doing Marina moved her own hand between her thighs and tentatively touched the spot that was almost driving her mad with desire.

Very gently Jerry removed her hand, ignoring her groan of protest. 'In a moment,' he promised her, as his roaming fingers strayed over her breasts, moving in circles around her hard little nipples.

Marina closed her eyes and savoured every moment of the seduction. Her body was swollen and tight, the pressure steadily mounting towards the moment of release, and she seemed to be drifting on a cloud of blissful eroticism. 'How shall I take you?' he asked against her ear. 'Tell me what you like best.'

Marina had no idea; she simply wanted him to continue pleasuring her as he was now, to keep the tension the same until the actual moment of explosive release. 'You choose,' she said softly.

Jerry was so aroused himself by the way Marina had responded to every touch that he knew he'd come very quickly, and had to choose a position that would trigger her climax swiftly as well.

'Once I'm inside you I want you to tense your buttocks,' he said quietly, continuing to massage her breasts. 'Then thrust upwards as you swivel your hips. When you move your hips downwards, tighten your internal muscles, as though you're trying to milk me.'

His words made her shiver with anticipation, and as he eased himself into her, his erection rock hard, she obediently tensed the cheeks of her bottom and immediately felt the walls of her vagina tightening about the thickness of his shaft. Strange coiling sensations ran up through her lower abdomen from behind her pubic bone.

'Lift now,' he reminded her and she did, swivelling her hips at the same time so that the swirling quivers of pleasure intensified into a stronger sensation that seemed to take over. On the downward movement she tightened her internal muscles automatically in order to add to her own pleasure.

Suddenly all the pressure seemed to draw in on her, until it was centred right behind her clitoris and there it merged into a heavy throb that was driving her out of her mind as it beat out its message of urgent need.

'Again,' said Jerry, his voice tight with his own efforts at self control. 'Do it all again, and move more quickly this time.'

Marina was past caring about anything but her own needs. She heard his words and obeyed them, but only because she sensed that this way lay her one chance of release. Even on the second movement the elusive climax refused to come and she was left teetering on the edge of the final shattering explosion that she so desperately needed. Frantically now she thrust up and down. At last the pulse quickened, every muscle in her body grew hard and tight and then, on her fourth downward pull, her entire body was pierced with unbearably intense shards of pleasure that caused her to buck mindlessly on the bed, and she flung her arms out to the sides as even her hands tingled with the force of her orgasm.

As she climaxed, her muscles gripped Jerry with an almost cruel force and he felt his semen rushing upwards through his penis and the muscles around his rectum tightening just before the moment of release. He heard himself groaning as his orgasm went on and on. The final wrenching moments were nearly painful for him, but at last they were both finished and he sank down beside her, pulling her sweat-covered body against his.

'I've never been so happy,' said Marina, pressing herself against him in order to feel every inch of his wonderfully masculine body and savour the hardness of his young muscles.

'Nor have I,' admitted Jerry. 'The only thing that worries me is whether I'll always be able to make you happy. You'll soon tire of living in a tiny cottage, no matter how good the sex is.'

Marina laughed. 'We don't have to live here for ever. I have a lot of money of my own. In the past I've spent it on Leyton Hall, but from now on I shall use it for us. We'll set up a stud farm somewhere. You'd like that, wouldn't you?'

There was nothing Jerry would have liked better but he hesitated. 'I don't want to be a kept man,' he said firmly.

'You won't be,' Marina assured him. 'It will be in both our names, and since I know nothing about horses its success or failure will depend on you.'

'But what will you do? Stud farms need a lot of hard work.'

'We'll be able to afford some help! I'll be happy looking after the house and knowing that we'll be together every night.'

'What about Lord Corbett-Wynne?'

'I intend to divorce him,' Marina said firmly. 'He won't cause any trouble: he'll be too frightened I'll talk about his penchant for the girl grooms.'

'You've got it all planned, haven't you?' Jerry exclaimed. He was surprised.

Marina let her hands stray down his body until she touched his penis, now shrunken and still between his legs. 'Yes,' she said with a throaty laugh. 'I've decided that I've earned some happiness at last.'

To his astonishment Jerry felt himself begin to stir as her fingers softly played over the thin area of skin behind his penis. 'I just hope you leave me with enough strength to run the stud farm,' he said with a muffled laugh, and then he was moving her up and down against him, restimulating her whole body until she felt the stirrings of desire begin again. At that moment she knew for certain that she would never miss Leyton Hall.

In Crispian's bedroom the activity had restarted as well. Tania had gone into the bathroom to change and re-emerged wearing a black leather strapsuit. The straps circled her breasts, plunged in a V-shape to her thighs and then split so that the tops of her legs were also circled, while her inner sex-lips were revealed by the tightness of the two straps that pulled on each side of her vagina.

Walking across the room she handed Matthew a leather cat-o'-nine-tails. 'Use it on me,' she said imperiously. 'I want you to cover my breasts with it. Don't worry, I enjoy the pain.'

Matthew shook his head. 'Sorry, Tania, that's not my scene.'

For the first time since she arrived at the Hall, Annabel saw Tania look taken aback. 'What do you mean?' she asked after a moment.

He smiled. 'I mean, I'm not into whipping women.'

'But it's what I want!' she said angrily. 'It turns me on.'

'I'm sure one of the others will be pleased to oblige. I really think it's time that Annabel and I left now.'

'Steady on,' said Crispian, who'd been watching the interchange with interest. 'You can't take Annabel away. She works here.'

Matthew turned to Annabel. 'What do you think, Annabel?'

Annabel picked up her evening dress and began to put it on. 'I think it's time I handed in my notice,' she said with a smile.

Matthew helped her pull her dress over her head, his hands caressing every available inch of her skin as he did so. 'I want to make love to you again,' he said thickly. 'I want to make you come and come until you're begging for mercy. I want to take you in every position and every way possible. I'm going to –'

'What about my mother?' Tania asked icily. 'Do you imagine she'll forgive you? And then there's David Crosbie. He'll be the laughing-stock of London once people learn that his personally recommended assistant was not only hopelessly inadequate but also thoroughly unprofessional.'

'What does it matter to you what your mother thinks?' Matthew demanded angrily.

Tania smiled. It was a very thin smile. 'It doesn't really, but I can always pretend. I tell you what, if you're so anxious to protect Annabel's good name, use the whip on me and then I'll keep quiet.'

Crispian watched as Matthew struggled to keep his temper in check. It was obvious the man had no desire to indulge Tania, but neither did he want David's career to suffer as a result of their involvement. He hesitated, his hand slowly moving towards the outstretched whip, and at that moment Amanda spoke.

'I saw your mother leaving the Hall with a suitcase a short time ago, Tania,' she said innocently. 'Perhaps she's going to be away for a while, so it won't matter what Annabel does, will it?'

Tania shot her a look of fury. 'My mother doesn't even get out of bed before ten in the morning,' she said.

'She did this morning,' insisted Amanda.

'Amanda's right,' confirmed Sheba. 'I saw her too, out of the alcove window there. She looked like a woman on her way to an assignation!'

Crispian laughed. 'Perhaps she's finally decided to leave Papa. How amusing; he'll be dumbstruck. Is it the stable manager, do you think? Surely not! Marina's far too well-bred for a rough-and-tumble in the hay, wouldn't you say, Tania? Unlike Annabel here, who thoroughly enjoyed it. Remember, Annie?'

Annabel did remember, remembered only too well, but it was the last thing she wanted to think about at this moment when Matthew was promising her so many sensual delights and her whole body was hot with desire for him.

'I didn't imagine you'd lived the life of a nun,' Matthew assured her, smiling at her anxious expression.

Losing patience with Matthew, Tania went over to Luke and handed him the whip. 'You use it,' she cajoled, thrusting her tightly encircled breasts forward.

Luke shook his head. 'Sheba and I are leaving now. Would you like to come with us, Amanda? I think we three might have some fun, and Sheba always prefers to have a second woman joining in, don't you, Sheba?'

The tall girl nodded, squeezing one of Amanda's breasts lightly between her unusually long fingers. 'I do,' she confirmed, 'and I adore your body, Amanda. It's so voluptuous. Why don't you come and stay with us in London for a few days. We'll go shopping as well, buy you some interesting underwear and some rather more flattering outfits.'

Amanda glanced at Crispian, but he was watching his stepsister, and while Amanda stared at him Tania walked slowly towards him, the whip held in her outstretched hand. She then let the ends rest against his taut stomach muscles for a moment before turning her hand so that he could take hold of the handle.

'You know what I want,' she said in a low voice. 'Only you can ever satisfy me. Do it now, Crispian, before they all go. I want them to watch.'

Matthew's grip on Annabel's hand increased in pressure, but he didn't move towards the door, and neither did any of the others. They all stood in silence as the fair-haired heir of Leyton Hall and his auburn-haired stepsister stood only a few inches apart, their eyes locked together, the physical desire between them crackling in the air like electricity.

At last Crispian grasped the whip and as he grasped it his face changed. The blue eyes turned cold and his mouth narrowed as he reached out with his free hand and tweaked one of Tania's nipples between his fingers. 'I want a better target,' he said, his voice almost contemptuous. 'Someone will have to prepare you for me.'

Tania was taking quick shallow breaths now and she looked appealingly at the others. 'Will one of you do as he asks?' she pleaded, desire making her desperate.

Luke nodded, and moving away from Sheba he took Tania by the hand then led her to the bathroom. Almost against their will the others followed, with the exception of Crispian, who remained in the bedroom, tapping the whip against the side of his leg.

Annabel watched Luke fill the basin with cold water from the tap and then he pushed against Tania's shoulders until her breasts were dangling just above the surface of the liquid. Tania hesitated, unable to make herself plunge them into the cold water, and so Luke did it for her, pushing once more until the leather-rimmed globes disappeared beneath the surface and everyone heard Tania gasp at the shock of the sudden coldness.

Once Tania's breasts had been fully immersed for nearly half a minute, Luke pulled her upright again, and now they could all see that her nipples were standing out proudly, tight and rigid from the cold.

'Put some water over her belly and back as well,' called Crispian. 'I like the sound of leather against damp skin.'

Tania tried to run back into the bedroom, but Annabel grabbed hold of her and kept her imprisoned until Luke could manhandle her back to the basin. He then held her still while Annabel plunged a sponge into the water and, holding it against Tania's ribs, she squeezed until tiny droplets of cold water ran down Tania's stomach and into the creases at the tops of her thighs.

As Tania shivered Luke turned her around and now the auburn-haired girl positively cringed as once more the cold sponge was held against her hot skin, and then squeezed until all the water had flowed down her spine.

Despite her protests, it was clear from Tania's shining

241

eyes and swollen body that this was what she wanted, what she craved more than anything, and when she was led back to stand in front of her stepbrother they stared at each other in a frenzy of mutual desire.

Crispian's tongue darted out and moistened his lips while Tania stood in front of him, her pale creamy skin covered in a sheen of water. Almost languidly Crispian raised his hand and then with a quick flick of his wrist the whip cracked in the air before falling across Tania's right breast, leaving it covered in tiny red lines.

Her body trembled so much at the moment of impact that Annabel thought the other girl was going to have an orgasm there and then, but she didn't, merely trembling on the brink as her stepbrother eyed her with satisfaction.

'Ask me to do the same for the other breast,' he commanded her.

Tania shook her head. 'You know you want to do it as much as I want it done, just get on with it,' she retorted, but Crispian refused. He continued to stand in front of her, the instrument of pleasure in his hand, and waited for her to speak.

Tania waited too, determined not to be the one to break, but in the end her body's urgent clamouring for this dark, bitter pleasure that meant so much to her proved too insistent to resist. 'Please, do the same again,' she begged Crispian.

'How hard shall I hit you?' he asked, prolonging her agonising wait.

'Harder than last time,' she implored him. 'I want to really feel it when the whip lands.'

'Like this?' he queried, and with a snapping sound the leather rose and fell in the air, landing right across the second nipple and causing Tania to scream with ecstasy.

'Yes! Like that, like that!' she moaned, and then she lay down on the floor, her legs spread wide. 'On my stomach,' she begged. 'Hit me there, and then take me, Crispian. Do it the way we like best. I need to feel the whip everywhere.

242

Nothing else can satisfy me, you know that. It's what we both live for.'

Matthew tugged at Annabel's hand. 'Come on, let's leave them to it. They don't need us any more.'

Annabel knew that he was right, but there was a terrible fascination about the scene unfolding in front of them, and she stayed where she was for a moment as Crispian moved to stand over his stepsister's body, his penis jutting out with an angry purple tip as he drew the leather thongs of the whip gently around each of Tania's breasts and then down the middle of her lower body, while she squirmed and cried out for him to let her feel the sting of it striking her.

A tiny drop of clear moisture fell from Crispian's penis and Tania jumped as it landed on her skin. But realising what it was, she laughed triumphantly and at the sound of her laughter Crispian raised his arm and let the whip fall across her belly.

It rose and fell several times and Tania's screams gave way to soft whimpering sounds of pleasure that slowly intensified until at last Crispian threw away the whip and hurled himself onto his stepsister's leather-ringed body.

He moved violently, angrily, but with skill and precision so that within seconds the pair of them were well on the way to a frenzied simultaneous climax, a climax that suddenly Annabel didn't want to see. Their desperation was frightening; it was as though they were capable of being consumed by this terrible need for each other, a perverted, dark obsession that, for the most part, they kept concealed from the outside world.

'I didn't realise it was quite like this,' she whispered as she and Matthew left the room, closely followed by Sheba, Amanda and Luke. The door was closed behind them by the footman, Michael. Forgotten by everyone once he was no longer needed, Michael was determined to stay until the very end, reasoning that the two young people on the floor would need someone they could trust in the house-

243

hold and certain that, after all he'd witnessed, he would be their automatic choice.

'I'd heard rumours to that effect,' admitted Matthew. 'All the same, it's different when you actually see it. Somehow I don't think Crispian will ever marry anyone else, do you?'

Annabel shook her head. 'How could he? They'll never be free of each other, and they'd never be able to keep apart even if he did marry, so what's the point? Besides, it isn't as though they're blood relations. It's only money that really stands in their way.'

'Money that Leyton Hall needs to survive,' Matthew pointed out.

'Crispian and Tania will probably spend their lives here in a blaze of sexual passion that only ends when the roof falls in on them!' laughed Luke.

'What's that noise?' asked Sheba as they walked along the landing.

Annabel listened for a moment. 'It's coming from Lord Corbett-Wynne's room,' she said. 'I can imagine what's going on in there, too!'

'What?' asked Amanda.

'I'll show you,' said Annabel with a smile. She turned the doorknob very carefully, and then pushed gently so that the door swung partly open.

In the middle of the room, naked except for a black blindfold and with his hands bound behind his back with a strip of black leather, Lord Corbett-Wynne was kneeling upright in front of Sandra, whose hands were pressing lightly on each side of his head, which was tilted slightly backwards. Between his thighs another girl, similar in appearance to Sandra but with dark instead of fair hair, was drawing his massive penis into her mouth and sucking on it. Every time he started to quiver and his testicles tightened, she would draw her mouth away, letting her teeth graze the sides of his erection as she did so.

From the landing the group watched in fascination as

this process was repeated four times until Lord Corbett-Wynne began making frantic gurgling sounds as he struggled to control himself. When the noises became too loud Sandra abruptly pushed him forward until his forehead was touching the ground and his naked buttocks were fully exposed to the secret spectators.

'Now for your treat,' said Sandra, and her sister Melanie giggled as she watched Sandra greasing the end of a riding crop. 'I'm going to do what you like best,' Sandra promised the bound and submissive man, 'but you mustn't come because you're going to make love to both of us afterwards, aren't you?'

Lord Corbett-Wynne groaned again, apparently unable to form any proper words. 'I'll take that as a yes,' continued Sandra, and then, as Annabel and the rest of them continued to watch with a mixture of astonishment and arousal, she eased the well-lubricated end of the crop into the opening between his buttocks, rotating it as she pressed upwards.

'Aagh!' gasped Lord Corbett-Wynne, feeling his climax rushing towards a conclusion.

Sandra's hand was still and she let go of the crop, leaving it sticking out from between his buttocks. 'Careful,' she cautioned him. 'Save something for us, or we'll be very angry with you.'

He mumbled something unintelligible and Sandra raised her right foot, clad in a high-heeled shoe, and placing it on his spine she allowed some of her weight to press against him. Lord Corbett-Wynne's excitement increased and when Melanie started to gently move the crop handle he made a sound of protest, knowing that he couldn't control himself for much longer.

'Take it out,' ordered Sandra, and with one deft hand movement Melanie obeyed, leaving him gasping as he breathed heavily through his open mouth in an attempt to quell his impending climax.

Amanda had never seen anything like it in her life. She

was totally fascinated. Luke's hands began to creep round her from behind. He pressed against her hips and lower stomach, his fingertips digging against the flesh above her pubic bone, and she found that she too was on the brink of an orgasm, an orgasm that she was helpless to control.

Lord Corbett-Wynne was in the same position. Pulled back into an upright kneeling position by the increasingly dominant Sandra, he felt the touch of the leather strap around his erection, and despite his overwhelming desire to make love to the two girls, that touch was fatal. As the strap tugged at the root of his penis he felt his glans tingling and then his sperm was gushing out of him and falling on to the carpet.

'What a shame!' laughed Sandra. 'Now Melanie and I will have to make love to each other while you just lie there quietly and listen.'

'No!' gasped her employer. 'That's it for today. It's time to release me. I'll see to you both another day.'

'Sorry,' said Sandra, who didn't sound sorry at all. 'Unless you can unfasten your own hands and get your blindfold off, you haven't any choice.' Leaving the helpless lord on his bedroom floor, she and her sister began to fondle each other, uttering tiny squeals of pleasure as they began their explorations.

'Don't worry,' Sandra called to the prostrate man as he remained helpless on the carpet. 'I'll tell you exactly what we're doing.'

As she began her vivid description Matthew reached across Annabel and pulled the door quietly closed. 'I think we'll leave this family to their own devices,' he commented. 'Personally I'd rather be taking part in some action myself than watching the occupants of Leyton Hall. Perhaps if they need money they should invite interested members of the public to watch them at play!'

Outside the front door Annabel and Matthew walked towards his car while the other three went off to Luke's. 'You're sure you'll be all right, Amanda?' called Annabel.

Amanda smiled. 'I've never had so much fun,' she called back. 'It beats breeding pigs any day.'

'I rather imagine it does,' murmured Matthew as he started the car. 'Now, let's get back to the Old Mill. It's time we were alone together.'

Annabel sighed with pleasure and settled back in her seat. This was what she'd wanted from the moment she first set eyes on Sir Matthew Stevens.

Chapter Thirteen

*A*nnabel sat up in the huge bed and moved several of the cream-coloured pillows behind her until she was more comfortable. She looked around the vast room, her designer's eye approving of the cream and beige colour scheme. Above the head of the bed, suspended from the high ceiling, ruched cream curtains were tied back to drape gently around the sides of the pillows and the matching curtains at the windows were partly opened to allow in some of the morning light.

Checking her bedside clock she saw that it was already ten-thirty. Since moving to the London apartment for the weekdays she and Matthew had been caught up in the London social whirl, and her intention of returning to work had begun to fade into the background, despite David's entreaties.

She liked the apartment. All the rooms were spacious and she'd been able to choose every item of furniture herself. Matthew liked nice things but style and colour schemes were of no interest to him. 'As long as you're here, I'm happy,' he'd remarked when she'd started consulting him, and that had been that.

Despite the six months that they'd been together his

sexual inventiveness could still astonish her. Every morning she would awake sated and aching from the excitement of the previous night, and often he'd take her in the day as well. Only the previous afternoon he'd made passionate love to her in the kitchen while one of his London friends had waited, blissfully unaware, in the library. He'd brought her to such a pitch of ecstasy that he'd had to muffle her final cries with his hand, leaving her exhausted while he'd gone off to his club with his friend.

It was all perfect, she thought, and yet somehow it wasn't. There was something missing, something that she couldn't explain, and couldn't even begin to identify. But it was there and sometimes it left her feeling hollow and frustrated.

She'd caught Matthew looking askance at her once or twice and knew that he sensed her vague dissatisfaction. But he didn't ask her any questions, for which she was immensely grateful – because she didn't have any answers.

She was still passionately in love with him, still felt a tug of physical desire every time she saw him. She couldn't understand why it was that she felt restless, when she should have been deliriously happy.

Today was her birthday. She had quite expected Matthew to wake her early, make love to her, and then give her his present, but there was no sign of him and the house seemed silent. Perhaps he too was wondering if their arrangement was really perfect, she thought, and felt a moment's panic. She didn't want to lose him; she loved their weekends at the Old Mill and their weeks in London. If only there hadn't been this sense of incompleteness that seemed to increase rather than diminish the longer they were together.

Getting up, she took a long lazy bath, after which she pulled on a turquoise silk kimono and wandered through to the library. The room was dominated by a scarlet brocade sofa with matching chairs, while scarlet and white rugs were strewn over the shiny wooden floor. The room usually soothed her. Entering slowly, she was surprised to find that there were people there already.

Matthew, who was standing by the sofa, turned and smiled at her. 'Good morning, darling. You were sleeping so heavily earlier I didn't like to wake you. Now that you're up I'd like you to meet Neil and Leah.'

Annabel pulled her kimono more tightly around her, suddenly very aware of the fact that she was naked beneath it, and smiled at the people standing at the far end of the room. The young man, in his mid-twenties, she thought, was tall and had long light-brown hair while his companion, Leah, was tiny with waist-length blonde hair and a fragile look.

'Hi!' Annabel said brightly. 'Sorry I'm not dressed, but Matthew didn't mention visitors.'

Neil's eyes fastened onto the deep-plunging neckline of the kimono, and as Annabel moved forward and the gown parted to reveal her thighs she heard his quick intake of breath.

'Neil's considering setting up his own interior design company and I thought you might like to help him,' said Matthew.

'Well, I could certainly give you some advice but I have to say that I've never run my own business,' said Annabel, aware that her nipples were suddenly hard beneath the silk fabric.

'As for Leah,' continued Matthew, crossing the room to stand behind the girl. 'As well as being Neil's girlfriend, she's also interested in breeding Dalmatians. I thought they might like to join us on our next trip to Wiltshire.'

As he spoke, Matthew let his right hand softly caress Leah's long, silky hair and desire shot through Annabel like a flame. Suddenly she understood exactly what she'd been missing, and why it was that she didn't feel contented. She needed the excitement and the stimulation that her stay at Leyton Hall had provided. Much as she loved

Matthew, he alone wasn't enough for her. But along with Neil and Leah it would be perfect.

'What a wonderful idea,' she said softly, and this time she deliberately let her kimono open a little more until the tops of her breasts were revealed. 'Do you live near here?' she added, moving closer to Neil.

'We're looking for a place at the moment,' he muttered, swallowing hard.

'Well, then you must use our spare room. This apartment's far too large for the pair of us, isn't it, Matthew?'

'It certainly is,' he agreed, his hands now resting on Leah's shoulders as his fingers massaged the flesh beneath her thin blouse.

Leah stood passively beneath his attentions, her large eyes expressionless, but when she looked at Matthew her adoration was obvious.

'What fun we'll all have!' enthused Annabel, brushing against Neil as she walked towards Matthew. 'I'm sure we'll all be great friends.'

'Yes,' said Neil, his mouth curving upwards in a knowing smile. 'I'm sure we will too.'

'Oh, yes,' agreed Leah, anxious as always to please him.

'I'll make us some coffee and then show you the bedroom,' said Annabel. 'If you like it then you can move in as soon as you like.'

She went into the kitchen and Matthew followed her. Sliding his hands inside the kimono, he cupped her firm breasts, teasing the rigid nipples with his fingers before lowering his head and tonguing them until she was frantic for him to possess her. 'Like them?' he asked softly.

'Very much!' laughed Annabel, her hands gripping him round the waist as she tried to pull his body against hers.

'They're your birthday present. I didn't want you getting bored with my company, and they're a very interesting couple. They come highly recommended.'

'I'm sure they do,' murmured Annabel, and as Neil and Leah waited in the library Matthew slid the kimono off

251

her, eased his straining erection inside her moist, welcoming warmth and brought her carefully to a blissful orgasm.

Annabel sighed, relaxed against him and knew that from now on everything would be wonderful because Matthew understood her needs and was more than happy to indulge them.

For a brief moment her thoughts returned to Leyton Hall and its occupants. She knew now that everyone had to find their own way to sexual fulfilment. But for her visit there, she would never have discovered her true self, nor met Matthew and started out on this exciting new life with him.

Slowly she pulled her robe back on, made the coffee, placed the cups on a tray and took them through to the waiting couple. 'So,' she said, her eyes bright and cheeks glowing, 'tell me all about yourselves!'

LOOK OUT FOR THE ALL-NEW BLACK LACE BOOKS – AVAILABLE NOW!

All books priced £7.99 in the UK. Please note publication dates apply to the UK only. For other territories, please contact your retailer.

To be published in June 2009

KISS IT BETTER
Portia Da Costa
ISBN 978 0 352 34521 9

Sandy Jackson knows a certain magic is missing from her life. And her dreams are filled with heated images of a Prince Charming she once encountered, a man who thrilled her with a breathtaking kiss touch. Jay Bentley is also haunted by erotic visions starring a woman from his youth. But as the past is so often an illusion, and the present fraught with obstacles, can two lovers reconcile their differences and slake the burning hunger for each other in a wild and daring liaison?

DOCTOR'S ORDERS
Deanna Ashford
ISBN 978 0 352 33453 4

Helen Dawson is a dedicated doctor who has taken a short-term assignment at an exclusive private hospital that caters for every need of its rich and famous clients. The matron, Sandra Pope, ensures this includes their most curious sexual fantasies. When Helen forms a risky affair with a famous actor, she is drawn deeper into the hedonistic lifestyle of the clinic. But will she risk her own privileges when she uncovers the dubious activities of Sandra and her team?

To be published in July 2009

SARAH'S EDUCATION
Madeline Moore
ISBN 978 0 352 34539 4

Nineteen year old Sarah is an ordinary but beautiful girl engaged to a wealthy
fiancé, and soon to be the recipient of all the privileges and opportunities marriage
into the upper class can bring. She is also a virgin but, at an exclusive party at
a hotel, loses her virginity to a man who is not her fiancé. In the morning she
wakes to find an envelope containing $2,500 on the bedside table; Sarah has been
mistaken for a high class call-girl. Soon, she is leading a secret life in top hotels
with strange and exciting men, until one of her clients turns out to be her professor
from university and a man she has long had a crush on. Their nights of passion and
journeys into erotic role-playing become an expensive obsession for each of them.
The biggest decision of all for their future has to be made when they are both
threatened with exposure. What will Sarah sacrifice for the passion of a lifetime?

GOING TOO FAR
Laura Hamilton
ISBN 978 0 352 33657 6

Spirited adventurer Bliss Van Bon sets off on a three-month tour of South America.
Along the way there's no shortage of company. From flirting on the plane to being
tied up in Peru; from sex on snowy mountain peaks to finding herself out of her
depth with local crooks, Bliss hardly has time to draw breath. And when brawny
Australians Red and Robbie are happy to share their tent and their gorgeous bodies
with her, she's spoilt for choice. But Bliss soon finds herself caught between her
lovers' agendas. Will she help Red and Robbie save the planet, or will she stick with
Carlos, whose wealthy lifestyle has dubious origins?

THE SEVEN YEAR LIST
Zoe Le Verdien
ISBN 978 0 352 33254 7

Newspaper photographer Julia Sargent should be happy and fulfilled. But flattering minor celebrities is not her idea of a challenge, and she's also having doubts about her impending marriage to heart-throb actor David Tindall. In the midst of her uncertainty comes an invitation to a school reunion. When the group meet up, adolescent passions are rekindled - and so are bitter rivalries - as Julia flirts with old flames Nick and Steve. Julia cannot resist one last fling with Steve, but he will not let her go - not until he has achieved the final goal on his seven year list.

To be published in August 2009

SEXY LITTLE NUMBERS
Various
ISBN 978 0 352 34538 7

Sexy Little Numbers is a choice cut of all new and original erotic stories and the latest addition to Black Lace's immensely popular series of erotica collections. This longer collection will contain even more variety and a greater range of female sexual desire than ever before. It will be the first of an annual collection of the best erotica stories written by women. Fun, irreverent and deliciously decadent, *Sexy Little Numbers* will combine humour and attitude with wildly imaginative writing from all over the world.

To be published in August 2009

UP TO NO GOOD
Karen S Smith
ISBN 978 0 352 34528 8

Emma is resigned to attending her cousin's wedding, expecting the usual
excruciating round of polite conversation and bad dancing. Instead it's the scene of
a horny encounter which encourages her to behave even more scandalously than
usual. When she meets motorbike fanatic Kit, it's lust at first sight, and they waste
no time in getting each other off behind the marquee. They don't get the chance
to say goodbye, however and Emma resigns herself to the fact that she'll never see
her spontaneous lover again. Then fate intervenes as Emma and Kit are reunited at
another wedding – and so begins a year of outrageous sex, wild behaviour, and lots
of getting up to no good.

THE CAPTIVE FLESH
Cleo Cordell
ISBN 978 0 352 34529 5

A tale of decadent orgies amidst the sumptuous splendour of a North African
mansion. 19th-century French convent girls, Marietta and Claudine, learn their
invitation to stay in the exotic palace of their handsome host requires something in
return – the ecstasy of pleasure in pain.

ALSO LOOK OUT FOR

THE BLACK LACE BOOK OF WOMEN'S SEXUAL FANTASIES
Kerri Sharp
ISBN 978 0 352 33793 1

The Black Lace Book of Women's Sexual Fantasies reveals the most private
thoughts of hundreds of women. Here are sexual fantasies which on first sight
appear shocking or bizarre – such as the bank clerk who wants to be a vampire
and the nanny with a passion for Darth Vader. Kerri Sharp investigates the
recurrent themes in female fantasies and the cultural influences that have
determined them: from fairy stories to cult TV; from fetish fashion to historical
novels. Sharp argues that sexual archetypes – such as the 'dark man of the
psyche' – play an important role in arousal, allowing us to find gratification safely
through personal narratives of adventure and sexual abandon.

THE NEW BLACK LACE BOOK OF WOMEN'S SEXUAL FANTASIES
Edited and compiled by Mitzi Szereto
ISBN 978 0 352 34172 3

The second anthology of detailed sexual fantasies contributed by women from
all over the world. The book is a result of a year's research by an expert on erotic
writing and gives a fascinating insight into the rich diversity of the female sexual
imagination.

Black Lace Booklist

Information is correct at time of printing. To avoid disappointment, check availability before ordering. Go to www.blacklacebooks.co.uk.
All books are priced £7.99 unless another price is given.

BLACK LACE BOOKS WITH A CONTEMPORARY SETTING

☐ AMANDA'S YOUNG MEN Madeline Moore	ISBN 978 0 352 34191 4	
☐ THE ANGELS' SHARE Maya Hess	ISBN 978 0 352 34043 6	
☐ THE APPRENTICE Carrie Williams	ISBN 978 0 352 34514 1	
☐ ASKING FOR TROUBLE Kristina Lloyd	ISBN 978 0 352 33362 9	
☐ BLACK ORCHID Roxanne Carr	ISBN 978 0 352 34188 4	
☐ THE BLUE GUIDE Carrie Williams	ISBN 978 0 352 34132 7	
☐ THE BOSS Monica Belle	ISBN 978 0 352 34088 7	
☐ BOUND IN BLUE Monica Belle	ISBN 978 0 352 34012 2	
☐ CASSANDRA'S CHATEAU Fredrica Alleyn	ISBN 978 0 352 34523 3	
☐ CASSANDRA'S CONFLICT Fredrica Alleyn	ISBN 978 0 352 34186 0	
☐ CAT SCRATCH FEVER Sophie Mouette	ISBN 978 0 352 34021 4	
☐ CHILLI HEAT Carrie Williams	ISBN 978 0 352 34178 5	
☐ THE CHOICE Monica Belle	ISBN 978 0 352 34512 7	
☐ CIRCUS EXCITE Nikki Magennis	ISBN 978 0 352 34033 7	
☐ CLUB CRÈME Primula Bond	ISBN 978 0 352 33907 2	£6.99
☐ CONTINUUM Portia Da Costa	ISBN 978 0 352 33120 5	
☐ COOKING UP A STORM Emma Holly	ISBN 978 0 352 34114 3	
☐ DANGEROUS CONSEQUENCES Pamela Rochford	ISBN 978 0 352 33185 4	
☐ DARK DESIGNS Madelynne Ellis	ISBN 978 0 352 34075 7	
☐ THE DEVIL AND THE DEEP BLUE SEA Cheryl Mildenhall	ISBN 978 0 352 34200 3	
☐ THE DEVIL INSIDE Portia Da Costa	ISBN 978 0 352 32993 6	
☐ DOCTORS' ORDERS Deanna Ashford	ISBN 978 0 352 34525 7	
☐ EDEN'S FLESH Robyn Russell	ISBN 978 0 352 32923 3	
☐ EQUAL OPPORTUNITIES Mathilde Madden	ISBN 978 0 352 34070 2	
☐ FIGHTING OVER YOU Laura Hamilton	ISBN 978 0 352 34174 7	
☐ FIRE AND ICE Laura Hamilton	ISBN 978 0 352 33486 2	
☐ FORBIDDEN FRUIT Susie Raymond	ISBN 978 0 352 34189 1	
☐ GEMINI HEAT Portia Da Costa	ISBN 978 0 352 34187 7	
☐ THE GIFT OF SHAME Sarah Hope-Walker	ISBN 978 0 352 34202 7	

- GONE WILD Maria Eppie ISBN 978 0 352 33670 5
- HIGHLAND FLING Jane Justine ISBN 978 0 352 34522 6
- HOTBED Portia Da Costa ISBN 978 0 352 33614 9
- IN PURSUIT OF ANNA Natasha Rostova ISBN 978 0 352 34060 3
- IN THE FLESH Emma Holly ISBN 978 0 352 34117 4
- IN TOO DEEP Portia Da Costa ISBN 978 0 352 34197 6
- JULIET RISING Cleo Cordell ISBN 978 0 352 34192 1
- KISS IT BETTER Portia Da Costa ISBN 978 0 352 34521 9
- LEARNING TO LOVE IT Alison Tyler ISBN 978 0 352 33535 7
- LURED BY LUST Tania Picarda ISBN 978 0 352 34176 1
- MAD ABOUT THE BOY Mathilde Madden ISBN 978 0 352 34001 6
- MAKE YOU A MAN Anna Clare ISBN 978 0 352 34006 1
- MAN HUNT Cathleen Ross ISBN 978 0 352 33583 8
- THE MASTER OF SHILDEN Lucinda Carrington ISBN 978 0 352 33140 3
- MIXED DOUBLES Zoe le Verdier ISBN 978 0 352 33312 4 £6.99
- MENAGE Emma Holly ISBN 978 0 352 34118 1
- MINX Megan Blythe ISBN 978 0 352 33638 2
- MS BEHAVIOUR Mini Lee ISBN 978 0 352 33962 1
- THE NEW RAKES Nikki Magennis ISBN 978 0 352 34503 5
- THE NINETY DAYS OF GENEVIEVE Lucinda Carrington ISBN 978 0 352 34201 0
- ODALISQUE Fleur Reynolds ISBN 978 0 352 34193 8
- ON THE EDGE Laura Hamilton ISBN 978 0 352 34175 4
- ONE BREATH AT A TIME Gwen Masters ISBN 978 0 352 34163 1
- PACKING HEAT Karina Moore ISBN 978 0 352 33356 8 £6.99
- PAGAN HEAT Monica Belle ISBN 978 0 352 33974 4
- PEEP SHOW Mathilde Madden ISBN 978 0 352 33924 9
- THE POWER GAME Carrera Devonshire ISBN 978 0 352 33990 4
- THE PRIVATE UNDOING OF A PUBLIC SERVANT ISBN 978 0 352 34066 5
  Leonie Martel
- RUDE AWAKENING Pamela Kyle ISBN 978 0 352 33036 9
- SAUCE FOR THE GOOSE Mary Rose Maxwell ISBN 978 0 352 34492 3
- SPLIT Kristina Lloyd ISBN 978 0 352 34154 9
- THE STALLION Georgina Brown ISBN 978 0 352 34199 0
- STELLA DOES HOLLYWOOD Stella Black ISBN 978 0 352 33588 3
- THE STRANGER Portia Da Costa ISBN 978 0 352 33211 0
- SUITE SEVENTEEN Portia Da Costa ISBN 978 0 352 34109 9
- TAKING CARE OF BUSINESS Megan Hart and Lauren Dane ISBN 978 0 352 34502 8

☐ TO SEEK A MASTER Monica Belle	ISBN 978 0 352 34507 3
☐ THE TOP OF HER GAME Emma Holly	ISBN 978 0 352 34116 7
☐ UP TO NO GOOD Karen Smith	ISBN 978 0 352 33589 0
☐ VELVET GLOVE Emma Holly	ISBN 978 0 352 34115 0
☐ VILLAGE OF SECRETS Mercedes Kelly	ISBN 978 0 352 33344 5
☐ WILD BY NATURE Monica Belle	ISBN 978 0 352 33915 7 £6.99
☐ WILD CARD Madeline Moore	ISBN 978 0 352 34038 2
☐ WING OF MADNESS Mae Nixon	ISBN 978 0 352 34099 3

BLACK LACE BOOKS WITH AN HISTORICAL SETTING

☐ A GENTLEMAN'S WAGER Madelynne Ellis	ISBN 978 0 352 34173 0
☐ THE BARBARIAN GEISHA Charlotte Royal	ISBN 978 0 352 33267 7
☐ BARBARIAN PRIZE Deanna Ashford	ISBN 978 0 352 34017 7
☐ THE CAPTIVATION Natasha Rostova	ISBN 978 0 352 33234 9
☐ DARKER THAN LOVE Kristina Lloyd	ISBN 978 0 352 33279 0
☐ WILD KINGDOM Deanna Ashford	ISBN 978 0 352 33549 4
☐ DIVINE TORMENT Janine Ashbless	ISBN 978 0 352 33719 1
☐ FRENCH MANNERS Olivia Christie	ISBN 978 0 352 33214 1
☐ LORD WRAXALL'S FANCY Anna Lieff Saxby	ISBN 978 0 352 33080 2
☐ NICOLE'S REVENGE Lisette Allen	ISBN 978 0 352 29984 4
☐ THE SENSES BEJEWELLED Cleo Cordell	ISBN 978 0 352 29904 2 £6.99
☐ THE SOCIETY OF SIN Sian Lacey Taylder	ISBN 978 0 352 34080 1
☐ TEMPLAR PRIZE Deanna Ashford	ISBN 978 0 352 34137 2
☐ UNDRESSING THE DEVIL Angel Strand	ISBN 978 0 352 33938 6

BLACK LACE BOOKS WITH A PARANORMAL THEME

☐ BRIGHT FIRE Maya Hess	ISBN 978 0 352 34104 4
☐ BURNING BRIGHT Janine Ashbless	ISBN 978 0 352 34085 6
☐ CRUEL ENCHANTMENT Janine Ashbless	ISBN 978 0 352 33483 1
☐ DARK ENCHANTMENT Janine Ashbless	ISBN 978 0 352 34513 4
☐ ENCHANTED Various	ISBN 978 0 352 34195 2
☐ FLOOD Anna Clare	ISBN 978 0 352 34094 8
☐ GOTHIC BLUE Portia Da Costa	ISBN 978 0 352 33075 8
☐ GOTHIC HEAT	ISBN 978 0 352 34170 9
☐ THE PASSION OF ISIS Madelynne Ellis	ISBN 978 0 352 33993 4
☐ PHANTASMAGORIA Madelynne Ellis	ISBN 978 0 352 34168 6

☐ THE PRIDE Edie Bingham	ISBN 978 0 352 33997 3	
☐ THE SILVER CAGE Mathilde Madden	ISBN 978 0 352 34164 8	
☐ THE SILVER COLLAR Mathilde Madden	ISBN 978 0 352 34141 9	
☐ THE SILVER CROWN Mathilde Madden	ISBN 978 0 352 34157 0	
☐ SOUTHERN SPIRITS Edie Bingham	ISBN 978 0 352 34180 8	
☐ THE TEN VISIONS Olivia Knight	ISBN 978 0 352 34119 8	
☐ WILD KINGDOM Deana Ashford	ISBN 978 0 352 34152 5	
☐ WILDWOOD Janine Ashbless	ISBN 978 0 352 34194 5	

BLACK LACE ANTHOLOGIES

☐ BLACK LACE QUICKIES 1 Various	ISBN 978 0 352 34126 6	£2.99
☐ BLACK LACE QUICKIES 2 Various	ISBN 978 0 352 34127 3	£2.99
☐ BLACK LACE QUICKIES 3 Various	ISBN 978 0 352 34128 0	£2.99
☐ BLACK LACE QUICKIES 4 Various	ISBN 978 0 352 34129 7	£2.99
☐ BLACK LACE QUICKIES 5 Various	ISBN 978 0 352 34130 3	£2.99
☐ BLACK LACE QUICKIES 6 Various	ISBN 978 0 352 34133 4	£2.99
☐ BLACK LACE QUICKIES 7 Various	ISBN 978 0 352 34146 4	£2.99
☐ BLACK LACE QUICKIES 8 Various	ISBN 978 0 352 34147 1	£2.99
☐ BLACK LACE QUICKIES 9 Various	ISBN 978 0 352 34155 6	£2.99
☐ BLACK LACE QUICKIES 10 Various	ISBN 978 0 352 34156 3	£2.99
☐ LIAISONS Various	ISBN 978 0 352 34516 5	
☐ SEDUCTION Various	ISBN 978 0 352 34510 3	
☐ MORE WICKED WORDS Various	ISBN 978 0 352 33487 9	£6.99
☐ WICKED WORDS 3 Various	ISBN 978 0 352 33522 7	£6.99
☐ WICKED WORDS 4 Various	ISBN 978 0 352 33603 3	£6.99
☐ WICKED WORDS 5 Various	ISBN 978 0 352 33642 2	£6.99
☐ WICKED WORDS 6 Various	ISBN 978 0 352 33690 3	£6.99
☐ WICKED WORDS 7 Various	ISBN 978 0 352 33743 6	£6.99
☐ WICKED WORDS 8 Various	ISBN 978 0 352 33787 0	£6.99
☐ WICKED WORDS 9 Various	ISBN 978 0 352 33860 0	
☐ WICKED WORDS 10 Various	ISBN 978 0 352 33893 8	
☐ THE BEST OF BLACK LACE 2 Various	ISBN 978 0 352 33718 4	
☐ WICKED WORDS: SEX IN THE OFFICE Various	ISBN 978 0 352 33944 7	
☐ WICKED WORDS: SEX AT THE SPORTS CLUB Various	ISBN 978 0 352 33991 1	
☐ WICKED WORDS: SEX ON HOLIDAY Various	ISBN 978 0 352 33961 4	
☐ WICKED WORDS: SEX IN UNIFORM Various	ISBN 978 0 352 34002 3	
☐ WICKED WORDS: SEX IN THE KITCHEN Various	ISBN 978 0 352 34018 4	

❑ WICKED WORDS: SEX ON THE MOVE Various   ISBN 978 0 352 34034 4

❑ WICKED WORDS: SEX AND MUSIC Various   ISBN 978 0 352 34061 0

❑ WICKED WORDS: SEX AND SHOPPING Various   ISBN 978 0 352 34076 4

❑ SEX IN PUBLIC Various   ISBN 978 0 352 34089 4

❑ SEX WITH STRANGERS Various   ISBN 978 0 352 34105 1

❑ LOVE ON THE DARK SIDE Various   ISBN 978 0 352 34132 7

❑ LUST BITES Various   ISBN 978 0 352 34153 2

❑ MAGIC AND DESIRE Various   ISBN 978 0 352 34183 9

❑ POSSESSION Various   ISBN 978 0 352 34164 8

❑ ENCHANTED Various   ISBN 978 0 352 34195 2

BLACK LACE NON-FICTION

❑ THE BLACK LACE BOOK OF WOMEN'S SEXUAL FANTASIES   ISBN 978 0 352 33793 1   £6.99

     Edited by Kerri Sharp

❑ THE NEW BLACK LACE BOOK OF WOMEN'S SEXUAL

     FANTASIES   ISBN 978 0 352 34172 3

     Edited by Mitzi Szereto